Red in the face

Nancy Louis was outraged. "You torture innocent animals in your research labs, and all in the name of vanity. And look at you—you're wearing dead minks on your back—in August! That's sheer human ego! Do you know how many animals died just to feed your vanity—"

"Enough!" Bebe leaned down until her face was inches from Nancy's. Her voice echoed through the room. "I guarantee you, I'll be filing for a restraining order this afternoon, and if you break that order, I'll haul your ass into court so fast you won't be able to spit, *little girl*."

As security made their way into the room, Nancy yelled out what sounded like a war cry. In unison, she and her friends reached into their pockets and came out with what I thought were guns. Oh my God, were they going to massacre Bebe's Belles?

Security moved in, but they weren't fast enough. Within seconds, I heard a loud noise, and the Belles at the table screamed as a spray of red hit the air . . .

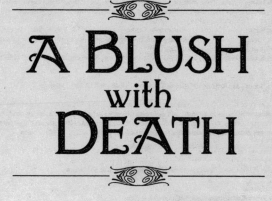

A BLUSH with DEATH

A BATH AND BODY MYSTERY

India Ink

BERKLEY PRIME CRIME, NEW YORK

THE BERKLEY PUBLISHING GROUP
Published by the Penguin Group
Penguin Group (USA) Inc.
375 Hudson Street, New York, New York 10014, USA
Penguin Group (Canada), 90 Eglinton Avenue East, Suite 700, Toronto, Ontario M4P 2Y3, Canada
(a division of Pearson Penguin Canada Inc.)
Penguin Books Ltd., 80 Strand, London WC2R 0RL, England
Penguin Group Ireland, 25 St. Stephen's Green, Dublin 2, Ireland (a division of Penguin Books Ltd.)
Penguin Group (Australia), 250 Camberwell Road, Camberwell, Victoria 3124, Australia
(a division of Pearson Australia Group Pty. Ltd.)
Penguin Books India Pvt. Ltd., 11 Community Centre, Panchsheel Park, New Delhi—110 017, India
Penguin Group (NZ), Cnr. Airborne and Rosedale Roads, Albany, Auckland 1310, New Zealand
(a division of Pearson New Zealand Ltd.)
Penguin Books (South Africa) (Pty.) Ltd., 24 Sturdee Avenue, Rosebank, Johannesburg 2196, South
Africa

Penguin Books Ltd., Registered Offices: 80 Strand, London WC2R 0RL, England

This is a work of fiction. Names, characters, places, and incidents either are the product of the author's
imagination or are used fictitiously, and any resemblance to actual persons, living or dead, business
establishments, events, or locales is entirely coincidental. The publisher does not have any control over
and does not assume any responsibility for author or third-party websites or their content.

A BLUSH WITH DEATH

A Berkley Prime Crime Book / published by arrangement with the author

PRINTING HISTORY
Berkley Prime Crime mass-market edition / May 2006

Copyright © 2006 by Yasmine Galenorn.
Cover art by Griesbach & Martucci.
Cover design by Annette Fiore.
Interior text design by Tiffany Estreicher.

ISBN: 0-425-20966-0

BERKLEY® PRIME CRIME
Berkley Prime Crime Books are published by The Berkley Publishing Group,
a division of Penguin Group (USA) Inc.,
375 Hudson Street, New York, New York 10014.
The name BERKLEY PRIME CRIME and the BERKLEY PRIME CRIME design are trademarks
belonging to Penguin Group (USA) Inc.

PRINTED IN THE UNITED STATES OF AMERICA

10 9 8 7 6 5 4 3 2 1

To Tiffany, my dear friend and shoe maven,
who understands my obsession with all things girly.

Acknowledgments

Forever and always, my eternal thanks and love to Samwise, loving and faithful friend and husband, and the best cheerleader I could have. And a fuzzy thank-you to my four riot gurlz, who purr me to sleep, meow me awake, and generally make life livable.

Thank-yous go out to: my agent, Meredith Bernstein; my editor, Christine Zika; and so many of my dear friends. And for this series, a nod and a thank-you to Aphrodite and Venus, goddesses of both inner and outer beauty. As always, to Mielikki, Tapio, Rauni, and Ukko.

To my readers: As always, thank you for buying my books, and I hope you enjoy this one. Even though I write this series under a nom de plume, India Ink is just another mask of mine. You can reach me via my Web site: www.galenorn.com.

If you write to me via snail mail, please enclose a stamped, self-addressed envelope for reply. Thank you.

The Painted Panther
Yasmine Galenorn aka India Ink

Foreword

The recipes in this book are my own concoctions. I've spent many years blending magical oils, and here I give you—perhaps not magical recipes—but ones to heighten your senses, to bring new experiences into your lives.

Essential oils can be expensive, so yes, you may use synthetics if you can't afford the pure ones, but bear in mind that the fragrance may end up differing slightly. However, this should not be a significant problem. Also, some oils may irritate the skin, so if I make a note to the effect of *Do not get on your skin*, I mean it. Cinnamon can irritate the skin. Black pepper and other oils can burn delicate tissue.

The oil and other bath recipes are obviously not for consumption, but I am stating it here to clear up any potential miscommunications: *Don't eat them or drink them.* They're meant to be used as fragrances, for dreaming pillows, sachets, potpourris, and the like.

"Opportunity makes a thief."
—Francis Bacon, 1561–1626

Prologue

My name is Persia Vanderbilt, and I bill myself as a sensory specialist. I blend custom fragrances at Venus Envy and generally help my aunt Florence run the shop.

Ever since I was a little girl, I've understood the subtle language of flowers and their scents. I can feel them talking, whispering, growing, can sense which essence might help lift depression or heighten self-esteem, and I use my talents to blend oils that bring these qualities to the surface. With my heightened sense of smell, I fine-tune each fragrance until it's just right. It's a far cry from professional perfumery, but I consider it an art in its own right.

In addition to working for Venus Envy, I oversee our gardens at Moss Rose Cottage, the thirty-acre estate and three-story, hundred-year-old Victorian mansion my aunt bought when I turned ten. With hydrangea gardens and lilac groves and bluebell thickets, with rose gardens and wildflower glades, Moss Rose Cottage is a veritable faerieland of flowers and paths.

A few months after I turned sixteen and graduated from high school, I left the thriving little community of Gull Harbor on Port Samanish Island for the big-city lights of Seattle. I gave the city fifteen years of my life and loved most of it until late last year when I went through a bad breakup with my long-term boyfriend Elliot, who turned out to be an embezzler, and after my job at the Alternative Life Center went belly-up. Discouraged and afraid Elliot's thug friends might come after me to pay him back for turning state's evidence, I called Auntie, who opened her arms and her home to me. And so I returned to island life. Now, both adults, Auntie and I've become friends as well as family.

Along with my custom blends, Venus Envy sells several lines of lotions, bath salts, oils, bulk herbs, crystals, scarves, and handmade jewelry from local artists. Aunt Florence offers facials, pedicures, manicures, and skin consultations by appointment.

The shop is thriving—a real success. Or rather, it was until Bebe's Boutique moved in a couple months ago. Bebe Wilcox is out to become the number-one beauty maven in town, and her concerted effort to force us out of business is having an effect on the books. A bad effect. And neither Auntie nor I are sure just what we're going to do.

Chapter One

The BookWich was hopping, every table jammed with summer tourists looking for a little local flavor. I spied Barbara in a back booth and maneuvered my way through the crowded café, skirting the waitresses as they scurried back and forth from the kitchen carrying platters of fish and chips, sandwiches, burgers, and a plethora of other goodies whose smells made my stomach rumble.

Barbara had sounded frantic on the phone when she called, begging me to meet her for lunch. The hint of panic in her voice had spurred me to cancel one of my appointments. If Barb was in trouble, I wanted to be there. As I slid into the booth, I immediately saw what her problem was. Barb had been the victim of a cut-and-run, and the results weren't pretty.

"What the hell happened to you?" I blurted out. "Nightmare on Scissors Street?"

Barbara Konstantinos, my best friend, was exceptionally pretty and petite. Standing next to her, I felt like the Jolly Green Giant because Barb barely topped five feet and

wouldn't rock the scales at one hundred pounds unless she
had just finished a seven course meal. I, on the other hand,
stood five ten and weighed one fifty. Granted, I was lean
and muscled, but still, I towered over her. Whether in her
baker's uniform or a slip dress, Barb was one of those
women who always looked pulled together and ready to
go. Her copper-colored bob exquisitely grazed her chin,
with not a hair out of place. Or it had, until today.

Her sassy European cut had been butchered into short,
jagged spikes, the color transformed into a brash calico of
brassy reds and tarnished blondes. To make matters worse,
the hairdresser hadn't even bothered to try to create an interesting pattern—say, tiger stripes, for example. No, instead, blotchy patches dappled her hair, making her look
like she had a bizarre case of ringworm.

My face must have belied my feelings, because she
moaned and rubbed her temples. "Oh, God, Persia. It's
bad, isn't it? I knew it! When they told me it was hip and
cutting-edge, I knew they were bullshitting me." She grimaced, and I could tell a migraine was incoming. Barb's
brow was pinched in that particular way that she had a few
hours before the blinding headaches struck. I winced,
wishing there was something she could do about them.

"Who did this to you?" I asked, unable to tear my gaze
away from the train wreck that passed for her hair.

She fidgeted with her napkin. "I tried a new stylist," she
mumbled. Then, tears springing to her eyes, she said,
"Please don't yell at me for going there! Venus Envy doesn't
cut hair, and I wanted to try something new, so I dropped in
there on an impulse, but I didn't buy anything except the
haircut. I really thought everything would be okay."

My aunt's shop, Venus Envy, catered to Gull Harbor's
yuppie set with herbal facials and soothing pedicures and

manicures, as well as being one of the best-stocked bath and beauty shops in the county, but we didn't offer haircuts, massages, or steam baths.

"Why on earth do you think I'm going to yell at you?" But even as I spoke, I flashed on why she thought I might be mad at her. There was only one place in town she could have gone that would piss me off. "Okay, spill it. You went to Bebe's, didn't you?"

She nodded, shamefaced. "Yes, I went to Bebe's Boutique," she whispered.

Nailed, right on the head. I sighed. "Barb, you do know they're trying to run us out of business, don't you? I can't believe you still went there. What kind of friend are you?"

"I'm sorry," she said. "I didn't realize things were *that* bad with Venus Envy."

She looked so contrite that I relented. She'd paid dearly for her indiscretion with that hideous haircut. I picked up one of the breadsticks and bit off the end. "I'm sorry, I didn't mean to yell. Don't worry. Your hair will grow fast, and you can have it dyed back to normal. Until then, maybe Auntie will let your borrow her hat." That cajoled a smile from her. She knew what Auntie's hat looked like. Everybody in town knew the fuchsia wonder my aunt wore, with the stuffed bird perched on the side—a real stuffed bird.

Though I managed to remain calm on the outside, inside I was fuming. When Bebe's Boutique had opened up on the other side of town a few months ago, it was soon apparent that they were hell-bent on putting us out of business. But their products were inferior, their sales techniques annoying, and their ethics nonexistent. They were aiming at regional domination, and we were their first target.

I'd heard through the grapevine that they were trying

some pretty underhanded tactics to steal our business, such
as telling people we used synthetic ingredients when we
actually used as many natural products as possible, and a
particularly onerous accusation—that my aunt didn't keep
Venus Envy's day spa up to Gull Harbor's health code regulations. We could prove that one wrong, but who was
going to bother to go down to City Hall to find out?

"What did they say when you complained?"

Barb squirmed a little, looking miserable. "The girl told
me it was edgy . . . hip. . . . I wanted to believe her because
I couldn't believe she'd butcher my hair on purpose. So I
didn't—"

"You didn't say anything. Good God, they really tried
to convince you that style is the hottest trend? Have they
seen a copy of *Vogue* lately?"

She blushed. "I feel so stupid. I'm ashamed to say that
I actually paid them. I should have argued, but the stylist
was so young . . . I didn't . . ."

Barb's self-esteem had been on the chopping block the
past few months. She was forty-one and convinced she
was losing her edge, which she wasn't. But I could easily
see her paying without complaint in a desperate attempt to
keep some snot-nosed young punk from thinking she was
old-fashioned and stodgy.

I held up my hand. "We all make mistakes. You were
probably in so much shock from what they did to you that
you weren't thinking straight." I had a nasty feeling that
Barb had paid through the nose for that cut. The words
"edgy" and "hip" guaranteed a high price tag in the worlds
of fashion and cosmetics. But I wasn't about to put her on
the spot by asking. "So, make an appointment with your
regular stylist and get it dyed back to your normal color."

"I can't." Barb bit her lip and stared at the table. "Not

for a week or so. I already consulted her and, fashion emergency or not, she's booked solid. I know she's pissed that I went somewhere else. I don't blame her."

Oops. Never good to make your hair stylist angry. "What did she say? Did she yell at you?"

"Not really, but she read me the riot act about going someplace else without finding out about their reputation first. I feel like a world-class heel. Anyway, after she was done lecturing me about fly-by-night operations, as she called them, she took a look at my hair and said that it's going to be awhile before it's back to normal. That little tart fried it, and the damage is pretty bad."

"So you're stuck?" I cringed, hoping she wouldn't have to live with the cut and color for much longer. Barb was meticulous about her appearance, and there's no way she could turn that mess into "classy."

"Not only do we have to re-dye it, but Theresa wants to cut it super short in order to allow the new growth to come in without frizzled ends. I can't believe I have to go out in public looking like this for over a week and then spend several months sporting a buzz cut!" She let out what was either a sob or a laugh, or possibly both.

"That must have been some powerful bleach." I shuddered, fingering my own waist-length braid. Thick and jet black, my hair was naturally wavy. I'd been blessed with good genes. Not a gray hair yet, and I was thirty-one. "Well, hell. I guess we'll have to keep you stocked with turbans for a few months."

"That about sums it up." She shrugged. "I deserve it, though, for sneaking around behind your back. And Theresa's. Believe me, I've learned my lesson. I'll never darken their door again, and I'm going to tell everybody just what they did to me."

Tilda dropped off our menus. "Sorry we're slow on the uptake today, girls," she said. "The place is so packed that we can't keep up with the rush." She did a double take when she saw Barb's hair but wisely kept silent.

I picked up my menu. Aunt Florence was supposed to meet us with some sort of news, but I was hungry and ready to order.

As if reading my mind, Barb said, "Let's talk about something else. You said your aunt is joining us?"

I nodded. "Yeah, she's got something up her sleeve. I can always tell. So, how's Dorian?" It seemed like ages since we'd gotten a chance to sit down and dish. Barb and I worked in adjoining shops, but the summer tourist rush had left us both scrambling for a moment to breathe, and we hadn't had time to duck out for a quick lunch in days.

She waited to answer until Tilda had taken our orders. I asked for a deluxe hamburger, a side salad, bag of chips, and a glass of iced tea. Barb ordered a bowl of gazpacho, grilled cheese sandwich, and a Diet Coke. Tilda returned with our drinks and then rushed off to another table.

"At least the BookWich and your bakery are doing good business. We've had a lot of customers, but they aren't spending as much." As I sipped my iced tea, a thought occurred to me. "Barb, why did you want a new hairstyle? You love the one you've got. Or, rather, the one you had."

Barb shrugged. "I guess I'm restless. Dorian and I got into an argument the other night because I wanted to go out to a movie and he wanted to sit at home and watch some stupid baseball game. We haven't gone out in over three weeks. I hate always staying at home."

Dorian and Barb were a wonderful couple with two exceptions: his mother was the MIL from hell, and Dorian liked to stay home and putter. Otherwise, he and Barb matched. Maybe too well. Sometimes I wondered, if couples didn't have any differences, what did they talk about?

"So you cut your hair because of an argument?"

She gave me a sheepish grin. "I know it sounds stupid, but I thought a change might get him moving again. He works hard all day, I know that, but so do I. And I still have the energy to get out in the evenings."

I played with my straw. "Barb, did you ever think that he might have a medical condition? Low thyroid, or something? Dorian isn't that old. Maybe he should see a doctor." I didn't want to scare her, but sometimes it was better to rule out medical problems first, then work on the issues that were left.

She tipped her head to the side, a quizzical look on her face. "You might have something there. It's about time for our physicals. I'll make the appointments tomorrow. Couldn't hurt either one of us to get checked out." She saluted me with her Coke. "Now, what about you? Bran and you still good?"

Bran Stanton and I weren't serious—neither one of us was looking for anything permanent—but we had developed a free and easy relationship. No ties, just lots of long talks and great sex.

"As good as we can be, considering that his leg's still healing. Not to mention the summer rush. He's been trying to keep his boat going, even though he's still using a cane. Tourist season brings in half his yearly income. He can't afford to spend the summer resting. The doctor told him if he's careful, he can go out on the boat, but I'm a little worried about him." Bran ran a tour boat during the summer and taught outdoor recreation classes during the winter. He was also the local urban shaman, which was actually more accepted by the locals than I would have thought possible.

"That's rough. At least he hired some help." She cleared her throat. "And Elliot? Has the albatross been around lately?"

I grimaced. "God, yes. Damned idiot doesn't seem to get it that I'm stacking up the evidence for a restraining order." My ex-boyfriend Elliot had moved to Gull Harbor after he got out of prison; he didn't want to listen to me when I told him we were done. Over with. Kaput. Or maybe he just wanted to make my life miserable, which was entirely possible. Either way, he was making a nuisance of himself. "At least he always stays out of my reach when he shows up. He knows I could break him like a twig."

Barb broke into a grin. "I love it that you're so macho . . . Not."

I snorted. "Hey, I'm no girly-girl, even if I do love makeup and perfumes and sexy clothes. But you have to admit, working out pays off. Elliot tries anything with me, and he'll find himself flat on his back, my knee in his nuts. Oh—here's Auntie."

Aunt Florence bustled over to the booth. A driving force in Gull Harbor, she was one of those unforgettable people, never easily ignored or dismissed. Five foot three, Auntie was as wide as she was tall, but she wore her size well. I couldn't imagine what she'd be like if she ever lost weight, though I knew she'd still be the same driving force she was now. Aunt Florence had presence. True, her fashion sense left a lot to be desired, but I'd learned never to underestimate her.

She slid into the booth next to me, her flowered mu'umu'u a splash of yellow against the green seat, and her ever-present fuchsia straw hat perched atop her head. She seldom left the house without it, and the hat came complete with a stuffed parakeet. Squeaky had once been part of the Menagerie—the eight cats, three dogs, and rooster—that shared Moss Rose Cottage with us, but the bird had ended up on the wrong side of a fight with an extension cord. Zap! He lost, the cord won, and Auntie had him stuffed and affixed to her hat. They made quite the pair.

Tilda deposited Barb's soup and my burger on the table and asked Auntie if she knew what she wanted.

"Ham on sourdough with provolone, mustard, and horse-radish. And a side of potato salad, please." She handed the menu back to Tilda. "Oh, coffee. Lots of it, and make it strong. Cream and sugar, please."

As Tilda left, Auntie flashed me a broad smile. "I'm going to grab dinner on the run, so you're on your own tonight, Imp." Aunt Florence had called me Imp since I was a little girl. Short for *impetuous*, the nickname fit.

"No problem," I said.

Barb sighed, and with one fluid motion, Auntie turned to her and said, "Child, what the hell were you thinking? You look like you just escaped from a band of rogue punk rockers."

With a grimace, Barb repeated her story. Auntie's eyes flickered when she heard the name Bebe's Boutique, but she was more tactful than I, merely raising one eyebrow. "I see," she said. "And so you can't do anything about the color for another week or so?"

Barb shook her head. "No, and it's too hot to wear a hat."

"Nonsense," Auntie said, pointing to her own fuchsia wonder. "I wear a hat almost every day of my life. You run on over to Marianne's after lunch. She's bound to have something that will work. And as for Bebe's Boutique, I have a few choice things I could say about them, but I'm a lady, and this is no place for that kind of language."

Tilda returned with Auntie's coffee. She refilled my iced tea and Barb's Diet Coke, then scurried off. Barb spooned up her soup and I started in on my hamburger as Auntie pulled out a sheaf of papers.

"So, what's your news, Auntie?" I asked, thinking that we might be able to take Barbara's mind off her hair.

"That's what these are about," Auntie said, spreading out several flyers and brochures on the table. "There's a convention in town, which means more business for everybody." She picked up one and flipped it open. "Persia, I know you've been feeling worn out the past couple of weeks, so I've planned something new. A break, of sorts, though it's really a working vacation."

I perked up. About the only holiday I'd been counting on was my upcoming trip to a B and B in Port Townsend in September after Labor day was over and the tourists were gone. The trip sounded eminently better than a "working holiday," but in the meantime, a break was a break was a break.

"Great," I said between bites. "What is it?"

She handed me one of the pamphlets. "The Beauty Bonanza Cosmetics Convention opens at the Red Door Convention Center on Saturday, as you know, and I decided that we have to be there. Venus Envy's going to have a booth, and I signed you and Tawny up. You can take turns manning it." She beamed.

The Beauty Bonanza Cosmetics Convention? She had to be kidding.

Not sure I'd heard her right, I said, "You mean you want me to hang around a beauty convention?" Subject myself to a week of giggling, simpering models and cosmetics mavens? As much as I loved my work, I couldn't stand the backbiting that I'd seen in the industry.

Aunt Florence stared at me, silent. I squirmed in my seat and tried to finish my hamburger, but her gaze drained any will I might have to protest. I finally pushed my plate back and sighed.

"You know I'm not cut out for that sort of thing. Can't you just send Tawny instead? I'll be glad to fill in for her at the store."

She shook her head. "Imp," she said, a warning note in her voice.

"But, it sounds so boring," I started, then stopped. I could hear the edge of a whine droning in my voice. That put an end to my temper tantrum. "All right, I'll go. Just so long as you know I'm not happy about it."

"Trust me, I knew what your reaction would be." Auntie laughed. "I have to balance the books, or I'd go in your place." The twinkle in her eyes told me she was full of hogwash. At least about the "go in your place" part.

I rolled my eyes. "You lie and you know it."

She winked. "Caught me red-handed. Oh good, here's my lunch. I'm starved." Tilda set Auntie's sandwich in front of her. As Auntie unfurled her napkin, I leaned back and leafed through the brochures. Like it or not, I was headed for hell-week.

"I know you think you'll be bored, but maybe you'll have fun. Think of it as one of your responsibilities. For the good of the shop," my aunt said, peeking at one of the brochures over my shoulder.

She frowned. "Venus Envy has to keep abreast of what's going on in the industry. We must keep pace with what's in style, and you can do that by going." Polishing off the last bite of her sandwich, she wiped her fingers on her napkin. "Persia, you know how much Bebe's Boutique is cutting into our business. We can't let them shut us out." She shook her head. "I just can't believe so many of our loyal clients are are stabbing us in the back."

"Their prices are lower, at least on their products," I said, glancing at Barb. "I think they're making it up in the salon. Anyway, I guess it comes down to money in the end."

Auntie hadn't been the only one surprised by how quickly our friends had turned away. Oh, not everybody had deserted us for Bebe's Boutique, but enough so that it smarted. Even if we manage to regain our customer base, it was going to be hard on me to be as friendly as I had been, though I knew better than to take it as a personal insult. Like it or not, I was learning that I had to separate business from my friends. It wasn't easy.

Auntie sighed. "Their prices are lower because they use such crappy ingredients. People just don't care about quality anymore if they can save a buck or two. I know that it makes a big difference with groceries, but let's face it, the people who patronize our shop aren't exactly hurting for money. No, they're listening to those awful rumors going around."

Barb looked like Auntie had just smacked her one. "I'm so sorry. I never meant to take business away from you! I just got my hair done there; I didn't buy anything. I never thought about it, but if people saw me there, they might think I prefer Bebe's to your shop, too. I'm so ashamed."

"It's okay, child," Auntie said, patting her hand. "I'm not blaming you. Besides, you're right. We don't do hair at Venus Envy. But I suggest you stick with your regular girl. That look . . ." She shuddered. "Honey, it isn't good."

I broke in. "So what do I need to be on the lookout for at this shindig?"

Auntie shook her head. "Just use your intuition, Imp. Since Venus Envy will be yours one day, it's time you get used to dealing with the industry mavens and wheeler-dealers." She leaned in. "Not to mention the fact that Bebe Wilcox is bound to have a booth there. You can scope out just what they're doing to subvert our usual clientele. They can't be going for the haircuts," she said, grinning at Barb.

"You know, I think it might be fun to go to this gig," Barb said. She picked up one of Auntie's brochures. "At least you'll get out of the shop for a day or two. I'd love to get away. The bakery's been busy nonstop this summer. I'm about to implode from overwork." Her eyes flashed. "Especially since it's being held at the Red Door Convention Center. That place is gorgeous."

I stared at her, an idea forming in the back of my mind. "Auntie, is the entrance fee steep?" When she shook her head, I asked, "Would you be willing to front Barb to go with me?"

Barb sputtered. "I can't leave Dorian stuck with the bakery!"

"Yes, you can. Dorian won't mind. You know he gives in on just about anything you ask!" I wheedled. If Barb could go along, it might not be so bad. We could sit in the booth and tell jokes and gossip to pass the time. "Please? For me? I need my best bud there."

After a moment, Barb rolled her eyes at me and broke into a grin. "Oh, okay, if your aunt agrees, then I'll ask Dorian. I could use the break, and maybe I can find something to help distract my attention from this god-awful hair."

Auntie glanced from me, to Barb, back to me again. "You two are as bad as a couple of teenagers." She laughed. "Barb can go in as your assistant, and it won't cost a dime. Anything to ensure you'll be there."

I threw my arm around her shoulder, giving her a big hug. "It's a deal. Thanks, Auntie. So, tell us more about the convention. What should we expect?"

She sipped her water. "Three hundred saleswomen, cosmetics manufacturers, models, and store owners are about to descend on Gull Harbor for five days of workshops, lectures, and discussions. That doesn't count the local traffic—it's open to the public for a fee. You can rest easy, though. I've only signed you up for the weekend, so don't get too bent out of shape. Tawny will handle the remaining time."

"Three hundred guests? Want to bet the Chamber of Commerce is ecstatic? They'll be able to use this as advertising to attract even more conventions next year," Barbara said, an edge in her voice. As much as Gull Harbor's economy profited from the tourist boom each year, there was always a love-hate relationship between the summer visitors and the locals.

"You're right about that," Aunt Florence said, handing me one of the brochures. The pictures were a jumble of crowded booths and photos of flawless faces, bright with lipstick and shimmering shadows.

I loved makeup as much as the next woman, but for some reason, the photos gave me the creeps. "They look like automatons," I said, pointing to a group shot of at least a dozen women, all with brilliant, eye-popping smiles. Clad in golden blazers and cream-colored skirts, they reminded me of a field of buttercups.

Auntie squinted at the page. "You're on the money," she said. "Those are Bebe's Belles."

I glanced up at her. "The same Bebe who owns Bebe's Boutique?"

"One and the same. And the same Bebe who owns the Bebe's Cosmetics factory on the outskirts of town. Her saleswomen are scary." Aunt Florence shook her head, frowning. "I swear, those women aren't right in the head."

"That bad, huh?" But I already knew the answer. I'd witnessed firsthand the trouble their fearless leader had stirred up for us this summer.

Auntie heaved a sigh. "They are the most hideous group of brainwashed, cackling hens you've ever met. The company directors are bad enough, but Bebe's Belles—Persia, it's like a cult."

Barb broke in. "I've chased them away from my house before. They're like the Jehovah's Witnesses, only instead of pushing religion, they're pushing makeup. And it's not very good. I tried it a couple times and threw it away, before she opened up the boutique."

I frowned. "You mean they go door to door, like Avon or Mary Kay?"

"Yeah, but without the class or products worth buying," Barb said. "Their stuff is crap and it hasn't gotten any better since they opened up the boutique. Just like their haircuts."

Auntie nodded. "Barbara's right. The company uses low-quality ingredients, and I suspect they don't always adhere to industry specifications. I seem to remember that they were investigated last year, but nobody could find any specific violations to shut them down. Bebe Wilcox is bent on pushing her way into the larger markets. They're local right now, but their eye is on the national scale. Don't underestimate her. She's ruthless."

I began to see why Auntie wanted eyes and ears at the convention. "Okay, I'll find out what I can."

Auntie scooted out of the booth and grabbed the check, giving me a grateful look. "I knew you wouldn't let me down. Lunch is on me, girls." She started toward the cashier, then turned back. "Oh, one more thing. I almost forgot—I signed you up to give a lecture on Sunday at the convention, Persia."

My stomach lurched. "Okay . . . what's the topic?"

Auntie laughed. "Get that hangdog look off your face, girl. You're an expert on the subject. The name of your workshop is 'The Fragrance of Desire: Driving Men Mad With Your Scent.'" Before I could protest, she tossed the waitress thirty dollars and was out the door like a light.

I sputtered. "How on earth am I going to host a workshop with that name? That's positively embarrassing."

Barb chuckled. "Face it, Persia. Your aunt plays to win, and she seldom loses. You know it, I know it, everybody knows it. Bebe's got her work cut out for her, that's one thing in Venus Envy's favor. So if I were you, I'd get started writing that speech, because I have a feeling you're not going to escape this one."

As I gathered my purse and keys, I knew she was right. "Yeah. I'd better get back to work," I said, glancing at the time. "Since Bebe Wilcox is out to usurp Venus Envy, I suppose I have to make sure I'm not late for any more of my appointments. Bebe's Belles can ride out on the same turnip wagon they rode into town on." But, despite my bravado, I had the feeling that the Wilcox woman was going to be more of a pain in the neck than I wanted to deal with.

Barb grinned. "Come on. Ever think the convention might not be so bad?"

"You're annoying," I said, but gave her a grumpy smile.

"Lighten up," Barb said, but she gave me a long look. "Persia, do you really think Venus Envy's future is in trouble?"

"I think it might be," I muttered. "We thought our customers were loyal, but I guess you can't mix business and friendship. Auntie's an incredible entrepreneur, but somebody's been bad-mouthing our products around town, and word gets around. Business has dropped off. I'm still getting a lot of clients looking for an individualized scent, but most of our customer base seems to be out-of-towners lately. That doesn't bode well for the rest of the year, especially the Christmas season."

Barbara sobered. "That does sound bad. Now I feel horrible about setting foot in that boutique."

I gave her a weary smile. "Stop beating yourself up, Barb. I'm more pissed that you paid for that atrocity, rather than the fact that you actually went there. But, you know, maybe it's time Venus Envy looked into hiring a licensed stylist. We do manicures and pedicures. Why not hair?"

As we passed through the door into the sunlight, Barb held up the brochure with the Belles on it. She shook her head. "They look like a bunch of Stepford Wives."

"Bebe's Belles," I muttered. "I sure wouldn't want to be one of them." And with that, I headed back to Venus Envy.

Chapter Two

꧁ ꧂

I had just wrapped up my last fragrance consultation for the afternoon and was looking forward to a quick swim before going home, when Tawny hurried over to my station. She flashed me a brave smile—bearer-of-bad-news brave—and slipped into the vacant seat opposite me, leaning her elbows on the counter. Her silver nose stud mirrored the platinum Euro trash cut she'd received from a trendy salon in Seattle. The coloring—or lack thereof—washed her out, but I wasn't about to say anything. Unlike Barb's fiasco, Tawny liked her look, and far be it from me to dash her self-esteem.

I leaned back, a thin layer of perspiration beading along my skin. Even my crop top and miniskirt couldn't keep me cool. "What's up?"

"I booked three more appointments for you today. At four, four thirty, and five." She winced. "Sorry, but you didn't tell me if you had any plans, so I went ahead and scheduled them."

"Ugh. I was planning on heading out to Driftwood Loop

before I went home, but I guess that's out." I desperately longed for a swim out at Spindrift Bay. The riptides seldom crashed to shore there, and the area was considered fairly safe for swimming. It was also one of the few tourist-free spots; nobody wanted to pick their way over the good half mile of pebbled beach that stood between the road and the thin spit of sand.

I pushed back my chair. "All right, but no more today, and don't book anything more than I have tomorrow. I'm beginning to feel the pressure," I said, grinning. Even though we needed the business, a lot of it was falling on my shoulders, and I needed a break.

She blinked, then smiled back, popping her gum.

"And don't let Aunt Florence hear you doing that—you know the sound drives her crazy."

"Gotchya," Tawny said. "God, I'm hot."

"I'll see about getting a couple more fans in here tomorrow," I said. With our usual weather, there was no need for air conditioning. "Listen, I'm going to run next door to the bakery for a few. I'll be back before my next appointment."

Tawny peeled herself off the chair. "Okay, boss. Say hi to Ms. Konstantinos for me."

"You got it."

I stepped out onto the sidewalk, plunging into the mad rush of foot traffic spilling through the streets. Tourist season was in full swing, with people flocking to the island to get away from the smog and noise of Seattle. Port Samanish Island—and Gull Harbor—might just be a ferry ride away across Puget Sound from Seattle, but we offered an uncluttered alternative to the urbanites who made their home in the sprawling metropolis that hugged Elliott Bay.

Barb had been telling the truth. The Baklava or Bust

Bakery was jammed. I pushed through a crowd of tourists who looked to be on a day tour and found myself squashed against the counter, where I was instantly assailed by the exquisite smells of yeasty bread and piping-hot doughnuts and cookies. The glittering display cases offered enough delights to tempt anybody's taste buds. Even though I wasn't all that hungry, I immediately fixated on the bear claws.

Dorian Konstantinos, Barbara's husband, was manning the counter. He gave me a harried wave and yelled out, "Barbara, Persia's here." Within seconds, Barb came racing out from the back. She zipped around the counter, deftly weaving between the customers, most of whom towered head and shoulders over her. As I leaned in to catch what she was saying, she put her hand on my arm.

"Dorian says no problem; he doesn't mind if I go to the convention. Ari will take over for me while I'm gone, and we have Ronette and Colin, of course."

"Great! I'm so glad you're coming with me."

She glanced at the back room. "I've got to go—I've got a batch of rolls about ready to come out of the oven. You want anything while you're here?"

I decided to surprise Auntie by bringing home dessert. "Give me one of your peach pies," I said, holding out a ten.

Barb pocketed the money, slid the pie into a box, then scurried away again before I had a chance to thank her. I headed back to Venus Envy to finish what was shaping up to be a long afternoon.

⁂

By the time I locked the door to the shop, it was too late to go swimming, so I headed home. As I pulled into the driveway, I saw Baby sitting there, and cringed. Our neighbors, along with Kyle Laughlin, the police chief, hated that car. Auntie was forever promising to get the muffler fixed, but for some reason, she never got around to it. The way she meticulously took care of everything else clued me in that my aunt might be subconsciously flaunting her rebel nature via one gas-guzzling, exhaust-belching convertible.

Moss Rose Cottage was a thirty-acre wonderland. The house, an exquisite three-story white elephant—excluding attic and basement—had been built over a century ago by Captain George Bentley, a retired naval officer. He'd spent the latter years of his life here, surrounded by family, and the house passed down through his children and their children until my aunt bought it.

I was ten years old when we settled here. Captain Bentley, or the Cap'n, as we called him, had remained with the house. Doorknobs rattled at night, soft footsteps fell in the attic, and shadows moved where there shouldn't be shadows. I knew it was the Cap'n, watching over the house. And over us.

The mansion brooded over the acreage like an eagle in its aerie. Even though Auntie had all the latest gadgets and cable, with walls crafted from stone and mullioned windows, Moss Rose Cottage seemed to exist outside of time.

The door was open, the screen tightly shut, keeping the Menagerie safely inside. Not a dog or cat in sight, but as I slipped into the foyer, barking broke out from the living room as Beauty and Beast raced up to greet me. Beauty, a gorgeous black cocker spaniel, was as delicate as her name. Beast, on the other hand, looked like a breeding experiment gone awry. He had a heart as big as his head, even though he fancied himself a guard dog. I looked around for Pete, but the golden retriever was nowhere in sight.

"Yes, I'm home, you two mutts," I said, giving them each a quick hug after hanging my purse on a hook. I wandered into the living room, where the curtains were open, exposing the floor-to-ceiling windows that provided a panoramic view: a vast wash of ocean breakers crashing against the shoreline. A hop, skip, and a jump across Briarwood Drive, a short incline, and a narrow stretch of rocky sand was all that separated the lower edge of our property from the ocean. In the evenings, Auntie and I sat and watched the rolling surf that curved along the edge of the island.

"Persia? Is that you?" Aunt Florence peeked around the corner. "Good, you're home early." She held a bowl that smelled suspiciously like crab salad. My eyes lit up.

"Is that dinner?" I asked, staring at the food. Always hungry, I was grateful that my workouts staved off worry about my weight. "I brought dessert—peach pie."

She took one look at my expression and snorted. "Set the table. Let's eat outside. It's a beautiful night. We're having crab salad on croissants, with vichyssoise. And that pie will go mighty fine with the vanilla ice cream I bought."

I followed her into the kitchen, where I retrieved the china and linens and headed out to the deck. The warm salt air streamed by, and I inhaled deeply, feeling the tang of the ocean settle deep into my lungs.

Auntie spooned the crab salad onto the sliced croissants and added a garnish of parsley, brilliant green, and a sprig of mint to the plates. I carried the tray out to the patio table, careful to close the screen door behind me to keep the bugs out and the Menagerie in. She followed with the tureen, and we settled in at the table. While she ladled the soup, I filled our goblets with white Zinfandel.

"So, how was your afternoon?" I said, reveling in the quiet that descended on us as dusk grew near as I tasted the vichyssoise. The chilled soup was rich and creamy. I let it roll around on my tongue for a moment, reveling in the smooth taste of potatoes, cream, and leeks. She'd added a bit of dill, which gave it a nice zest.

Auntie sipped of her wine. "Not bad, not bad at all. I spent the afternoon over at Winthrop's." Winthrop Winchester was her lawyer, a crafty old codger. He was good, so good that he was worth a small fortune in fees.

"What were you doing over there? Figuring out a way to sue Bebe's Boutique, I hope?"

"Don't I wish." She smiled gently. "I asked Winthrop to draw up the papers that will make you an official partner in the business. That way, if anything happens to me, there won't be any hassle over what happens to Venus Envy. The forms will be ready to sign at some point next week." She flashed me a quick smile as my jaw dropped.

Partner? I already knew that I'd inherit the shop if—heaven forbid—Aunt Florence died, but for her to make me a partner meant she really trusted me.

"I don't know what to say. I wasn't expecting that." I fumbled with my sandwich, dropping a bite of crab on the deck. I reached down and snagged it up, tossing it over the railing. Some creature would feast on it.

"You're going to inherit everything, anyway. You might as well be a full-fledged partner. We'll just keep doing things the same way as usual, but as you become more familiar with the business over the next year or two, I'll let you make more of the decisions."

The phone rang.

She motioned for me to stay seated. "You eat your dinner. I'll get it."

I stared out at the ocean as I ate. The sun was glinting off the horizon; storm season had abated and wouldn't start back up for another month or two. We'd had the most gorgeous summer in the past ten years of Gull Harbor's history, according to my aunt.

"Oh my goodness!" Auntie's voice startled me out of my thoughts. "Is it really you? I can hardly believe it."

I perked up, straining to listen without being obvious. After a pause, she said, "How about lunch tomorrow at the Lighthouse Café?" Another pause, then, "Yes, that's right. I'll meet you there at noon. And Kane, it's good to hear from you." After replacing the receiver, she returned to the deck.

My curiosity aroused, I said, "Who was that?"

"Kane Jimenez. I knew him when I lived in Hawai'i." She hesitated, in a way that made me think there was a lot more to the story than an old friend.

"Go on, please. You don't talk very much about that period in your life," I said. Auntie seldom discussed the years she'd lived in the island paradise.

She stared at her soup, then ground a little more black pepper into it. "It was a bittersweet time in my life. Do you remember the spring when Lydia was killed, how I told you I've only ever known two people who were murdered?"

I nodded. "Yes, I do."

Auntie rubbed her temples, then leaned back and stared out at the water. "When I first visited Hawai'i, it was on a whim. I stepped off the plane and never wanted to leave, so I cashed in my return ticket and settled down. I even opened a shop, a lot like Venus Envy but much smaller. I love the islands, they're in my blood."

I knew this and had often wondered why she never returned, even for a vacation. I snagged up the last bite of my crab croissant and finished my wine.

"While I was living there, I met someone. He was a wonderful man, part native Hawaiian, part Portuguese, part Hispanic, by blood. His name was Keola Manuel Jimenez and he was tall and strong, with long hair that he kept in a braid. His eyes were so dark that you could crawl in and never find the bottom. I fell in love, and he asked me to marry him."

I stared at her; Aunt Florence had never mentioned him before. I knew she had never married, but until now, I assumed that the thought had never crossed her mind. "You were engaged?"

She nodded. "This was back in 1970, a few years before you were born. I loved him more than I'd ever loved anybody in my life." Her blue eyes sparkled, mirroring the glint of the setting sun on the rippling currents.

"What happened?"

She forced a smile to her lips. "Keola was murdered. He was killed one day when he accidentally stumbled onto a *pakalolo* farm." At my confused look, she said, "A pot farm. The owner was a Vietnam vet who'd been discharged because he went crazy and tried to shoot up his unit. Keola was a biologist; he stumbled onto the operation while doing some fieldwork. Something triggered a flashback, and the guy lost it. Before Keola knew what was happening, the man shot him. Keola was dead before he hit the ground. He never had a chance."

I stared at my plate, digesting the information. My aunt

had been engaged, and her fiancé murdered. "Did they catch the guy?"

"Yes, they caught him. And put him away for good. But Keola was dead," she said with a shrug. "I couldn't stay there. I left, vowing to return someday. I never have. Not yet." She pushed herself away from the table. "The man who just called is Kane . . . Keola's brother. We've kept in touch over the years, and he recently moved to Seattle."

"Is this the first time you'll have seen him since you left Hawai'i?" I could tell that she was nervous; she kept fidgeting with her napkin.

She blinked. "Child, this will be the first time we've spoken face-to-face since the funeral. We've written letters, but somehow, neither one of us ever got around to making that first phone call." She turned, facing me square on. "I don't need to tell you how this makes me feel. Kane was the spitting image of Keola. They were twins, and I simply don't know how I'm going to react."

And with that, she hurried out of the house, down to the gardens. I cleared the table and stacked the dishes in the dishwasher. Dessert could wait until later. Auntie needed some time alone, and I wasn't about to bother her.

❧

I slept deep that night, long and hard and heavy. When I woke to the alarm, the corners of my eyes were crusted, and I felt like I had a hangover. Delilah, Auntie's daft seventeen-year-old white Persian, was curled on the foot of my bed. At first she'd considered me a rival; now I was simply her property, as was everything else in the house. A leo, Delilah rule the roost.

As I slid into my workout clothes, I reflected on what

I'd learned the night before. What would it be like to lose the love of your life to a bullet?

I'd thought I loved Elliot—after all, we lived together for years—but I was coming to realize that what I'd felt for the man had been fondness, not true love. I had my doubts that I even knew what love was. At least of a romantic nature. And maybe I never would. I was happy being single. Dating was a game to me, one that I enjoyed until emotions began to run too high, and then I backed away, worried that I might get trapped into something I couldn't handle. Or maybe I just hadn't met anybody who made me want to open up.

I opened the curtains, and light streamed through my bedroom as I slid the window up. A rush of fresh air billowed into the room. Breathing deeply, I raised my arms, stretching as high as I could, letting the air energize me before heading into my workout room.

Every day I went through *Ki No Taiso*, or Three-Minute Exercise, a grounding aikido routine that built and energized my chi. As I closed my eyes and settled my body, I could feel my energy strengthen. My aura flared as I flowed into the dance of movement. Inhaling deeply, I let instinct take over, tuning out everything except what was happening in my body.

As always, the moment my body started moving, I was lost in the exercise. After I finished the three-minute exercise, I transitioned directly into a Pilates workout, concentrating on my stability balls for core-strengthening, and then a lively jaunt on the treadmill finished my workout for the day. After cooling down with some light stretches, I padded back to my bedroom, where I stripped naked and let the breeze wash over my body, luxuriating in its caress. Time for a shower.

Under the pulsating water, I thought about my speech. The title sounded like something out of Godiva, or one of those other numerous soft-porn-masquerading-as-fashion mags. I read several in order to keep up on the latest trends in beauty products, but could never quite shake the feeling I was treading onto sleazy ground.

It wasn't that they discussed sex in frank terms. I liked sex. Sex was good, and I was of the firm belief that I didn't get my fair share. But the way they approached the entire subject of beauty made it sound like the sole purpose was to entrap a man. I wanted to see more self-empowerment articles in the pages, encouraging women to look long and hard at their lives, and to go after their dreams.

After slipping into a gold broomstick skirt and a diaphanous tank top, I hung chandelier earrings from one set of my ear holes and slid delicate little gold hoops into the other set. My bluebell faerie tattoo glowed bright as it wound its way up my left arm. I slid my feet into sky-blue runabouts that complemented the flower's color, then dashed downstairs where I found Aunt Florence making breakfast. She poured me an OJ banana smoothie. I slurped it down as I stood over the sink, then accepted one of the egg-and-ham pitas she'd whipped up.

"You're in a hurry, Imp. Big plans this morning?"

It was my morning off. "I thought I'd hit the library and get a start on that speech you roped me into giving."

She snorted. "You'll do fine, and you know it."

"But Auntie, it just sounds so . . . so . . ."

"So idiotic?"

I glanced up at her and was greeted with a rueful smile. "I wasn't going to put it that way but, yes, now that you mention it. Idiotic . . . lame . . . fluffy."

She finished off her breakfast and patted her lips with

her napkin. "Persia, I don't have to tell you that in this business, sex sells. That's a fact of life that we have to live with. We can use it to our advantage and still try to retain what dignity we can. Do you know why I agreed to sign you up for that speech?"

I shook my head. Other than make my life miserable—which I knew Auntie wasn't looking for—I couldn't figure it out. "Not really. To teach me how to cater to a mind-set of which I don't approve?"

With a sigh, she pushed herself out of her chair and deposited her dish in the sink. "No, though if you really want to run the business, sometimes you have to accept things you'd rather not. I signed you up for that speech because I knew you could actually do justice to the subject. I thought you might be able to elevate fragrance and aromatherapy out of the Beauty Bonanza gutter. You can avoid fluffing it up and yet make the talk interesting and informative."

I stared at the sink, suddenly feeling ungrateful. Here I'd been blaming my aunt for punishing me, when she actually was paying me a compliment. As I watched, a single drop of water dripped onto the skillet and carved a rivulet through the drying egg. I turned on the water, lightly scoured the pan, and stuck it in the dishwasher.

"I never thought of it that way."

She gave me a gentle peck on the cheek. "Sometimes, all it requires is a slight shift in perception to make the world seem a whole lot brighter."

I noticed that she was wearing one of her prettiest mu'umu'us, and then remembered: Kane Jimenez. "You ready for your lunch date?"

She paled slightly, then straightened her shoulders. "As ready as I'll ever be. I'll be gone when you get to the store, but I should be back around two or three. That is, if traffic's light."

For a small city, Gull Harbor had a tremendous gridlock problem during summer, thanks to the tourists. Most of the residents just took it in stride. A small but vocal percentage of the population depended on those tourism dollars to see them through the rest of the year. Locals took the back roads in order to avoid the biggest traffic jams, knowing enough to plan out their trips in advance.

I put my arm around her and squeezed, leaning down to kiss her head. "Auntie, you're wonderful. At least the two of you share a bond through the memory of someone you both loved. That's something not everybody has."

She wiped her eyes and leaned her head against me. "Imp, you are such a treasure. Now go on, scoot, and don't worry about me. I've seen enough of life's storms; I think I can weather the little squalls."

"Okay, then. I'm off. And I'll remember what you said about the speech. That's the only way I think I can make it through!" I grabbed my handbag, laptop, and keys, and headed toward my car. I'd left the top down, and after stowing my gear, hopped over the door into the driver's seat, taking care not to catch my skirt on the gearshift.

I decided to beat the traffic and turned right off of Beachcomber Drive onto Deer Tail Lane. The narrow street wound through some pricey homes that were nestled behind thickets of cedar and fir, and with the top down on my car, the scent of freshly mowed grass assailed my senses, making me want to stop and go wandering through a meadow somewhere. Vowing to get in a walk, if not a swim, before dinner, I took the S curves with ease, coasting to a halt at the stop sign near Johnson's Grocery & Gas.

I glanced at my gas gauge and pulled up to the island.

Climbing out of the car, I adjusted my skirt, making sure it wasn't caught in my underwear as it had a couple of weeks ago, and wandered into the tiny food mart. The Johnson sisters had opened up a burrito and taco bar in the store, and the smells were incredible, even at this time in the morning.

I paid for fifteen dollars' worth of gasoline. Mae Johnson leaned against the wall, wiping her hands on a grease rag. She was an incongruous sight, nearing seventy, with blue-silver curls and a grandma's face, and yet dressed like a grease monkey. She looked happy, though.

"Persia, right early this morning, aren't you?"

I nodded, tucking the change in my purse. "I have some errands to run and thought I'd take the back route to avoid the tourists downtown. How's your sister?"

Mae shook her head. "Emma hasn't been feeling too good lately, but I think it's all that crap she eats." Mae had no trouble calling things as she saw them. "But I told her, 'You go to the doctor, and this time you listen.' She's there right now," she said, glancing at the clock.

I pumped my gas, pulled out my shades—the sun had fully topped the tree line and was promising to chase away the wisps of night clouds that lingered in the sky—and headed for the library.

Two stories high, the Gull Harbor library was, for a small town, extremely well-stocked. The building itself was white brick, sturdy and weatherworn, even though it was barely ten years old. The town planners had voted to keep a coastal feel to the architecture of the city buildings, and so in one way or another, City Hall, the police station, almost every official building resembled a lighthouse or a cove cottage.

I pulled off my sunglasses as I reached for the door. A

rush of cool air swept over me as I entered the foyer, and the hushed sounds of turning pages and gentle conversation rustled through the stacks. I inhaled slowly; the scent of ink and paper from long-forgotten volumes swathed me in a dusty embrace. If I let myself dwell on the fragrance, it was almost as if I could smell the words, the knowledge locked within the volumes.

One wall consisted of floor-to-ceiling windows, the clerestory allowing the natural light to flow in through the building and diffuse the artificial fluorescents that glimmered from the ceiling. A row of carrels lined the back wall, but I chose a table near the window, where I could look out onto the lush lawn dotted with islands of wildflowers and roses.

I settled myself and pulled out my laptop. If I was lucky, I'd be able to knock out the speech by the time I was due at Venus Envy. If not, I'd be working on it this evening as well.

Auntie was right, I decided. Maybe I could offer a few nuggets of real knowledge along with the T & A advice. I plugged in my notebook and opened it, waiting while the machine fired up. Aunt Florence had just bought me the computer a few weeks ago, and I still wasn't used to it, considering most of my writing was limited to entries in my daily journal and my fragrance journal, both of which I wrote in with a Waterman's pen that I bought at the local Barnes & Noble. Neither one of us was comfortable with computers yet, though my friend Jared kept prodding us to take a layman's class at the community college. We kept meaning to, but hadn't got around to it yet.

As I stared at the computer, trying to compose my thoughts, a shadow fell across my screen. I glanced up. Elliot, my ex, was standing beside me.

"Go away," I said, not bothering with niceties. At least he looked sober and reasonably clean, two qualities that, as of late, he had been sorely lacking.

He leaned on the table and tried to read over my shoulder.

I blocked his view by closing the screen.

"Not very friendly, are you? That's no way to greet your long-lost lover," he said, giving me a cow-eyed look.

Great, he was going for the gag-me romance lines today.

"You're not lost, you're no longer my lover, and every time you bother me, you're one step closer to a restraining order. *Ding,* three strikes, you're out."

His eyes narrowed. "Miss Hoity-toity aren't we? All I wanted to do is ask you to come with me to a picnic next week. I've been invited by the guys at work and thought you might want to hang out, have a beer, talk about old times."

He really thought I'd say yes? His logic eluded me. However, I'd discovered the best way to get rid of him was to avoid asking more questions. "Not in a million years. Now, I repeat: Go away."

He leaned in so close I could smell his breath—not a good thing. Though he appeared sober, I could smell the residue of stale beer. "Still playing the bitch, aren't you? I hear you're seeing that spook guy, Bran Stanton? Got news for you, honey. He's never going to measure up to me."

Unable to stomach his presence another moment, I shot out of my chair, throwing him off balance. Elliot sprawled on the floor, narrowly missing hitting his head on a trash basket. Glaring, he picked himself up and brushed off his jeans.

"If by that, you mean Bran's never going to be an

embezzling, lowlife, son of a bitch, then you're right," I
said cheerfully. "He won't measure up to you in that way
because *guess what*? He's not pond scum! Now get the
hell out of my sight." I pulled out my journal and began to
record this little interaction, a procedure that Kyle, the
chief of police with whom I had a vaguely uneasy friendship, had recommended I do.

"By the way," I said, jotting down notes. "This is warning number five: Don't bother me again. Don't talk to me.
Don't come near me. I think we might be getting nearer to
that restraining order, don't you agree?" I flashed him a
snarky smile and, without a word, Elliot turned on his heel
and stomped away.

As I watched him go, I wondered what I'd ever seen in
him to begin with. But this side of him hadn't surfaced all
those years; at least not in ways so I would have recognized it. After he disappeared out the front door, I returned
to my computer, about to begin typing, when my cell
phone rang. I snatched it out of my purse before other pa-
trons could shoot me nasty looks, and flipped it open. It
was Trevor, one of our gardeners from Moss Rose Cottage.

"Hey Trev, what's up?"

"We have a problem with the roses," he said.

"What's wrong?"

"Can you meet me at the shop? It would be easier to ex-
plain there. But I'm afraid we may lose the entire harvest.
I'm not even sure we can save the garden itself."

Oh, hell. That didn't sound good. We depended on our
rose garden for the petals with which we distilled rose
water so pure it could be used in cooking. Venus Envy's
Rose Water Essence was a consistent best seller at the
shop. We couldn't afford to lose an entire crop. I told him

I'd be there in twenty minutes, packed up my laptop, and headed out of the building.

Trevor better be exaggerating, I thought as I pulled out of the parking lot and zoomed down the road toward Venus Envy. If not, then our financial worries had just gotten worse. And right now, money woes were the last thing we needed.

From the Pages of Persia's Journal

Evening in Summer Oil

❧ ❧

When I think about summer fragrances, long walks on dusty evenings come to mind, when dusk is just hitting the shaded lanes. Birds are settling down for the night, and the slight chill of our northwest autumn hasn't quite arrived, but the tang is there, on the horizon, waiting to take over.

And so I came up with Evening in Summer, a custom blend that makes me think of lovers strolling in a garden, of honeysuckle creeping over a gazebo, of ice cream cones and laughing children in the distance.

- Plan an outdoor midsummer's eve party. Invite close friends to stay up and watch for the faeries with you.

- Use Evening in Summer to scent potpourri, and keep several bowls of it around the patio. Use citronella candles to keep mosquitoes away; their fragrance won't interfere with the potpourri and won't add a chemical tang to your party like other insect repellents.

- Decorate with hanging lanterns and luminarias—decorate paper bags with stars and sparkles, fill with sand, and set protected votive candles inside to provide lighting around the edge of your patio. Always keep water on hand for any unexpected emergencies of the fiery kind.

❧ Serve a late tea—watercress and cucumber sandwiches with cream cheese, strawberries dipped in chocolate, salmon mousse and crackers, pâté, sparkling water, champagne punch, and if you are feeling extravagant, caviar.

❧ Play light classical music that inspires thoughts of drowsy evenings and faerie barrows.

❧ Encourage each guest to bring a poem or excerpt from a book that relates to the theme of the party—W. B. Yeats is a good place to start.

Blend and store this oil (as with all oils) in a small, dark bottle. You will need a bottle and stopper or lid, an eyedropper, and the following:

> *1/4 oz. almond or apricot kernel oil*
>   *(a good unscented base)*
> *50 drops silver fir oil*
> *50 drops rose oil*
> *25 drops white camphor oil*
> *15 drops sandalwood oil*
> *10 drops lemon oil*
> *10 drops French vanilla oil*
> *10 drops sweet orange oil*

OPTIONAL:
> *dried rose petals (2, torn in half)*
> *a small piece of garnet or peridot (you can use a chip*
>   *off a gemstone chip necklace)*

Using an eyedropper, add each fragrance oil to the apricot oil, gently swirling after each addition to blend the scent. After adding all the oils, cap and shake gently. At this time, add the rose petals and garnet or peridot to the bottle for added energy, if so desired.

Garnets promote passion and vitality, while peridot is reminiscent of warm summer evenings in a tree-shrouded grove. Keep oil in a cool, dark place—if left in the sun it will lose potency. As always, remind customers to avoid eating or drinking this oil, to check for allergies before using, and to keep it out of reach of children and animals.

Chapter Three

Trevor was waiting at the shop for me, seated on one of the mahogany benches scattered around the store. Venus Envy was a study in tranquillity, with sea green walls and mauve and gold trim. Even the furniture matched the gentle elegance that Auntie had established within the shop.

In his early twenties, Trev was a handsome young man, and a sweetheart, but today he wasn't sporting his usual good-natured grin. As I hurried through the front door, he jumped up and hurried toward me, holding up a paper bag.

"What's that?"

"I don't want to open it out here," he said. "We need to talk, and it better be in private."

Taken aback by his abruptness, I nodded for him to follow me and led him back to the office, where I shut the door behind us and turned on the fan. Hell, I'd forgotten to bring the extra fans I'd promised Tawny. The shop was going to be toast today; the temperature was already climbing into the mid-eighties. "Listen, after you're done, can you run out and pick up three sturdy standing fans and bring them back? Tawny's sweltering out there."

"Sure, but the heat's the least of our problems," he said.

"What's up?" I said. "You said there's trouble with the roses?"

He sighed. "You aren't going to be happy about this, I can tell you that. Where's Miss Florence?"

"She's having lunch with a friend, and I doubt if she'll be back before three, so you're stuck with me, babe. Spill it." I slipped into Auntie's soft leather chair and leaned forward as Trevor opened the sack and withdrew a smaller plastic bag from within. The bag was filled with rose petals. He set it on the desk in front of me. I started to reach for it, but he shook his head.

"Leave it shut, or you'll be sorry. Whatever you do, don't handle those petals," he said.

"Why? What's wrong?"

"Look at them, but don't open it up. Do you see anything suspicious?"

I squinted as I picked up the Ziploc and peered at the roses. There—a thin, white powder crusting some of the petals. "What's on them?"

"Organophosphates. At a dangerously high level. Somebody doctored the entire rose garden with pesticides—probably some form of insecticide. If you used these roses to make rose water, you could make your customers sick." He shook his head. "This wasn't an accident, Persia. Nobody accidentally spills that much pesticide on a plant. Besides, Miss Florence doesn't allow any pesticides on your property."

Pesticides? Auntie had worked for years to build up a natural environment for our flowers that both nurtured them and kept away the pests. We never used sprays of any kind. Our rose water was safe enough to use in baking, if people so desired. This was unthinkable.

"Who the *hell* did this? Auntie's going to be furious when she finds out."

"That's not the half of it, Persia. You're going to have to report this. And when word gets out . . . it's not going to be pretty. You also need to find out if the pesticides have seeped into the soil. At that level, it could taint the dirt for quite awhile. I'm pretty sure that all the bushes are affected. After I stopped to get the results this morning, I went back to Moss Rose and had a look at the rest of the rose garden. I'm almost certain that the entire crop was doctored."

He looked sick. Trevor took great pride in his work; he was a wonderful gardener, and both Auntie and I valued his contributions to our store. Without his help, we wouldn't have half the bulk herbs and floral waters that we sold.

"Well, hell. Auntie is going to be beside herself. She worked her butt off to make those gardens what they are. You should know, you worked right along beside her."

He nodded. "Yeah, and that's why I know this was deliberate. While I was there today, I did some checking. There's not a single container of this crap in any of the sheds, so whoever did it took the evidence with them."

I sighed. "How did you find out?" Or rather, I thought, *Thank heaven he'd found out.* If we'd gone ahead and processed the roses without knowing, we would not only have ruined our reputation, but we would have endangered customers. Or worse.

He opened his notebook and tossed a paper on the desk. "Here's the official analysis. I have a friend who works in a lab in town. When I was harvesting the floribundas two days ago, I noticed that my eyes and hands were burning.

And then i saw a crystalline residue on some of the petals. I thought something was up, but didn't want to worry you until I knew for sure. So I asked Dave to examine a sample from several rosebushes, and he had this waiting for me this morning. Organophosphates, in a high concentration."

I picked up the report and studied it, grateful for my background in botany. Organophosphates were highly toxic to humans and animals, and most often found in insecticides and pesticides. A number of them were under review by the EPA, but the government worked so slowly that it would probably be years before the majority were phased out. In high enough concentrations, they were deadly. And the levels that Trevor's friend Dave had found on the roses was dangerously high. If we'd processed these petals into rose water and somebody used it in their baking, we could have been looking at a disaster, both for whoever ate it and for our store. Even skin contact at this level was bound to cause irritation.

"Christ, this is bad," I dropped the report on the desk and glanced over at Trevor. "Are you okay? You handled those flowers."

He nodded. "I went to the doctor. Though I've got a rash and some burning, I was lucky. I stopped once I noticed the residue. But Persia, if the roses were tampered with, what about the rest of the grounds? We're going to have to go through every single garden to find out if anything else was touched. Including the herbs."

I stared at him, my understanding growing. This could have a considerable impact on Venus Envy's livelihood. If the roses were the only thing hurt, we could probably manage to get out of this without a major disaster, unless the soil was contaminated. If there were other casualties in our gardens ... I didn't want to think about what that might signify.

I glanced at the clock. Now, not only did I have to write that stupid speech and get my appointments out of the way, but I had to start figuring out what to do to cope with the current disaster. Auntie was going to need all the help she could get on this one. Or rather, I corrected myself, *we* were going to need all the help we could get. I was, after all, almost a partner.

"As soon as Auntie gets back, I'll talk to her. Meanwhile, call Sarah and let her know what's going on, then the two of you examine the rest of the gardens. Don't overlook anything. In fact, I'm just going to make the decision that we should have samples from each garden tested. If your friend Dave can do it within the next few days, all the better. Be sure to wear protective clothing. I don't want either you or Sarah dropping dead on me. Got it?"

He nodded. "Are you going to call the police?"

"Yeah, but I'll wait till Auntie comes back. No doubt Kyle will have questions for all of us, and I want Auntie here when he comes over."

"Who do you think could have done this?" Trev asked, pushing himself out of his chair, the look on his face gloomy.

I gazed into his eyes. "Trevor, I have a good idea of who might be behind it, but there's no way to prove anything. So I'm going to wait until we talk to Kyle to voice my suspicions. But you and Sarah, keep an eye out for anybody wandering our property. Maybe it's time we got a guard dog. Beast fancies himself one, but he's about as ferocious as a three-week-old puppy."

"Have you thought about fencing in the property? It would cost you plenty, but it might be a good idea. Right now there are any number of ways people can sneak onto your land."

We had thirty acres; there were always going to be ways people could gain access to our gardens. But maybe we were making it too easy. "I'll mention the idea to Auntie. As soon as she's back from her lunch, we'll head out to the house and meet you and Sarah there. I'll call before we leave."

As Trevor took off, leaving the bag of petals and the lab report with me, my thoughts turned immediately to the most likely culprit. Bebe Wilcox. It had to be her. Why she was so hell-bent on running us out of business, I wasn't sure. Maybe it was simply that we were stiff competition, and our merchandise was far higher quality than hers. Whatever the case, the attack on our roses was tantamount to industrial sabotage, and neither Auntie nor I were of the nature to let the matter drop.

I slipped out into the main shop and motioned to Tawny. As soon as she finished ringing up Mrs. Gentry, she made her way over to where I was standing, out of earshot of any customers who might be wandering by.

"Tawny, we've got a bit of an emergency on hand. I want you to cancel my appointments for today. Call them, make some excuse, just don't let them think anything's wrong."

"Nobody died, did they?" She glanced nervously at the back of the store, and I laughed gently, shaking my head. She'd never quite got over the fact that I'd found a body in the shop a few months back. "No, nobody died, but we have a crisis out at the gardens."

She glanced through the appointment book. "Juanita Lopez is probably on her way—she's due here in less than ten minutes. You want me to try her home number? She doesn't have a cell phone."

Juanita was one of my favorites. "No, I'll take care of her, but call everyone else, and do it right now. Leave messages if you can't reach them. And the minute Aunt Florence comes in, tell her I need to talk to her. Immediately."

ॐ

Juanita Lopez was not the woman she'd been a few months ago when she feared her husband was cheating on her. One of the lucky ones, she'd discovered the supposed affair was all in her imagination, and with the help of a fragrance oil I'd blended for her and a lot of work on her self-esteem, she'd blossomed from a woman worrying about wrinkles to the epitome of confidence and contentment. She'd changed from jeans and tee shirts to pantsuits, and now an elegant but simple application of makeup graced her face instead of the brilliant sheen of pink lipstick she used to wear. Her hands were still rough from the work she did, but she held her head high, and her eyes sparkled.

"Juanita, you're positively glowing! Have a seat. What can I do for you today?" If I hadn't been so worried about the roses, I would have been happy to see her. Over the months, Juanita and I'd developed an easy friendship.

She winked at me. "Give me a new fragrance, Persia. I still have half a bottle of Narcissus Dreaming, but I want something a little lighter and more playful—and I also want it in a custom blend of bath salts and lotion."

"Summer fragrance," I murmured, knowing exactly what she meant. I'd concocted Narcissus Dreaming for her when she feared for her marriage, and it had been perfect to elevate her mood and strengthen her perception of herself, but the scent was too heavy for the summer heat.

I pulled out my oils. Summer was all about the beach and waves and salt spray and strolling along the pier. But Juanita's body chemistry couldn't carry a crisp, breezy fragrance. I turned my thoughts away from the water toward the long, shady lanes that skirted the island, the parks and dusky evenings during which couples strolled hand in hand.

Starting with a base of apricot oil, I added an undertone of silver fir, then heady amounts of white camphor and rose. After that came a subtle but spicy mix of top notes: sandalwood, French vanilla, lemon, and sweet orange. One whiff told me it was perfect. I dabbed a drop on her wrists, asking her to walk around the shop for five minutes in order to get a clear idea of how the fragrance would blend with her body chemistry.

When she returned, she was lit up brighter than the rays of sun glinting through the arched windows over the door. "I love it! And so will my husband."

"You wanted that in bath salts and lotion?" I asked.

She nodded. "Yes, and could you add a cologne base to this so I can use it as a spray? I like oils for winter, but in summer . . ."

"Not a problem." I blended the oil into a cologne base and poured it in a spray bottle, labeled it Evening in Summer, then wrote up her order and invoice. "I'm in a bit of a time crunch. I don't think I can have the bath salts and lotion ready before Wednesday. Will that be okay?"

"Of course," she said, giving me a quick hug, after which she took her order to the counter, paid Tawny, and left.

I glanced at my watch, wondering just how long Auntie was going to be. Might as well use the time to work on the speech, I thought, but had to nix that plan before I could make it halfway to the office. Sharon Wellstone breezed into the shop, stopping me in my tracks.

Whoa. Sharon had been our model for the life-sized replica of *The Birth of Venus* that covered one entire wall of the shop, and her voluptuous figure was usually draped in a chiffon floral dress, nipped in at the waist and tied with a satin ribbon. Likewise, she usually wore her shining blonde hair held back by a wide velvet band. The ultimate Stepford Wife, albeit sexier than the all-American-woman image. But today, Sharon looked anything but dreamy.

Poured into a butt-hugging, thigh-showing, boob-boosting power suit, she carried a nifty briefcase—the type that turns into a shoulder bag. Her hair had been swept up into a chignon held by two black lacquer chopsticks, but it pulled at her temples, giving her that taut, face-lift look of surprise. I didn't quite know what to say as she quick-stepped her way up to me, her heels tapping smartly against the floor. The noise made me regret the fact that Auntie had taken up the carpet a month ago and had tile laid in its place.

"Persia! I'm so glad to see you!" Her voice had taken on a burr, and her enthusiasm immediately set me on edge. Usually I found Sharon congenial, but I wasn't up for perky today.

"Sharon, you look so . . . different." When in doubt, find a neutral word.

Just as I hoped, she took it as a compliment. "Thank you! I love my new look. It really suits me, don't you think?"

I didn't think, but refrained from commenting. "What can I do for you? A new fragrance to match your new style?"

She glanced around. "Persia, is your aunt around?"

"Still out to lunch, I think. Why, did you need to talk to her about something?"

A canny look crept into her eyes. "No, actually I wanted to talk to you. Have you given any thought to your future?"

My future? What was she doing, selling insurance? I cleared my throat. "I've made arrangements; I have my will, as well as all the insurance I need to cover emergencies or accidents."

Confusion flashed across her face for a moment, then understanding. She shook her head and laughed with a light, almost giddy giggle. "No, no—I'm not trying to sell you anything."

Good thing, I thought, because with that getup and her new persona, I doubted if Sharon Wellstone would have many takers unless it was to a lonely man looking for a bit of thigh with his policy.

"Can we sit down?" she asked.

I glanced at the clock. "I'm sorry, I'm so busy—"

"Please! This will only take a moment."

With a sigh, I led her to my station and motioned for her to take a seat. "What's up?" As she leaned over the counter, I began to tidy up, straightening my brochures, card, and fragrance journal.

Her eyes glittered with an unnatural brilliance, and I thought she might be high on something. "We want you."

Huh? What the hell was she talking about? Not amused, I shook my head. "I don't have time for riddles, Sharon. What are you talking about? Get to the point, please."

She flushed as her words tumbled out like boulders caught in a rockslide. "I belong to Bebe's Belles as a sales associate and HR person. Bebe wanted me to recruit you. Your expertise with fragrance isn't going unnoticed in this town, nor in Seattle, either. You've made a name for yourself, and Bebe's interested in negotiating a contract with *you*." She settled back, a triumphant look on her face. There was something else there, but I couldn't quite catch it. Envy? Irritation? Whatever it was, the look vanished, and she beamed again, her smile not rising to meet her eyes. "I promise, it will be worth your time."

What the hell? "Sorry, not interested. I have no intention of stabbing my aunt in the back, and I would have hoped you'd realize that, but apparently I was wrong. Now, if you'll excuse me, I've got work to attend to—"

"Think about it before you answer," Sharon said, standing. Her gaze flickered over my station, over the store. "Venus Envy's on the way down. And this is the kind of opportunity women long for. It could totally change your life. Get in with the right people, and your career will skyrocket. If you brought your lines over to Bebe's, we would start advertising immediately. We could really get your name out there."

I pushed aside my fragrance journal, wanting nothing more than to kick her butt out the door, but I managed to keep my voice even. "Asking me to betray my aunt is pretty much the last thing I ever expected to hear out of your mouth. I suggest you turn around and walk out the door before I tell you just where you can shove your offer, because my patience is wearing thin."

"I can't believe you'd pass this up. Think of the money you could make." Sharon seemed miffed, but did I detect a slight hint of triumph behind her effervescent voice? Whatever the case, she was breathing so hard that the material across the front of her jacket strained, and I had a nerve-racking vision of buttons popping and boobs exploding out of the push-up bra she'd crammed them into.

"I choose to keep discussions of my monetary situation

between me and my banker. And my loyalty isn't for sale."
As I turned to leave, she dashed around the counter and
caught my arm. I firmly grasped her hand and applied a little force, and she paled and let go.

"One last chance, Persia. You're going to be sorry you
turned us down. We're offering you a chance to grow, to
become a major force in the fragrance industry."

I whirled on her. "At whose expense would that be? The
expense of Venus Envy? Of my aunt and our relationship?" I jabbed her shoulder with my finger, not hard
enough to hurt her, but enough to startle her into taking a
step back. "Aunt Florence raised me as her own daughter.
Yet you suggest I just toss her aside? I wouldn't work for
you if I was out on my ass in the pounding rain." I pointed
to the door. "You'd better go."

Her cheerful demeanor disappeared like hot dogs at a
Super Bowl party. She grimly shouldered her bag. "You're
making a mistake, Persia. We're going to put Venus Envy
out of business, and if you're still here when that happens,
good luck in finding a new job. If you come to your senses,
give me a call, and I might be able to talk Bebe into re-
considering."

And with that, she hightailed it out of the store.

Disconcerted, I motioned to Tawny. "I'll be in the office. Send Auntie in as soon as she gets here."

On my way to the office, I couldn't help but wonder just
who had applied that insecticide to our rosebushes. Could
it have been Sharon? One of her cronies? Or was it Bebe
Wilcox herself? I wanted to call Kyle, but Auntie needed
to hear about this first.

An hour later, I had about one hundred words written,
and was thoroughly depressed. I couldn't get the problem
with the roses off my mind, but the conference started

tomorrow—on Saturday—and my speech was scheduled for Sunday. I'd better get on the ball. I sighed, knuckled down to work, and wrote an outline, highlighting the points on which I'd touch.

The use of scent harkened back to basic biology. Pheromones produced by insects and animals were the love potions of the natural world, drawing together those seeking romance and reproduction. Unfortunately for some of the creatures, their love code had been broken and mimicked by others in order to catch an unwary, love-struck dinner. Ants seemed to have particularly bad luck in this area.

And plants played their own form of deception. A few species of orchids—tropical in nature—had broken the code of wasps, inviting the creatures into a bizarre mating attempt that succeeded only in helping the orchids pollinate one another as the frenzied males went from flower to flower, seeking gratification.

While the existence of human pheromones was still in question, hormonal responses had been noted in experiments done to stimulate menstruation in women, whose cycles notoriously swung into synch when exposed to other females on a daily basis. However, since nature's romantic calling card definitely existed in insect and mammal populations, it was probably only a matter of time before biologists discovered the secret within our own human realm. Until then, all the pheromone-promising perfumes worked on what was, most likely, a psychological level, since it wasn't clear just what type of pheromones the companies were using.

I paused, leaning back in my chair as I stared at the words on the screen. Would my audience be interested in all this? I'd have to jazz it up, of course, anthropomorphize the ants and wasps and orchids, but when speaking about fragrance and desire, there was no way to avoid the subject of pheromones. Not unless I wanted to go for pure fluff. The world of scent was so complex, so incredibly intricate, that a two-hour lecture wouldn't even touch on the basics.

It was easy to discuss fragrances that had specific correlations. *This perfume has undertones of vanilla,* or *that perfume has a top note of roses and lilies.* But then we got into more esoteric discussions—what does a freshly mown lawn smell like? What does grass smell like? There, vocabulary lagged and inevitably the conversation fell into comparisons. Cut grass smelled like sunshine. What did sunshine smell like? Warm, yellow chiffon.

The intercom buzzed, startling me out of my thoughts. It was Tawny, telling me that Auntie was on her way back. I sighed, dreading the upcoming conversation. I saved my file and shut down the laptop. As the door opened and Auntie came in, a quizzical look on her face, I vacated her chair and motioned for her to sit.

"You'd better sit down. I've got something to tell you, and it isn't good." As I launched into the news about the roses, the look on her face changed from puzzled to angry, and I knew we'd just entered a war.

Chapter Four

As I sped along Beachcomber Drive, the top of my convertible down to allow the breeze and sun to pour in, I hoped to hell that Kyle would take our complaints seriously. The chief of police was stubborn, and usually he managed to irritate the hell out of me, but I had to give the man credit. He wasn't blind, and he wasn't stupid. The official report from the lab would help. Both it and the tainted rose petals sat in the passenger seat of my car, held down by my purse to keep them from blowing away.

Auntie had been furious, after the shock wore off. She immediately called Kyle and informed him that he should meet us at our house as soon as possible. Then, while she talked to Tawny, I called Trevor.

"How'd she take it?" Trevor asked.

"You know that steamroller look she gets?"

He grunted. Everybody in town knew when Auntie went on the warpath. When she was angry, nobody went up against her. Nobody until Bebe Wilcox, that is. "Yeah, so you guys on your way?"

"We'll be there in fifteen minutes. Both you and Sarah stay put until we arrive. We've called Kyle and he'll be over in awhile."

I grabbed my keys and purse.

Tawny waved me out. "Your aunt's taken off already."

Sure enough, by the time I jumped in my Sebring, Auntie was already on her way, with Baby smoking up the road.

As I pulled into the driveway, I noticed that Kyle hadn't arrived yet. I headed around back, where I found Auntie, Trevor, and Sarah standing in the middle of the rose garden, staring at one of the bushes. Some of the roses had burnt edges on the petals, others looked good, but a faint crystalline powder was visible if you looked very close.

Our rose gardens covered over two acres and were filled with all different colors, both antique and hybrids. We had been thinking of selling some at the shop, but that was out of the question now.

I poked at the roses, frowning. "Have you had a chance to look through the other gardens to see if they're contaminated?"

Trevor nodded. "Yeah, but I can't tell by looking at most of them. I'm hoping that if I can't see residue, there won't be any, but don't go by my word. You need to have everything tested."

"Well, this just takes all," Auntie said. "Trevor, take clippings from every garden on our land to your friend's lab today. Tell him to run whatever tests he needs to and to run them stat."

"Already done." He held up a box of baggies he'd tagged with labels showing what the plants were and where they were gathered from. "I also gathered soil samples from around the acreage. If you don't want any contamination, there can't be any residue in the dirt."

Auntie glanced at her watch. "Kyle's supposed to be here any minute, but he's late, as usual. Why don't you run those over to the lab, then head straight back? The sooner we get the results, the better. We need to know exactly what we're facing."

"Sure thing, Miss Florence." Trevor picked up the box and took off.

Auntie gazed at the roses sadly. "This is just horrible. Sarah, I need you to come in this weekend and help Trevor uproot every plant. We simply can't take a chance of those chemicals leaching into the soil. I hate to think about it, but we're going to have to replace every rosebush we own."

"That's going to run a pretty penny," I said.

Sarah scuffed the ground with one of her Birkenstocks. "I know this isn't the best time, but I have to leave tonight. I'm going to Chehalis this afternoon and won't be around tomorrow. I'll be back Sunday though." At Auntie's look, she added, "There's a llama show, and I have to pick up some new breeding stock."

I sighed. Sometimes I rued the day Auntie had hired Sarah. She was a wonderful employee in many ways, but running her own business was starting to compete for her time. She was skimping on her hours and wasn't even getting in twelve out of the twenty she'd promised to give us. It wasn't that I begrudged her success, but it was becoming apparent that her loyalties were divided.

One look at Auntie's face told me she wasn't pleased.

"Sarah, we have to get rid of those roses," Aunt Florence said. "And we have to do it before the weather changes. We can't count on the sun. Why, if we had a good rain, it would make a mess of things. Trevor can't do all the work by himself. If you skip out on us, Persia and I are going to be out here in the middle of the night digging up flower bushes. And I'm too old to be out here with a shovel."

Sarah grimaced. "I know I'm putting you in a spot—"

Auntie interrupted. "Why didn't you bring this up earlier? At least then we would have had prior warning."

"I would have," Sarah said, blushing. "It's just that . . . I've been having some problems at home, and I forgot. If I don't go to the show on Saturday, all the best stock will be taken."

I squinted, shading my eyes from the light with my hand. The sound of a car in the front yard told me that Kyle had just pulled in. Either that, or we had unexpected company.

Auntie let out a large sigh of exasperation. "Go then, if you must. But Sarah, you need to think about what your job with us means to you. We simply can't make do with one gardener every time you decide you need some time off. I hired you part-time, on the agreement that you'd be here twenty hours a week. This week, you've logged about eight, according to Trevor."

Oh boy, Auntie was ticked. Sarah knew it, too, but she just ducked her head and nodded. "Thanks, Miss Florence. I'll try to do better." She stripped off her gloves and tossed them in the cart. "Let me know what happens with those tests!" Her voice trailed behind her as she jogged down the path toward the front of the house.

I dared a glance at my aunt. Thunderclouds. Not good.

Auntie crossed her arms. "What do you think we should do about her?"

She was asking me? I grimaced. "I have no idea, though I'm tempted to say we need to replace her."

"The reason being?" she asked. I knew that Aunt Florence wasn't being contrary. She was testing me and truly wanted to know my reasons. She'd been doing this more frequently as she handed over more control of the shop.

I sighed. "I don't know whether we can rely on her anymore. The problem has been getting worse as the summer's progressed. I suppose . . . we could hire another part-time gardener and cut down Sarah's hours?"

Auntie shook her head. "You'd only prolong the problem. If Sarah truly isn't pulling her weight anymore, what should we do?"

My voice dry, I whispered, "Fire her?"

"That's what a good businesswoman would do." She patted me on the shoulder. "Don't feel so bad, Persia. Sarah's hinted to me that she's thinking of expanding her business to full-time. I've been expecting a resignation any day now. Rather than fire her, tell her we need her to put in more hours. My guess is that she'll gather her courage and quit. That way she won't have a termination on her record. If she accedes to the extra hours, make sure she knows we expect her to be on the ball."

"Do you want me to talk to her?"

Auntie gave me a gentle smile. "You are in charge of the gardens, so you oversee the gardeners. If this was Tawny, I'd do the dirty work, but I think you need to take the reins on this one."

I let out a long breath. "I'll talk to her as soon as she gets back."

Just then, Kyle came striding down the path. "Sorry I'm late. I thought you were going to meet me in the backyard," he said. "It took me a few minutes to figure out where you were." He was covered with dust, and cobwebs clung to his back.

"You seriously need a lint brush, Kyle. What the hell have you been doing?" I blurted out. "Creeping around in somebody's basement?"

He ran his hand through his hair. "You're close. I was over at Mary Margaret's house."

Mary Margaret was Gull Harbor's official cat lady, and a recluse. She was also the sister of Eva, my ex-nanny, although I knew the two had endured some sort of falling out years ago, shortly before Eva left Gull Harbor to marry her sweetheart.

Mary had twenty cats. All were well cared for, but she lived in a house that should have been condemned long ago. On the few occasions my aunt and I'd dropped over, stacks of newspapers had filled the rooms, along with boxes of unopened merchandise that blocked all but the narrowest of walkways through the high-ceilinged chambers of the broken-down Victorian.

"Did Suzy call you?" Auntie asked. Suzy was Mary Margaret's daughter, and every now and then she called Kyle when she hadn't heard from her mother for awhile. Mary Margaret was a little touched in the head; she wouldn't let anybody from her immediate family set foot in the house because she thought they were out to kill her so they could inherit her "fortune." My aunt and her friends took round-robin turns visiting, making sure Mary had everything she needed and that she was okay.

Kyle glanced at Auntie. "Actually, Mary Margaret called me herself. I had to break in through the front door, then crawl through all that dust-laden crap in order to find her."

Auntie paled. "Is she okay?"

He sighed, then shook his head. "Mary had a mild stroke. I called nine-one-one, and the paramedics took her to the hospital. She'll probably be all right, but she can't go home for awhile, and she's asked me to find someone to look after her cats. I'm thinking this would be a good time to have the humane society take a look at the animals and make sure they're all okay. I don't think Mary's a typical hoarder, but we want to make sure everything's on the up and up."

Auntie leaned against one of the fence posts and fanned herself. "You might also call the health department to take a look at Mary's house—she really needs some psychiatric help, Kyle. The woman's a compulsive spender, and I'll bet you she's gone through her life savings buying crap from the TV shopping channels. I'm afraid there might be toxic mold in the house, or hobo spider nests, or something else equally nasty."

Kyle's cell phone rang, and Auntie paused for a moment while he moved aside to take the call. In the sunlight that glimmered down through the trees and foliage, a bevy of jays let loose with a scolding chorus, and I closed my eyes for a moment, trying to find a little peace of mind for the day. Fridays were supposed to be good, but today had been a rotten way to end the week.

When Kyle returned, he apologized for the interruption. "That was my office. We're trying to line up help for Mary, but social services won't act until they know her income, and she hasn't a clue what her assets are."

Auntie nodded. "I don't think you're going to have an easy time finding out, either. I know the pastor of Mary's church—Reverend Timothy Layton. I'll contact him and see what they can do. Meanwhile, I suggest you call Nanny-Goat's Pet Sitting Service for the cats. They're reliable and bonded." She gave him a rueful grin. "Tell them I'll cover the cost if she can't. At least for now."

Kyle jotted everything down in his notebook, looking relieved. "Thanks, Miss Florence. Now, what can I do for you?"

Trevor appeared at the head of the trail, and we motioned for him to join us. Once we were all together, Trevor ran down what he'd found out about the roses, and I showed Kyle the lab report.

"This has to be a malicious act. It destroyed our entire crop. In fact, we're going to have to replace every bush we have," I said.

"You don't think it could have been teens out for kicks?"

"Using toxic doses of insecticide? Come on, Kyle. I could see vandalism from a group of bored kids if they had ripped the flowers off the stems, or if they'd TP'd the trees, but to deliberately apply a near-fatal dose of insecticide to our roses? That isn't a prank. That's downright dangerous, and fits right in with the other crap that's been going on."

"What's the 'other crap' that you're talking about?" Kyle's brow furrowed.

We told him about Bebe's Boutique and the rumors they'd been spreading about our shop. "And, Auntie doesn't even know this yet, but today, Sharon Wellstone tried to steal me away from Venus Envy to go work at Bebe's—the actual company, not the boutique. They want me to hand over my fragrance lines to their company. Sharon threatened that they had every intention of shutting down our store, whatever way it takes."

Auntie gaped. "I had no idea they'd go that far."

At her worried look, I reached out and patted her arm. "Well, I had a mouthful for her, believe me."

Kyle sighed. "I'll see what I can find out, but I can't promise much. We don't have a lot to go on. Meanwhile, if I were you, I'd consider fencing in the rest of your property and getting a guard dog." He flipped his notebook shut and shoved it back in his pocket.

Auntie closed her eyes and let out a small sigh. Then, forcing a smile to her face, she said, "Thank you, Kyle. At least we've reported it. Meanwhile, since both you and Trevor are here, I want to invite you to a barbecue I'm planning for tomorrow evening."

Trevor licked his lips. "Sounds good to me. Would you mind if I bring Cindy Andrews? She and I are . . . we're kind of seeing each other now, I'd be happy to pay for the extra food."

With a "Tsk, tsk," Auntie shook her head. "Don't you worry about the cost. We'd love to meet her."

Trevor flashed her a grateful smile. "I'll be at the shed if you need me. I want to get started on digging up these flowers. I hate to do it, but you're right, we have to get them out of here before any of the insecticide has a chance to leach into the soil." He frowned, staring at the ground around the roses. "That is, if it hasn't already managed to." With a quick shrug, he took off, jogging down the path.

Auntie turned to Kyle. "What about you? Can you make it to our shindig?"

He grinned. "Wouldn't miss your barbecued burgers for anything, Miss Florence. I'll be here with bells on." He took the bag of roses and the lab report for evidence and headed toward the front of the house.

After he left, I glanced at Auntie. "You know I invited Bran tomorrow night. Those two will be butting heads all evening." Kyle wasn't happy about the fact that I chose to date Bran over him. First, he'd lost me to his cousin in junior high, and then hadn't been thrilled when I'd politely rebuffed his renewed attempts after I moved back to Gull Harbor.

Auntie shrugged. "You made your choice. Kyle has to live with it."

I sighed. Maybe it sounded simple, but the fact was that whenever the two were in the same room, sparks flew, and they weren't the kind that made my knees weak. "Let's talk about something else for awhile. Why don't we go get some iced tea and cookies, and you can tell me about your lunch with Kane," I said, putting my arm around her shoulder, and we headed back to the house.

❦

"Well, Imp, going to that lunch was one of the hardest things I've had to do in a long while. I almost didn't go in, but then I thought, *Kane's waiting for me, and I can't just stand him up.*"

The refrigerator hummed as Auntie filled two glasses with crushed ice. I stirred the tea I'd made that morning, added sugar and lemon, and poured it over the ice. Cool beads of condensation trickled down my hand as I settled in at the table, waiting for Auntie to join me.

"Are you okay?"

She joined me, a pensive look on her face. "It was good to see Kane again. Even with all the intervening years, he still looks so much like Keola. At first it was hard, but after a few minutes it got easier. Kane is a fine man, but he's not my Keola, and I was able to separate the two in my mind, and my heart, once we got to talking. We had a good lunch and caught up on the intervening years. He does make me miss the islands. But at first, when he walked through that door . . . Oh, Imp, it brought back all the memories."

I took her hand in mine. "You've never loved anybody else, have you? Not in that way."

With a little shake of the head, she said, "Never. With Keola, it was like tumbling off a tall building. I was afraid, but I couldn't help it. The first day we met, I thought he was nice. The second, I thought he might make a fun date. The third, I decided I was going to marry him. It took him several months to catch up, but he did, and on our six months' anniversary, he proposed. We were engaged for a year. Then it was all over, just like it had never happened. His family wanted me to stay in touch, but I couldn't. Kane, though, he kept tabs on me. Eventually I began writing back."

"And you never met anybody else?"

"No, not really. I dated, but nothing special ever came of anyone I met. And I didn't need to get married. I'd inherited a tidy sum from my grandfather when he passed over, and I'd learned from my father how to make money work for me. I invested wisely and, well, here I am. Sixty-four and suddenly facing a past that I had hoped to forget."

She stared at the table for a moment. "They say you can't run away from your pain; I guess it caught up to me after all these years." And with that, she smiled, and I knew the subject had been dismissed. "Tell me, other than the roses and Sharon, how did the day go? Did you get your speech written?"

"Almost. I'll finish it up tonight. Are you hungry? I was thinking of ordering pizza for dinner."

"Go ahead, child. I think lunch will keep me, and if I'm hungry later, I can make myself a sandwich. I'm going to call Winthrop and let him know what's been going on. If we ever get to the point where we can file charges, he needs to know in advance what's happened." She paused on her way to the den. "By the way, I invited Kane to the barbecue tomorrow night."

I smiled, but she merely twitched her lip and left the room.

~

Delilah woke me up at seven by tapping my face with her paw—her claws ever so gently extended—until I opened my eyes. She was quite the curmudgeon, and even though we'd finally made peace, she delighted in playing games with me that were more for her amusement than mine. The minute I opened my eyes, she bounced away, happy as could be.

I rummaged through my closet. What to wear? Something cool but professional. I didn't want to look stodgy or—worse—even remotely resemble one of Bebe's Belles. I finally decided on a gauze skirt that fell about three inches above my knees and a mint green tank top with a matching sheer silk shirt over the top. Cool, and yet not overexposed. Flirty, but professional enough to get by. I slipped on three-inch spiked sandals, and packed a pair of black jeans and a crop top in my bag in case I wanted to change later, then headed for the kitchen, where I polished off the last of the cold pizza for breakfast, along with a pint of fresh strawberries.

By the time I made it downtown, the streets were starting to fill out, but it was still early, and I managed to find a parking spot in front of the shop. Venus Envy was quiet. I glanced at the clock. Tawny wouldn't arrive for another half hour.

Auntie and I'd packed the samples in sturdy quilted tote bags. I slung two of them over my shoulders, and then picked up the remaining two and lugged them out to the car. They were heavy, filled to the brim with trial-sized bottles of oils, lotions, bath salts, creams, and other goodies. We weren't looking to make a lot of sales at the convention, so much as to expose potential buyers to our lines. Hence, small samples that we could give away or sell for minimal cost.

As I stowed away the bags and locked the trunk, a tantalizing array of smells drifted out of the Baklava or Bust Bakery to capture my attention. I glanced over at the bakery. The stress over facing the upcoming convention and speech left me with an unusual craving for sweets. Hmm, we'd need fuel for the day, I thought, dashing through the door.

Dorian was behind the counter; he waved when he saw me. "I thought Barbara was supposed to meet you at the convention center?"

"I had to pick up the sample cases, and in the process, I smelled cookies." I grinned. "I see Barb finally talked you into a haircut." His shaggy locks had been transformed; now he sported a smoother cut, like Tom Selleck's hair in *Magnum P.I.* And his five o'clock shadow had disappeared along with the tangle of curls. "Shaved your beard, too?"

He raised an eyebrow. "My darling wife threatened to call Mama Konstantinos and tell her that I refused to shave or brush my hair."

Good way to bluff, I thought. The only reason Barbara would ever willingly call Dorian's mother was if her news would be a thorn in Mama Konstantinos's side. In that case, she'd dial the phone and grin from ear to ear as she dropped the bomb on her meddling mother-in-law. But apparently Dorian hadn't realized that after all these years, and the threat worked.

"Well, you look great. Give me a dozen peanut butter

cookies, would you?" I pulled out my wallet, fished out a
ten dollar bill, and handed it to him.

He handed me the bag and my change. "A baker's
dozen, as always, and one for the road. Tell my lovely wife
I miss her."

I promised to deliver the message and blew Dorian a
kiss. Time for the conference, as much as I dreaded the
thought.

⁂

The temperature was climbing as I hugged the curves on
Seguamish Road. When I passed by Willow Wand An-
tiques, the thermometer on their reader board stood at a
balmy seventy-three. I coasted down the slope toward the
beach to a four-way stop, where I turned right onto Dego-
bar Drive.

Another block saw me to the valet entrance of the Red
Door Convention Center, which was conveniently located
on the waterfront, a mere three blocks from the ferry ter-
minal. A spacious six-story hotel with valet parking and a
four-star restaurant, the Red Door was home to most of the
conventions and VIPs who journeyed to Gull Harbor.

The doors were actually lipstick red with gold trim,
while the hotel itself sported a modern look in polished
marble facade. I shook my head at the bellboy's offer of
help; Auntie had impressed on me not to trust anybody
with the sample cases. Anyway, by the time I gave the
valet my car key, Barb appeared at my side. She gathered
up two of the bags, and I swung the other two over my
shoulder, along with my hobo bag.

"How do you do it?" she asked. "Your hair is in perfect
shape—and the wind's up."

I grinned. "Try a braid so tight it makes you wince," I said, swinging my butt-length braid around to show her.

She grimaced. "I think I'll stick with hair spray. I haven't got enough hair to braid, anyway." She tried for a smile, and I glanced at her head. She'd done a remarkable job hiding the atrocious cut. The spikes were nowhere to be seen. Instead, she'd smoothed it back into a sleek, head-hugging style and lacquered it with enough hair spray to hold an army in place. Two glittering green combs, one on either side, took the eye's focus away from the calico color.

I galvanized myself as we approached the door. "So, how bad does it seem? Is it as awful as I was afraid of?" I dreaded going in, already imagining a buzzing foyer filled with wild-eyed cosmeticians, anorexic models, overzealous saleswomen, and dozens of start-ups eager to home in on the market.

"Bad enough," Barb said. "This is going to be a long two days."

As she fell in beside me, I winced. She smelled like a brothel gone bad. "Barb, I hate to tell you this, but that perfume reeks to high heaven. What on earth is it? It's not one of mine, that's for sure."

She coughed. "I am not wearing any of yours. I'm wearing six perfumes, to be precise, including the one I arrived in. I've already been spritzed five times by crazed testers. They're hiding all over in there, waiting to pounce. I tried to fend them off, but they spray and run." She shook her head. "I smell like a skunk, and I know it."

Great. Given my hyperactive nose, the next few days were going to play hell on my olfactory senses. I'd probably end up with a massive sinus headache. As we approached the door, the doorman—in a red and gold uniform—opened it for us. I steeled my nerves and, resigned, plowed through into the foyer.

The lobby of the Red Door was a bustling network of women—with a few men mixed in for good measure. Women in starched white coats, women in floral dresses, women in power career suits, women who could only be models drifting through in a breeze of gauze and linen.

The lobby had been decked out with gold and red ribbons hanging from the ceiling. The registration and information tables were covered in red cloths trimmed with gold lace. And over the double doors leading into the main convention hall hung a huge banner that read, Beauty Bonanza Cosmetics Convention Welcomes You to the Red Door! The letters were red on white, with a golden halo, and paintings of what I could only assume were supposed to be lipsticks and eye shadows scattered in a haphazard manner around the banner.

What the hell had Aunt Florence gotten me into? I could be home now, working with Trevor, taking care of a real problem.

"Persia? Persia?"

"Huh?" I said, startled.

Barb nudged me with her elbow. "I've been trying to get your attention for the past couple of minutes. What on earth is wrong? You look really upset."

I frowned. "We've got a serious problem at home. I'll tell you in a little while. First, let's get registered."

We shouldered our way through the crowds to the registration desk, where I produced the forms Auntie had given me.

The attendant was perky. Perky-annoying, not perky-cute. "Persia Vanderbilt, of Venus Envy, and Barbara Konstantinos. Very good—here you go; here are your badges. Now, be sure to wear them at all times; we don't want security to think you're sneaking in!" Her voice trilled over the words, and I tried not to cringe. She was, after all, just doing her job.

"Where's our booth?" I asked.

She pointed through the double doors where people were milling about. "Through there, to the left in the Garden of Beauty."

"Garden of Beauty?" I mumbled, confused. "I thought this thing was taking place inside." Maybe there would be some saving grace, if they were holding it outdoors.

"Oh," she lowered her voice to a whisper, "that's what the BBCC is calling Conference Room A. But we're supposed to refer to it as 'the Garden of Beauty.'" She gave me a secretive wink that told me she was onto just how bad it sounded, and I grinned, feeling like a jerk for having judged her too quickly.

"Okay, so what else do we need?"

She handed me a packet of information. "Here are your handouts. Keep your ticket stub with you—the BBCC has a number of door prizes planned for the next few days. And you can't get away without wearing a name tag, as well as your badge."

Though it seemed redundant, I accepted the sticky tag and scrawled my name on it, elbowing Barbara to get her attention.

"Huh?" she said. She'd been craning her neck, watching a group of young women who were obviously models, as they shared a single doughnut, cutting it into tiny pieces and handing it around amongst themselves.

I handed her the marker. "Name tag. You have to wear a name tag."

She must have been off in the ozone, because she said,

"But you just gave me my badge," and held it up for me to see.

I snorted. "Name tag, too. Get with the program, Konstantinos." Within another moment, we were badged, tagged, and ready to go. "Here goes nothing," I said, feeling a sense of dread as I took a deep breath and led the way toward the double doors. I couldn't wait to get this weekend over with.

Chapter Five

The room was packed with presenters, at least six rows of ten booths each. The space assigned to Venus Envy was halfway down the third row. Each booth was spacious, big enough for three people, and had a canopy ceiling, lending a Moroccan feel to the room. A privacy panel in front of the table hid locking storage bins that rested beneath. Most of the booths were already taken, draped in silk, satin . . . almost every material imaginable.

Auntie had packed a sea foam cloth for our table, and a mauve shawl to drape over the top, reflecting the colors of Venus Envy, and I shook them out, spreading them across the tabletop while Barbara checked the banner we'd been given to make sure Venus Envy was spelled correctly. I had images of some snot-nosed wiseass substituting a *P* for the *V*.

After we'd tacked it to the top of the booth, we organized the samples into the display holders and stood back, gazing at the tiny bottles that lined the miniature display cases, making sure everything was symmetrical and invit-

ing. I added a stack of brochures and business cards, then
looked around, sighing.

"Now, I guess we just wait. The opening ceremonies are
scheduled for ten o'clock. We've got twenty minutes until
then." I arched my back, stretching my arms over my head.

Barb snorted. "That sounds delightful. Do you want me
to watch the booth while you go? It won't hurt my feelings
to miss out on the inspired speeches they must have
planned for us."

I glared at her. "Not a chance, Konstantinos. If I have to
go, you have to go. Anyway, they have security guards to
watch over the merchandise during presentations. Here, I
brought treats." I held out the bag of cookies, and Barb's
face lit up. "Dorian said to tell you he misses you. You sure
lit a fire under him about the beard and hair."

A blast of music ripped through the hall. Apparently
festivities were getting under way. Blondie blared through
the loudspeakers with "Rip Her Apart," and I had a sinking feeling the song was a presage to what was to come. As
if on cue, a bustle of activity and shrill voices echoed from
a few stalls down. Barbara and I peeked down the row to
see what was going on.

Heaven save us from idiots. A gaggle of Bebe's Belles
were air kissing each other in a major love fest, letting out
excited squeals as they staged a hyper meet-and-greet,
jumping up and down in their thigh-hugging power suits. I
grimaced, thinking they looked like escapees from some
deranged motivational meeting. The Belles hadn't even
opened their booth to customers yet, but they were about
as psyched as they could get. I pulled back as Sharon Wellstone popped into view. She hadn't noticed Venus Envy's
booth, and with luck, she'd be too busy to bother with us
when she did.

As the group of women blurred into a semicircle around their booth, an elegantly coiffed Belle that I vaguely remembered as being Mimi Carter, the wife of our butcher, suddenly charged out of the elevator, up to the group, and gave one of her sisters a nasty bitch slap. So much for camaraderie.

"You stole my sale with Carla Willis—she lives in my territory, and you know it!" Mimi's voice was so loud it echoed through the auditorium. "I'm telling Bebe!"

"Mimi, don't be so quick to assume the worst!" An older woman strode up and separated the sparring partners. As God was my witness, she was wearing a fur coat in the middle of a hot August day. Indoors. The convention hall was air-conditioned, yes, but watching her prance around in a mink was on the far side of surreal. "Maybe Linda didn't realize Carla lives in your area. Remember our motto: When Belles bond, Belles bloom."

Mimi sniffed. "But Tammy, she moved in on my territory. She's trying to sabotage me because she knows I only need fifty more in sales to win the car!" She burst into tears and glared at her rival.

Linda, her opponent, launched into a high-pitched protest. "I deserve that prize. I've had a hard year. Don't be so selfish—you're rolling in money! Your husband could easily afford to buy you a new car."

Apparently the befurred Tammy had run out of patience, because she straightened her shoulders and began tapping a stiletto-heeled foot against the floor. "Knock it off. How do you think this looks? People count on us to set an example of confident, competent career women. Now, both of you, up to the main suite. Bebe will take care of this matter." She pointed toward the elevator, following as the two dissidents marched toward it, glaring at each other the entire way. As the three disappeared, the crowd of Belles dispersed quietly, the love fest apparently over.

I turned to Barb, openmouthed. What on earth could I possibly say about the spectacle? "Surrealistic catfight?"

Barb shuddered. "More like the American dream gone horribly wrong. I wonder what they were fighting over."

"A sparkling lemon yellow convertible." The voice was smooth as velvet.

I whirled to find myself facing a tall, red-haired, bearded man. He was the most gorgeous man I'd seen in ages, and to my chagrin, I let out a little gasp. Tall and lean, he wore a pair of black jeans and a tweed, leather-elbowed suit jacket over the top of a black tank top. His hair was short and just ever so slightly spiky. As I stared into his eyes, I slowly extended my hand.

He slid his own over it. His skin was warm and smooth and set me to tingling. Grinning, he said, "Didn't mean to startle you. Forgive me?"

I blushed. "No problem," I said.

Barbara cleared her throat. "I'm Barbara Konstantinos, and this is Persia Vanderbilt. She's with Venus Envy. I'm just along for the ride."

"How do you do?" He nodded to her, but his gaze remained fastened on me. "I'm Killian Reed, owner of Donna Prima Cosmetics. And I'm very pleased to meet you. I've heard a lot of good things about Venus Envy." His lips were full and ruddy, and I couldn't take my eyes off them—or that brilliant blue gaze that searched my own.

Trying to shake off the feeling that I was two seconds away from making a fool of myself, I asked, "So they're fighting over a car?"

"That's about the whole of it." Killian relaxed then, pulling back just far enough to allow me to breathe. "Every

year, one of the Belles wins a yellow convertible. It goes
to the sales associate with the highest profit record. Second, third, and fourth prizes are shoddy fur coats. Those
women are like a pack of hyenas. Not only do they hunt
their quarry but each other as well." He laughed then, and
my self-consciousness slipped away.

"That sounds about right, from what my aunt told me
about them. They're like some maniacal cult. I think
they're all brainwashed."

Barbara cleared her throat. "You're not far off. I hear
they do use some common programming techniques
among their sales staff. How else could they manage to sell
so much lousy merchandise?"

Killian glanced over our display. "Well, you certainly
have a better display than they do. Their booth is so garish
that it positively reeks."

"You said you're with Donna Prima?" I asked. "That's
a new company, isn't it?"

He shrugged, hooking his thumbs on his belt loops.
"We've been around for awhile, but we keep a low pro-
file." Industry jargon for *we haven't hit it big yet*. He shot
another look at the gaggle of Belles, who were now snip-
ping at one another in yet another hissy fit. "They never
give it up, do they?"

I thought I detected a frown on his face, which deep-
ened as Sharon Wellstone turned around. Oblivious to our
presence, she was glaring at one of her coworkers. I was
troubled by the sly look on her face. Though we'd never
been close friends by any shot of the imagination, Sharon
had always seemed very nice until she approached me in
the shop about leaving Venus Envy. Now, her whole demeanor seemed downright vicious.

Sharon was cornering a tall blonde, and the two looked

like they were really getting into it. I couldn't catch what they were arguing about, but another woman, petite and looking ready to pounce, stepped in and with a short word or two, quelled the discussion. The blonde headed toward the entry, while Sharon stared after her, glaring.

I glanced at Killian again. "So, what do you think about Bebe?" It would be interesting to hear his take on the group.

"Can't stand her or any of her ilk." He shook his head. "That one in particular," he muttered, jabbing a thumb Sharon's way. "Listen, be careful what you say around here, and who you say it to. There are spies in the mix."

"Spies?" Barbara perked up, looking around as if she expected to see James Bond wandering down the aisle.

I snorted. "Put your eyes back in your head. Sean Connery is not going to come rambling through to sweep you off your feet."

She snorted. "Says who? He was the only real Bond, you know."

"I happen to agree, but that's beside the point, so shush!" I wanted to know what Killian meant. "Were you joking, or do you really believe there are spies running around Gull Harbor's convention center? I don't mean to be flippant, but that sounds like a tall order."

He leaned close and lowered his voice. "I don't mean military spies. I'm talking about corporate espionage. It happens a lot, or didn't you know that?"

Bingo, now it made sense. I nodded. "Actually, yes, I've been reading about a few cases lately in my aunt's business magazines. Corporate crime is more widespread than people think." I decided to forgo mentioning that our roses may have been the latest victims in the corporate wars. "You think there are people here trying to ferret out company secrets?"

Killian looked grim. "I don't just think it, I know it. But there's no way to dig up any proof at this point. Just watch your back, watch who you talk to, and don't say anything too confidential."

The loudspeaker announced the opening ceremonies were about to begin. As the convention hostesses herded us toward Auditorium C—or as they were calling it now, the Gardenia Grove—I tapped Killian on the arm. "So, why are you telling me this? Why trust me?"

"First," he said, "it doesn't matter if my feelings get back to her. Bebe already knows I think she's scum, along with all of her little prima donnas." Then, with a flicker of a smile, he added, "Second, I know you're Florence Vanderbilt's niece. She has a reputation for scrupulous honesty in the business, and she wouldn't hire you on—relative or not—unless she trusted you implicitly. She's an honorable competitor, and I have the highest regard for her."

Just then, an older woman scurried over and whispered something in his ear. "Shit," he said. "Crisis time. I hope I'll see you in the auditorium," he hastily called back to me, racing away.

As I watched him go, I realized that I wanted to see more of Mr. Killian Reed. Doubly glad that I'd shooed Sharon Wellstone out of the shop when I had, I decided that Auntie's reputation reflected on me, and I wasn't about to endanger that trust. I straightened my shoulders, linked arms with Barb, and strolled into the hall.

⁂

The opening ceremonies were as bad as I thought they were going to be. Boring and drawn out, they were basically a gushing welcome to over three hundred attendees from all sides of the beauty aisle.

We'd already spent an hour listening to introductions for the models and distributors when they finally got around to introducing the representatives for each company. They went in alphabetical order so, naturally, Venus Envy came last. I tried to keep focused, but it was difficult. My thoughts kept drifting away as I craned my neck, trying to catch a glimpse of Killian. However, at the mention of two companies in particular, I snapped to attention.

The first was Bebe Wilcox. She reminded me of Mrs. Simone, one of my English teachers, a bat from hell who had terrorized most of the students. Though I'd never intimidated easy, even *I* pussyfooted around her.

Bebe was dressed in a Calvin Klein suit, and she could have been anywhere from fifty to seventy. Her hair was pulled back in a sleek wheat-colored bun, and though I was fairly certain she'd undergone a round or two of Botox, she couldn't get away from the prison-matron sturdiness that some women have from the moment they're born.

As she took the podium, I felt an instant revulsion. On the surface she seemed nice enough, but when I looked into her eyes as she gazed over the conference, I sensed a shark. Not a nice nurse shark who would most likely let a curious diver go about his business, but the dead eyes of a great white, trolling for her next meal. I fought the urge to slip out of the audience and head back to the shop.

"Thank you for welcoming Bebe's Cosmetics and Boutique to the convention, ladies. I just know we're going to have a wonderful time. If you get a chance, drop over to our company headquarters for information on becoming a consultant or one of our Belles. And don't forget to visit Bebe's Boutique, over on Vicar's Drive. Bebe's Boutique is the *only* store in town that can fulfill every need you might have."

Next to me, Barb snorted, and I knew she was thinking about her haircut. As if on cue, she leaned close to me and whispered, "Do you know how hard it is to keep from jumping up and asking her what level of hell her stylist came from?"

I glanced at her, grinning. If it had been me, I might not have managed to be quite so diplomatic. I'd probably be onstage, making a scene.

Shortly after Bebe stepped down, Killian Reed took the podium. He looked a little haggard, and I had the feeling that he had yet to avert whatever crisis his friend had dragged him off to solve.

"Thank you for welcoming Donna Prima Cosmetics into your lineup," he said. "We represent a new face in the world of cosmetics, a more natural look. All our products are made with organic ingredients, and we don't test on animals. Thank you for inviting us to the convention." Killian was clearly distracted, and though I tried to catch his eye, he looked distant and preoccupied.

Eventually, they worked their way through the entire alphabet, and it was my turn. I took the stage and looked over the audience. Most were women, though a few men stuck out in the bunch. Company employees tended to sit together; you could almost segregate them by dress and style. The group of Bebe's Belles were easiest to spot— there must have been a half-dozen fur coats in the bunch, and a handful wearing bright yellow dresses or tight little skirt suits.

"My name is Persia Vanderbilt, and I represent Venus Envy, a bath and beauty shop from right here in Gull Harbor. We're local, and we offer various day spa services by appointment. I'm in charge of our line of Persian Rose Fragrances—custom blended to your every sensory need." I'd recently applied for my own business license; Auntie had encouraged me to. "Thank you for inviting us to participate. I'll be giving a speech tomorrow about the power fragrance plays in attracting a mate. You're all welcome to come listen." I cleared my throat. The hostess had asked me to include a little blurb about my upcoming speech.

After another interminable round of speeches and notes, during which Barb and I surreptitiously played solitaire on her PDA, the meeting broke up, and we filed into the dining hall for lunch. I was pleasantly surprised to see that Barbara and I had been assigned to the same table where Killian and his retinue were eating. He brightened up as we approached, hurrying to pull out my chair for me.

The older woman who'd waylaid him in the hall was named Trish Jensen, one of Donna Prima's research assistants. Other members of his company who were there included Betsy Sue, a receptionist, and a thin, gawky man named Julius Skye.

"My mother had a thing for Caesar," he said with a grin as we shook hands. Julius and Trish were both wearing tailored green lab coats, and they were the primary members of research and development.

"Looks like we got the short-end-of-the-stick table, ladies," Killian said.

I glanced around and immediately understood what he meant. We weren't anywhere near the bigwigs' tables; in fact, we were situated next to the door. Bebe's Belles hadn't fared much better; they were stationed nearby— near the kitchen—and nobody in the group looked happy about it.

Trish raised her eyebrows. "I cannot believe they are wearing fur coats in this weather. They're insane."

Killian chuckled, "Bebe would probably hang them from the rafters if they didn't show up in full regalia. Her nickname's Attila, if you didn't know." He scowled again. "You can't trust her. She's a vulture."

"Yeah, I know," I mumbled, thinking about her campaign to shut down Venus Envy. "She's spreading rumors about my aunt's shop." And quite possibly resorting to corporate espionage, I thought, if she was the one behind doctoring our roses with insecticide.

Killian glanced at me, a concerned look on his face. I told him about Bebe's Boutique's attempts to drive us out of business, and Barbara tipped her head to show them her haircut. I was about to ask him what experience he'd had with Bebe when the waitress deposited our dinners at the table—chicken breasts with parmesan noodles and asparagus spears.

As we started to eat, there was a ruckus from the door.

"Oh God, time to watch the fur fly," Killian said, rolling his eyes. "I may not like the Belles, but that woman is just as bad. Won't she ever get over herself?"

Somebody as bad as Bebe? I glanced over to see who he was talking about. A tall, young twenty-something in jeans and a flannel shirt, the woman's hair was yanked back in a tight ponytail, and her face was devoid of both makeup and smile. She barged through the door, followed by several young men and women dressed in various stages of wannabe hippie garb. Next to me, Barb groaned.

"Who are they?" I asked.

"Nancy Louis and her crew of environmental roughnecks," Barb spoke up. When I shot a questioning look at her, she added, "The Animal Freedom Association? Remember, I told you about Patty Ann, my niece?"

I rolled my eyes. "Yeah, I remember."

"Nutnick extremists," Trish said. "Don't get me wrong, I support a variety of environmental causes, but these fruitcakes are fanatics, and they go to extremes to make a point." She shook her head as she patted the corner of her lips with her napkin.

"Tell me about it," Barb said. "We've been trying to coerce my niece to leave the group for months. She's the brunette in the flannel shirt and cutoffs." She sighed, obviously not happy about the fact. "Bullheaded little brat."

"What are they doing here?" I asked as they strode into the room, past our table, and directly over to the Belles, all of whom looked uneasily up at the group.

Bebe rose. She was tall, at least as tall as me, and she towered over the group. "I thought I made myself clear at our last meeting, Ms. Louis. If you continue to harass my staff, I'll take out a restraining order and file charges against you for stalking."

This was promising to get interesting. I looked around for security, but apparently the convention organizers had assigned them to watch over the display tables, and no one was minding the dining hall. A well-groomed woman I recognized as one of the event planners slipped out the door, no doubt to summon assistance.

"You torture innocent animals in your research labs, and all in the name of vanity. And look at you—you're wearing dead animals on your back! That's sheer human ego! Do you know how many animals were slaughtered just to feed your vanity—"

"Enough!" Bebe leaned down till her face was inches away from Nancy's. Her voice echoed through the room.

"I guarantee you, I'll be filing for a restraining order this afternoon, and if you break that order, I'll haul your ass into court so fast you won't be able to spit, *little girl*."

As security made their way into the room, Nancy yelled out what sounded like a war cry. Acting in unison, she and her friends reached into their pockets and came out with what I thought were guns. Oh my God, were they going to massacre the Belles?

Security moved in, but they weren't fast enough. Within seconds, I heard a loud noise, and the Belles at the table screamed as a spray of red hit the air. Oh shit—blood?

"Hit the deck!" I grabbed Barbara and dragged her under the table as the room erupted in chaos. Killian, Trish, Julius, and Betsy Sue dove for cover along with us, and we all huddled together, trying to fit under the tablecloth. Trish was praying quietly, and I saw her hand move to the crucifix hanging around her neck. Betsy Sue pressed up against Julius, and his arm automatically pulled her close.

Something seemed off to me—no sound of bullets. Just as I was about to comment, a voice boomed over the loudspeaker.

"Please return to your seats, ladies and gentlemen. Everything is under control. You aren't in any danger. We repeat, you are not in any danger."

We slowly crawled out from under the table. As I stood up, I saw that security had taken control of the situation. Nancy, Patty Ann, and the rest of the group were sitting on the floor, cross-legged, looking sullen. Bebe's Belles were in a state of disarray, covered with patches of brilliant crimson. A light went on in my head, and sure enough, I knew what had happened. Not blood, but spray paint. Red spray paint. What I'd thought were guns were actually spray cans.

Barbara took in the situation and pushed past me, her face set in an angry mask. She stomped over to where security was holding the young people.

"Patty Ann! What the hell do you think you're doing here? Does your mother know you're causing havoc?"

Patty registered shock when she saw Barb leaning over her. "Aunt Barbara—I didn't know you'd be here—"

"You know this young woman, ma'am?" One of the security officers took out his pad and pencil. I moved up behind Barb and placed a hand on her shoulder for support.

"I most certainly do," Barb said over Patty's protests. "Her name is Patty Linden. She's my niece, although at this moment I'm ashamed to admit it." She stared down at Patty, who remained seated. "I can't believe you'd act this way. It's one thing to follow your conscience, another to terrorize and destroy property—"

"Your niece is a grown woman and can make up her own mind," Nancy Louis broke in. *Bad idea,* I thought. Barb was a tough customer when she was riled, and right now, she was about as furious as I'd seen her in ages.

Barbara whirled on Nancy. "Take your propaganda and shove it. You're the worst of the lot. You use your influence to turn these kids into criminals. You're only looking for publicity! You're no better than any terrorist group, and I hope *you* end up in prison."

"Aunt Barbara! How can you talk to us that way?" Patty struggled to get to her feet, but the guard waved her down again.

Barb set her hands on her hips. Her voice carried through the entire dining room. "You should be thankful I'm talking to you at all. I'm ashamed of you, and I'm going to call your parents. You have to learn to take responsibility for your actions." She pushed past me, back into the vendor's chamber, her mouth set in a grim line.

I was about to go after her when Kyle, along with three officers, entered the room. He took in the situation in one glance and nodded to his men, who produced handcuffs and began reciting Miranda rights to the members of the Animal Freedom Association. *So much for lunch,* I thought, reaching to grab my dinner roll before we were all herded back out of the dining room.

Somehow, we managed to survive the rest of the afternoon, though not much went on—people were too busy gossiping about the attack on the Belles to pay much attention to the booths. I tried to spot Killian, but he was busy somewhere, so Barb and I spent the rest of the afternoon handing out samples and making small talk. I could see she wasn't in the mood to discuss her niece's fiasco.

Around five, people started to drift away. There weren't any major events the first evening, so I felt no obligation to stick around. Barbara helped me pack up the samples, and we headed out.

"Thanks for coming with me today," I told her as we stowed the bags in my car. "It would have been unbearable without you. You and Dorian coming to the barbecue tonight?

"We'll be there around seven thirty. See you then."

As Barb drove away, I headed for the shop where I knew Auntie would be waiting for a full report. The downtown area had cleared out; at this time of day, the tourists were dining, and since most of the restaurants—the nice ones—weren't directly in the town center, the traffic was relatively light.

I pushed through the doors of Venus Envy, carrying the bags with me. Tawny looked up and waved me over to the counter. "Let me take those. You go talk to your aunt. She's frantic."

"What happened? Is she okay?"

"Yeah, she's fine, but the store's computer is not."

Uh-oh. That couldn't be good. I headed back to the office, where I found Auntie, her brow knit with worry, hunched over the keyboard, cursing a blue streak under her breath.

"What happened?"

"I don't know—Persia, I can't get this to work. I don't know what happened, but I can't find most of the store's records." She scooted out from behind her desk and let me squeeze in.

Neither one of us were very computer literate, though with my friend Jared's help I was making the attempt. I brought up the My Computer screen, and clicked on My Documents, where most of our files were stored. It took forever, but finally the folder opened, and I stared at the blank screen, a growing sense of dread creeping up my spine. Where were all our documents? Our letters, our inventory lists, our spreadsheets?

With a deep breath, I began poking through all the other files. It was as if something had plunged our computer into mud—it was running so slowly. And what little I knew to look for was nowhere to be seen. I remembered a little trick that Jared had shown me and clicked on the Start button, then on Search. "Auntie, do you remember the name of any of the documents we had in the folder?"

She thought for a moment, then said, "Yes, actually. I wrote a letter to Pete Stephens last night when I was answering e-mail. He wanted to know if we were interested in some fish for the freezer, and I sent him a letter in Word, saying yes. I called the file *Pete1.doc*, then copied and pasted it into the body of the e-mail."

I ran a search for *Pete1.doc* but came up with nothing. Nada. If it had ever existed, it was gone now. I opened the recycle bin, wondering if Auntie had somehow managed to delete the folder, but the bin was empty.

I glanced up at her. "I don't know what's wrong, but Auntie, all our inventory sheets, our spreadsheets and files . . . they're all gone."

"Gone?" she repeated. "Persia, what are we going to do?"

I stared at the blank screen, wondering the same thing.

Chapter Six

I stared at the computer for a moment, then inspiration struck me. "Let me call Jared and see if he's home." Jared, one of my close friends, had worked for Microsoft once upon a time before returning to Gull Harbor, where he took a job with the community college, teaching computer science. He also ran a consulting business on the side. He kept after Auntie and me to let him check out our system and update it, but with the summer rush and the worries over Bebe's Boutiques, we hadn't had time.

His life partner, Rod McKinley, a local artist, answered the phone. "Hey Rod," I said. "Is Jared there?"

He sighed. "No, he's not back from Seattle yet, and he won't be until Monday. What do you need?"

"I don't suppose you know anything about computers?" I asked, hoping he might say yes. My wishes were destined for disappointment, however.

"Me? No, Jared's the whiz. What's wrong? Should I take a message?"

I debated. Even if Jared was back on time Monday,

there was no guarantee he'd be able to hurry down to the shop and check out our problem. "No, but do you know what computer store he goes to? We have a nasty glitch here and need to get it fixed."

"Hold on," Rod said, and there was a muffled noise that sounded like flipping papers. "Yeah, he goes to a place over on Devonshire Point called In-A-Fix Computers. Their number is 555-8822."

I jotted it down and thanked him, then called the computer store. They were open until eight and said we could drop off the computer. Auntie and I carefully shut everything down, then unplugged the box, and I hauled it out to my car. I hurried back into the store to change into the jeans and crop top I'd tucked in my tote that morning before heading back to the car, my hobo bag slung over my shoulder.

Auntie was waiting for me next to Baby. "I'll go home and get the barbecue started. I already wasted enough time on that damned machine today."

"No problem. I'll tell them it's a rush job," I said. "Do you know when the problem started, just in case they ask?"

She shrugged. "Last time I used it was yesterday when I was answering e-mail. Everything seemed normal then. There was a lot of spam, but after I checked them to make sure they weren't anything important from our usual vendors, I deleted them."

As I sped over to Devonshire Drive, a nasty headache began to creep up on me. The stress of the summer had been increasing with the temperature, and I was starting to look forward to cool weather. If we could just solve the problems Bebe's Boutique was causing us, then maybe things would get back to normal.

In-A-Fix Computers was in a minimall, next to a Starbucks and Jumping Joe's Burger Joint. The aroma coming out of the hamburger shack made my mouth water, and I could hardly wait to get home and chow down on Auntie's barbecue. Lunch at the convention had been more adrenaline rush than sustenance. As I pushed through the door, carrying the computer, I heard a voice that was all too familiar.

"Persia! Whassup? How's it hanging?"

Andy Andrews, slacker extraordinaire, sauntered over to take the computer from me. He was still wearing low rider shorts two sizes too big, but at least his tee shirt was clean, and he'd lost the backward baseball cap in favor of a retro mullet with one thin braid down the back. Maybe this time he wouldn't make a pass at me. His last attempt had been less than spectacular.

"Andy? What are you doing here?"

He shrugged. "Had to make some bucks to pay the rent after I got fired from the aquarium, you know? Can't eat forever off the food bank. I know a lot about computers but never thought of putting it to use for cash until my old man talked to Brian, the owner of the shop here. He gave me this gig, and it's working out pretty good. So what's the problem?"

I explained what was going on, and he shook his head. "Did you back up your files?" As I shook my head, he let out a groan. "No? That figures. You don't know how many people screw up on that. Okay, when do you want it by?"

"As soon as possible. Is there any way you can look at it tonight?"

Andy shrugged. "Can do, but it'll run you an extra fifty bucks. Store policy," he added, pointing to a sign that promised expedited service for a fee. "Otherwise, I'd do it for free, for such a hot chick like you."

I fought back a grin. Andy was Andy was Andy, whether he sprawled in his apartment watching TV or working behind the counter in a computer store. "That's fine. We need this ASAP. Call us when you know what's wrong. You have my home number, right?"

He gave me a receipt and, before I could head for the door, caught up with me. "Whoa! I didn't know you had such awesome tattoos—and you pierced your belly button! Too cool." He leaned over, looking a little too closely at my belly-button ring. I wasn't about to mention my nipple ring. That would probably be too much for the poor boy to handle.

"Hey, Andy, shake out of it, dude. I've had my belly button pierced since you were still covered in pimples."

He gave me a salacious grin. "You sure you don't want to get together for coffee, or something? I'm not that much younger than you."

By his emphasis on the word *something* I knew what he had in mind. "Andy, let me give you a business tip. While you're working, you shouldn't hit on your customers. Not good for the store, not good for you, not good for your pocketbook. Just chill out, dude, put the tongue back in the mouth, and go work on my computer." At his puppy dog look, I relented and smiled. "Don't try so hard. I'm just not available." *At least not to you,* I thought.

"Gotchya." With a sheepish grin, he turned back to the counter, and I slipped out of the shop. As I drove along Beachcomber Drive, I thought it would be a good night to take the dogs out for a late-night walk. Maybe Bran and I could slip away from the barbecue and hit the beach. The moon would be waxing a bare sliver, working its way toward first quarter, and I could really a quiet wind-down to the day.

I pulled into the drive and dropped off my things in the living room before heading into the kitchen for a glass of iced tea. As I entered the room, I stopped cold. Buttercup, Delilah, Beast, and Pete were standing in the midst of chaos. The door to the pantry was open, and somebody had spilled a forty-pound bag of dog food all over the floor. The kibble was scattered all through the kitchen, and the bandits hadn't stopped there. Packages of potato chips, pretzels, and dry cereal had been shredded and strewn across the floor. At least they couldn't use a can opener. Yet.

As I turned from right to left, taking in the damage, I groaned. Not only had they gone on a munchies rampage, but somebody had also gotten into the flour. Where the kitchen merged into the back hall, a torn package rested on the floor, ten pounds of flour spilling out in a powdery trail. Paw prints—both big and small—were everywhere. In the midst of the mess, Hoffman came strutting in, clucking like the proud cock he was.

I counted to ten before turning on the guilty group. "You are the dumbest nitwits I've ever known! Wait till Aunt Florence sees this . . ." As I babbled on, Pete began to wag his tail and Buttercup batted a piece of kibble across the floor, a look of sheer delight on her face. I growled, then stalked out the back door and through the yard, over to Auntie's side. She looked up from manning the grill.

"What did the computer shop say?" She was basting chicken with a sauce that smelled like pineapple and mint. The burgers and hot dogs would come later, after everybody was here.

I shook my head. "Nothing yet, they'll let us know

tonight or tomorrow morning. Auntie, did you leave the pantry open?"

She frowned. "I don't think so, but I was in there getting supplies for the party. Maybe . . . why?"

I grinned. "The Menagerie decided to have a little party of their own."

A suspicious look clouded her face. "Uh-oh. What did they do now?"

"Maybe you'd better come see."

Auntie closed the grill and followed me back to the house. The moment she saw the havoc, she let out a little cry and grabbed the broom, gently swatting everybody who had four legs or wings out of the kitchen.

"Oh Persia, what a mess! I can't believe they did this." She looked like she might be going to cry, but then just shook her head. "Well, that's about par for the course. We have to clean this up before anybody gets here," she said, starting to sweep up the mess.

I gently took the broom from her hand. "You go watch the chicken. I'll clean it up. It's not so bad, really, just a few boxes of cereal, some chips, flour, dog food . . . a bag of jerky."

As Auntie left the kitchen with Pete, Beauty, and the Beast in tow, I stared down Delilah and Buttercup, both of whom were eyeing the pile of food. "Don't even think about it. Go find your buddies and curl up or have a hissy fit or go find a mouse or something. You've caused enough trouble for one day."

⚓

Once the kitchen was clean, I set out food for the troops. Maybe it would keep them out of our dinner. The doorbell rang as I finished up washing the counters, and Barbara and Dorian paraded in, bearing dessert—a huge sheet cake. While Dorian carried the cake out into the backyard, to the picnic tables Auntie had set up, Barb and I got started on the salad. Barb washed and tore the lettuce while I sliced tomatoes, radishes, and carrots. She dried the leaves in the vegetable spinner and then set about mincing garlic and dicing onions.

"Tonight should be interesting," I said. "I invited Bran, and Auntie invited Kyle."

Barb stopped, knife in midair. "Not really the wisest choice, you think?"

"No, really?" I grinned at her. "Well, both of them have to get over it. Bran's a good friend and lover, and Kyle's . . . well . . . Kyle is Kyle." I tried to focus on my work, but my thoughts drifted back to the convention and Killian's face. I glanced at Barb. "What do you think about Killian?"

Barb's lip twitched. "I thought I noticed a spark between the two of you. "

"I don't know what to think. There's just something about him . . ."

She scraped the onions and garlic into the big wooden bowl. "What's going on with Bran and you right now?"

I shrugged. "We date. We sleep together on occasion. We've already had the 'where is this leading' conversation and decided that while we enjoy each other's company, there's no long term in our future, except for friendship."

Barb began blending a vinaigrette. "Then you have leeway, if you really are interested in Killian?"

"Yeah, I do. And I'll be honest with Bran. We agreed that honesty is the only way a relationship . . . friendship . . . like ours can work."

As I put away the leftover veggies, I remembered that I

had another talk to face. Sarah had called and left a message that she'd returned early. She'd be over to work tomorrow morning as planned. I groaned and leaned against the fridge.

"What's wrong?" Barb rinsed the sponge and handed me a paper towel to wipe my hands on. "Here, dry your hands."

"Sarah's been slacking off. I'm supposed to talk to her about it tomorrow morning, and I have to fire her if she won't shape up. I've never fired anybody in my life."

Barb empathized. "We had to have 'the talk' with Ari last year. He was trying to branch out into construction on the side and got so unreliable that Dorian finally had to issue an ultimatum. He could either stay with the bakery or go into construction full time. He chose the bakery. It's hard. You want to encourage people to follow their dreams, but you can't let it interfere with your own business."

"You're right. I never thought about this side of being an employer, but now that Auntie has made me co-owner of the shop, I have to start paying more attention to the administrative issues. Which I hate."

"But which you'll do, because you're such a good niece."

I grinned, ducking my head. "Yeah, you nailed it. Auntie has faith in me. Venus Envy's a good shop, and I'd miss working there. Since she has put this much trust in my abilities, I can't and won't let her down. I just hope Bebe Wilcox won't drive us into the ground in the meantime."

A glance out the window told me that Bran and Kyle had arrived, and they both looked a little ruffled. "Uh-oh, time to go break up the testosterone match. Come on," I said, lifting the salad. "Let's go charm them into submission."

⁘

By the time we joined the group, Kyle and Bran were nose to nose over the death penalty. I didn't want anything to do with the debate, so I slid my arm through Bran's, gave Kyle a wide smile, and said, "Enough. No politics at dinner. Kyle, I see you brought your guitar. Why don't you play something? Bran, please help Auntie carry the platter of burgers and dogs over to the picnic table."

Kyle opened his guitar case. He was surprisingly talented and had a good voice, although I didn't really like his choice in music. But anything was better than listening to their bickering.

Having played a good game of détente, I moved on to welcome Trevor and his new girlfriend, Cindy. To my relief, Cindy Andrews was a far cry from Lydia Wang, Trevor's ex. Cindy was pretty, rather than stunning, but she was funny and witty, and I liked her immediately.

We were about to gather round the tables when our last visitor showed up: Kane Jimenez. As I watched him come through the gate and greet Aunt Florence with a kiss on the cheek, I had the sense of déjà vu—a sense that I'd seen all this before, but yet I knew I hadn't. They seemed right together, their energies meshed. In fact, as I watched them walk, arm in arm, I realized that even though she might not know it, she had the chance for happiness standing by her side.

I slowly approached, not wanting to encroach on their intimacy. But Auntie glanced at me, and her face lit up in a way that made me feel warm and loved.

"Kane, this is my niece, Persia."

The tall, salt-and-pepper-haired man held out his hand. He was dark, his hair long and braided in back. He wore a Hawaiian shirt and a pair of Bermuda shorts, and his grip was warm and sure. "I've heard so much about you through your aunt's letters. It's a pleasure to actually meet you in person."

"Thank you, the pleasure's likewise." I turned to Auntie. "Dinner's ready, it looks like. Should I get everybody started?"

She gave me a grateful smile. "Would you? I want to take Kane on a tour of the gardens while it's still light enough to see."

As they wandered off through the trellis and down the path, I headed over to the picnic table and began directing the ravenous crowd. But my thoughts lingered with Auntie and her caller, and I had a feeling that we'd be seeing a lot more of Kane over the next few months. And that thought, unlike the worries over the shop, made me smile.

While everybody was engaged with their food, Bran and I managed to find ourselves a private moment in the kitchen. He slid his arms around me, pulling me to him, his lips seeking mine. After a lingering kiss, which left me wonderfully distracted and horny as hell, I pulled away.

"Bran, we promised to be honest with each other, right?"

He nodded, waiting for me to go on.

"The thing is . . . I think I've met someone I'm interested in." I spoke delicately, not wanting to step on his ego, even though we'd already discussed this possibility.

He leaned against the counter. "Are you lovers with him?"

I shook my head. "No. I don't know if this will even lead anywhere past a friendship, but I wanted you to know. We already agreed that we wouldn't be exclusive, but I don't want to just spring it on you if something does happen. I know you're seeing Victoria, and I don't mind."

And, in truth, I didn't. Victoria only came over to Gull

Harbor once a month or so, and I knew she and Bran had been seeing each other on a casual basis for over two years now. We'd had the safe sex talk, and when I searched my heart, I couldn't find a shred of jealousy.

Bran ran his fingers down my face. "Who is it? I hope not Kyle? That's the only man on this island that I'd have a problem with you dating, and only because he's such a jerk about us."

I snorted. "I have no intention on sharing my love life with Kyle. No, this is someone I met at the convention. I'll tell you about him later. Right now, if you're interested, I'd like to get back to what we were doing?" I wrapped my arms around his waist, and he drew me in, searching my mouth with his tongue, setting me on fire. "Would you like to take a walk down by the water after dinner?" I murmured.

He nudged me in the hip, and I grinned, feeling his desire grow. Oh yeah, sex on the beach. Always fun, if a little sandy.

❧

The sun had been up for forty-five minutes by the time I made my way out into the garden, where I planned on meeting Sarah when she arrived at six. The sky was so clear I felt like I could fall into the vast stretch of blue, and early sunbeams cut through the lingering shadows, creeping like slow tendrils waking from the earth. An echo of birdsong pierced the air, and I inhaled deeply, pulling the tangy chill into my lungs. There—on the edge, peeking around the corner, lurked a presage of autumn. A few more weeks and we'd be heading into the rainy season, and the glorious summer would fade.

I settled at one of the picnic tables, pushing away a lingering crumb from last night's barbecue. I'd brought out a plate of Danish and a pitcher of iced tea with lemon to soften the impact of my impending talk with Sarah, but I knew they were only window dressings. At the last minute, Auntie had offered to join me, but I declined. She was right; I had to learn how to handle this like an adult.

The sound of a car pulling into the drive told me Sarah had arrived. At least she was on time. During the summer, she and Trevor started work early in order to beat the morning light. Watering flowers under the hot sun led to burned petals and skin, so they got the watering and weeding out of the way before noon.

I waited nervously as she popped around through the side gate into the backyard. As she shaded her eyes from the sudden glare of sunlight, I sprang to my feet and made my way over to her side.

"Hey Persia," she said. "What's up? You usually aren't awake this early."

I sighed. *Here goes nothing,* I thought. "Sarah, we need to talk." I gestured to the umbrella-shaded table.

Sarah hesitantly took a seat and accepted a glass of tea. I settled down across from her. "This is about me missing so much work, isn't it?" she said, saving me from making the first move.

I let out a long sigh. "Yes, it is."

"I warned your aunt when I first came to work here that I have my own business, too—"

Holding up my hand, I gently shook my head. "We know that. Auntie knows that. But Sarah, we need someone who's going to be here on a regular basis. Your business seems to require more and more of your time, and that's a good thing—for you. But it interferes with our operations. You haven't put in a full twenty-hour week this summer. Can you see that?"

She stared at her glass, swirling her straw around in the lemon-flavored tea. "Yeah, I know. I guess I just haven't wanted to face this moment. I've been hoping that I could squeeze in more time for my own affairs without affecting the job here, but I guess it's reached a point where I have to make a decision. Either I go full time on my own, or I scale back and resume my work here. Shit or get off the pot time, you know?"

I gave her a rueful nod. "That about sums it up." Maybe Auntie was right; maybe Sarah had just been looking for an excuse to quit in order to pursue her own dream.

She glanced up at the house, then over her shoulder at the gardens. "I love this place. I love working here, and I adore your aunt. You, too, Persia. I wasn't sure how I'd feel when Miss Florence first told me you'd be overseeing the gardens, but I'm glad you came. You know what you're talking about, and you're easy to work for."

"I try," I said, a hint of a smile springing to my lips. When I first arrived, Trevor seemed amicable enough, but Sarah had taken a while to win over. I knew she didn't like me interfering, since Auntie had pretty much left things up to the two of them. But we'd worked it out. I refilled our glasses.

Sarah leaned back, playing with the condensation on her glass. "While I was at the llama show, I started talking to one of the breeders there. She's been raising llamas for years. Last year, somebody snuck into her barn and killed one of her favorites. Just gutted the poor thing. She doesn't know who did it, doesn't know why. Police haven't got a clue. I asked her what she planned on doing to prevent a repeat. She just stared at me blankly and said, "Oh, I doubt that it will happen again. We're just making sure the barn door is locked tight at night."

She lifted her gaze to meet mine. "She really doesn't care enough to take any extra precautions. Made me wonder how she can call herself an animal lover." Sarah lifted a Danish and bit into it, closing her eyes against the first burst of sweetness. "You guys are going to need a lot of help to shore up security, especially after what happened to the roses. I'll be here."

I let out a long sigh. "What about your own business?"

She shrugged. "I've made the decision to scale back. I knew this was coming, and I thought long and hard over the past few weeks. The llama show just brought it home to me. I didn't buy any new stock. The truth is, I'm not making enough money to branch out full-time. And I love working in the gardens. So I'm cutting back the amount of spinning I do, and I'm going to raise my prices a little. There's leeway for me to do that and still bring in customers. I'm also going to take more custom work—fewer orders, but pricier goods."

My relief must have shown on my face, because she laughed.

"Oh Persia, you look like you just escaped a fate worse than death. Don't sweat it, okay? I know you had to talk to me about this, and I'm fine with that. So, should you and your aunt and Trevor and I get together and discuss security?"

I flipped open my Day-Timer. "Yeah, but let me talk to Auntie first and find out her schedule. Either she or I will let you know. I suppose it's about time we ironed out some interim measures, as well as plan for long-term strategies."

She pushed herself out of her chair. "Sounds good. And now, I'll see what's left to do in the rose garden. Trevor worked his ass off because of me, and I'll repay the boy in kind. Trust me, whoever did this has their head up their butts . . . or will, once we get hold of them." With a wink, she headed through the trellis, down the path, into the gardens.

I closed my Day-Timer, breathing a deep sigh of relief. Thank God that had worked out. Now, one day left of the convention, and then I could get back to focusing on important issues. Like whoever trashed our gardens. Sarah had nailed it on the head. If I found out who destroyed our roses, I'd shove their head up their butt so fast they wouldn't have time to even squeak.

Chapter Seven

Buoyed by the satisfactory resolution to the first problem of the day, I hoped everything else would go as easy as my talk with Sarah. I decided to stop off at In-A-Fix Computers before I forced myself back to the convention. Just one more day and I'd be free from the clutches of the beauty barons. Of course, first I had to make it through my speech, but I didn't foresee any problems. I picked up Barb on the way, thinking she'd be a good foil to Andy Andrews and his handy hands.

"So good old Andy is working here?" she asked. "That must have come as quite a shock."

I shook my head. "Yes, and the little twit tried to put the make on me again. One of these days I should surprise him and say yes—he'd be so scared, he'd piss his pants. I honestly think he wouldn't know what to do with me once he got hold of me. Andy doesn't strike me as the go-getter type."

Barb suppressed a snort. "Yeah, or at least he'd be

scared of you *after* you got done with him. There he is," she pointed to the service counter.

We sauntered in his direction as he motioned us over to the desk. "My computer working yet?" I asked, giving him a lazy smile.

He winked, but then actually let his professional side come out and the smarmy look disappeared from his face. "Hey Persia. Listen, you have some seriously bad shit going on with your machine here. I can't believe you didn't have any AV protection on it."

"AV? What do you mean?"

"Antivirus software. You picked up a nasty virus, and it wiped out your files. What were you thinking? Nobody in their right mind should be without AV protection in this day and age." He grumbled something I didn't catch, and I had the same feeling I would have if I'd been caught having sex without a condom.

I frowned. Computer virus? Great, just great. Served me right for not listening to Jared and learning more about computers. "So what do I do? How do we get the information back?"

Andy gave me a look that read, *You're out of the loop,* then shook his head. "You don't. Not unless you kept a floppy or burned a CD of your data. Since you told me you didn't back up your files, I don't suppose you managed that?" I had the feeling he was enjoying this in some perverted way. Unfortunately for me, he was also correct in his assumption.

"Guilty as charged. I guess we should have, right?"

"Uh . . . it's pretty much standard if you want to be sure you're okay," he said. "I can't believe you made it this far without something like this happening."

"All right," I said, unable to take being scolded by

slacker-boy anymore. "We screwed up. Big time. What do we do now?"

"Your registry files are all messed up. I need to reformat the hard drive, which means most of your data's going to be toast because the virus already deleted a good share of it. Pretty much, you start from scratch. I'll save what I can and slap on a good AV software and a firewall while I'm at it."

"A firewall?"

Barb spoke up. "Firewall. It keeps hackers out of your computer."

"That's another thing," Andy said. "I think somebody has been browsing around through your data. I can't be sure, but I checked the log files . . ." At my questioning glance, he held up his hand. "Don't ask. What I think happened was that somebody sent you a virus through e-mail and you—or your aunt—opened the attachment. This created a back door in your computer, which allowed whoever sent it to sneak into your files and look around, then destroy them."

I grimaced. *A back door?* "That sounds deliberate."

And right up Bebe Wilcox's avenue. For a brief moment, I realized that I was sounding paranoid, even to myself. Next thing I knew, I'd be placing the blame for the federal deficit and world hunger on her shoulders. But the old adage, "Just because you're paranoid doesn't mean they're not out to get you," kept running through my head.

He shrugged. "Could be, or could just be some joker. You have no idea of the number of wannabe hackers out there, just looking for an open port. I can't tell you whether it was deliberate or just random."

Barb tapped me on the shoulder. "The roses? The computer? Are you thinking what I'm thinking?"

I glanced at her. "Yeah, I am, but let's talk about it later. Okay," I leaned on the desk. "Here's the deal, Andy. Fix the computer, clean it, protect it, do whatever you have to in order to ensure both our privacy and the safety of our information. Can you have it ready by tomorrow?"

He saluted me. "Will do. Say, you sure you won't come over and hang out? We could have a rockin' time. I could show you my hard drive." Again with the grin. Apparently Junior Lecher was back.

I had to hand it to him; the dude had perseverance. "Andy, I guarantee you, your hard drive just wouldn't be big enough for me, but thanks for the invite. You're all right." Leaving him openmouthed, I turned on my heel and led Barbara out of the store.

᠉

Once we were at the convention, we got right down to business. We'd almost sold out of samples when a *ding, ding, ding* echoed through the hall. The loudspeaker blared to life. "Ladies and gentlemen, we are pleased to announce the winner of our first door prize for the day—a boxed set of Bedroom Beauty Delights graciously donated by the Inner Beauty company! And the winner is . . . Persia Vanderbilt, of Venus Envy!"

I almost choked on my lemonade. Bedroom Beauty Delights? Oh God, that meant body paints and edible gels. Barb snorted as I groaned.

"Wonderful—probably full of dyes and chemicals and preservatives," I muttered as the leader of the prize patrol marched my way, a gift wrapped box in her hands.

"Persia, congratulations, you lucky girl!" The hostess presented the boxes to me and scrunched in too close for comfort. I winced as her voice spiraled into the upper register. "Now, if you'll hold up the box, we'll just take a picture for our brochure—"

"Picture? Of me holding up a box full of body paints? I don't think so," I said, arching my eyebrows. "Why don't you pick another winner? I shouldn't win; I'm one of the vendors."

She stared at me blankly. "But why not? You're part of the convention. I suppose if you don't want your picture taken we can't force the issue, but you'd be such a good sport if you'd let me."

I grimaced and shook my head. Even Auntie wouldn't berate me for saying no in this case. The girl backtracked, leaving Barbara and me alone again, both of us staring at the box full of tubes and tubs.

"What are you going to do with it?" she asked.

I shrugged. "Garbage. Unless you want the kit?"

She snorted. "Oh yeah, I can just hear what Dorian would have to say if I brought this home. He'd laugh me out of the bedroom." She opened one of the tubes of edible body shimmer and stared at the squiggle on her finger. "I wonder if it tastes any good?"

I shook my head. "We're not going to . . . oh all right, here." I opened another tube of what was supposed to be cherry flavor. Unable to believe we were actually going to do it, I hesitantly licked the gel off my finger.

As the thin film of fruit flavor hit my mouth, I glanced around, wildly looking for my bottle of water. Pure sweetener and neon flavor. I chugged, trying to wash the metallic taste out of my mouth. Barb was doing the same.

"Shit, that tastes bad," she said, gasping after she downed an entire bottle of San Pellegrino. "I feel like I just rotted out half the teeth in my head. Man, I wish I had some of your aunt's barbecue to take away that taste. Last night was a lot of fun, wasn't it?"

I nodded, still trying to wash away the lingering flavor.

"Yeah, everybody seemed to enjoy themselves. Did you notice Auntie and Kane? I think there's romance brewing." I grinned at her. "Speaking of romance, this crap isn't it." With one sweep, I gathered up the box, marched over to one of the trash bins, and dumped it in. As I turned around, the sound of applause hit my ears. Killian was clapping, a grin a mile wide on his face. I let out a muffled groan and joined him.

"So, you aren't into kink?" Killian asked, leaning over my shoulder to whisper in my ear.

Once again, I found myself short of breath. His eyes were sparkling, and I wanted to reach up and smooth out the wild mop of spikes that covered his head.

"I didn't say that." I winked at him. "But body paints aren't part of the food pyramid. So, you coming to hear me give my speech today?"

"Wouldn't miss it for the world," he said, giving me a long look. "Persia Vanderbilt, would you join me at the hors d'oeuvres table?" The way he said it made me think it was an invitation to something more than a bite to eat.

I hadn't felt this nervous since my first date. "I think I'd like that," I said, glancing over my shoulder at Barb. "Can you watch the booth for a few minutes?"

She gave me a wicked grin. "Are you sure it won't take longer than that?"

I stuck my tongue out at her, then followed Killian toward the buffet that had been set out for the vendors. We'd barely gone two yards when Sharon Wellstone sauntered past. She flashed us a snide look and headed in the direction of Bebe's booth. Beside me, Killian tensed.

"Excuse me for a moment," he said, gritting his teeth. "I'll meet you at the buffet. There's something I have to discuss with Ms. Wellstone." He hurried to catch up with her, catching her arm to whirl her around. "How can you just swish your merry little way past like that without even saying a word? I demand that you return what you stole."

I blinked. What was this? Sharon had stolen something from him?

She yanked her arm away. "Killian, you're a loser. You always have been, and you always will be. I've got nothing to say to you. Why don't you face facts? You just can't cut it in the business. We're smarter and faster than you."

Just then, Trish strode up to drag Killian aside. She leaned close, cupping her hand around his ear. Whatever she whispered to him only infuriated him even more. He spun on one heel, and leaning close, snarled in Sharon's face.

"I warned you before, *little girl*. Mess with me again, and you're in trouble. You're a thief, Wellstone. A thief and a spy. Maybe you think you can bring down Donna Prima, but you and your cronies had better think again. If you so much as blacken my door, I'll kick your butt to the curb! Now, go tell your owner to prepare for a lawsuit because baby, I'm going to slap a doozy on Bebe Wilcox."

Sharon laughed. "Try and make it stick." She sashayed over to her booth, where a group of her yellow-jacketed sisters were tittering behind their hands. The look on Killian's face was one of sheer hatred, and I edged my way back to Barb's side as he stomped through the door into the gardens, our trip to the buffet obviously forgotten in the heat of the moment.

"Jesus, what was that about?" Barb asked.

I shrugged. "Don't know. But man, did you see the look

on his face? And what did he mean about her bringing down Donna Prima? I'm going to find out." I started to go after him, but Barb tapped me on the shoulder.

"You don't have time. Look at the clock—you're due to give your speech in less than ten minutes. Here comes Tawny to take over the booth." Sure enough, Tawny was jogging down the aisle toward us.

She stopped, panting. "Sorry I couldn't get here sooner. Traffic. But you can go now. You don't want to be late for your presentation."

I wanted nothing more than to blow off the speech, but I'd promised. I couldn't let the shop down. Not that I really thought they'd be paying much attention once they found out it wasn't going to be a scintillating treatise on hog-tying a man. With a regretful look at the doors leading to the hotel gardens, I headed toward Conference Hall C, followed by Barb.

The room was packed. If the convention had three hundred attendees, at least two-thirds of them were in my audience. I swallowed a lump in my throat and headed toward the stage, where I faced the mass of expectant women. The expressions on their faces made me think of a group of starved alley cats, waiting to pounce on a mouse.

Wendy Bartleby, the chair of workshops and presentations, was playing hostess. She tapped the microphone to make sure it was working, then introduced me. "Please welcome Persia Vanderbilt, from Venus Envy. Persia is a sensory specialist who custom blends fragrances for her clients." After leading everyone in a polite round of applause, she stepped aside.

Taking a deep breath, I glanced at my notes as I took the podium. "Thank you, Wendy, and many thanks to the Beauty Bonanza Cosmetics Convention for asking me to speak on this subject. Welcome to 'The Fragrance of Desire: Driving Men Mad With Your Scent.'" There were a few titters from the audience. As I stared into the sea of faces, two hours promised to stretch into eternity. I suddenly had doubts that my speech would cover even a fraction of that period.

"Since the beginning of time, our sense of smell has served us by protecting us against potential dangers, fed and nurtured us by leading us to food and water, and propagated our species by leading us to the proper mate. . . ."

And I was off and running. With the exception of a few bored yawns, my audience seemed more appreciative than I'd given them credit for. Perhaps they were in the mood for more than just the fluff that made up most of the fashion and beauty magazines, because by the time I finished the Q and A period, I'd not only worked up a sweat keeping up with the flurry of questions, but I was besieged by a bevy of women asking how they could make an appointment with me. Auntie had the foresight to remind me to bring my Day-Timer, and I scheduled a week's worth of consultations before Barb and I managed to edge out of the room. *Take that, Bebe Wilcox,* I thought.

The minute we were back in the Garden of Beauty, I looked around for Killian, but he was nowhere to be found. Tawny was manning the booth, and finally, unable to locate him, I left instructions with her to give Killian my number if he should ask for me. Barb and I headed out. I was relieved the convention was over for me but couldn't help but wonder about the fracas between Killian and Sharon. And about whether Killian was seeing anybody or not.

❧

The next morning started out just fine but deteriorated rapidly. While Tawny was at the convention, Auntie manned
the counter at Venus Envy. I reached the shop an hour before my first appointment and, chatting brightly with her,
went to organize my station. As I set out my oils and eyedroppers and rubbing alcohol, it struck me that something
was off. I glanced through the drawers, trying to pinpoint
what seemed out of kilter.

The oils were all there, everything I needed to create a
new blend, the measuring cups and spoons I used to make
the bath salts . . . and then it dawned on me. I knew what
was wrong. I pushed back my chair and dropped to my
knees, peering under my desk. Nothing. Another glance—
nope—clean and neat and tidy. Not a dust bunny in sight.
At least the new cleaning woman we'd hired was doing her
job.

I rummaged through every drawer, piling stuff on my
countertop. Auntie noticed what I was doing and mean-
dered over. I looked up at her. "It's gone."

"What's gone?"

I dropped back into my chair. "My journal of recipes for
my oil blends. I'm pretty sure that I put it in the upper left-
hand drawer on Friday, but now, I can't find it anywhere."
And if the journal was gone, I was hip deep in trouble.

Auntie frowned. "Have you looked in my office?
Maybe Tawny moved it for some reason."

"I doubt it, she never touches my things."

"Go look anyway. I'll search the counter."

As I headed back to her office, I had the sinking feeling
that my quest was useless. But I dug through the desk
drawers and looked under the desk and in the wastebasket
and everywhere else I could think of. After that, I tore
apart the area we reserved for the facials and manicures.

Auntie managed to pull herself away from the crowded shop long enough to ask me if I'd found anything.

I shook my head. "Nothing. It's not here."

"Why don't you go home and look? Maybe you tucked it into your purse or tote bag and forgot. Stranger things have happened. Go on; I'll reschedule your appointments for this afternoon. You have to find that notebook."

I grabbed my purse and keys and headed out to the car, fretting. Auntie was right; I didn't dare lose the journal. I'd stupidly ignored all warnings to make a copy, although I'd been gearing up to store a backup of the recipes on my new laptop. Hindsight was a bitch. I dropped into the bakery before I took off for Moss Rose Cottage to fill Barbara in on the problem. She offered to help me out by continuing the search at Venus Envy while I was away, since Auntie had her hands full. Grateful, I took her up on it.

The roads were packed and, where it usually took me fifteen minutes to make it home, this time it took me over forty. By the time I pulled into the driveway, I felt like I was balancing on a razor's edge. Seeing Elliot's car there didn't help matters any. He was waiting on the porch. I stomped up the steps, glaring at him.

"What the hell are you doing here?"

He frowned. "Is that any way to greet an old friend?"

"You aren't my friend, old or otherwise." I pointed toward the driveway. "Make tracks. Now. Or I'll call Kyle again, and you'll have one more incident on the track record we're keeping."

Elliot pulled out an envelope and handed it to me. "I brought you a card."

I sighed. "Listen, Elliot, and listen good. I'm in a bad mood, and you know better than to get on my bad side. Hey, speaking of cards, did that marker ever come off your chest?" I'd written a nasty note on him while he was drunk one night, after he'd insisted on sliming all over me. In permanent marker. Last I heard, he still had a faded crimson note imprinted on his chest, warning all comers to avoid dating him because he was such a jerk.

His eyes narrowed, and I knew I'd struck a nerve. "Want to find out?" He reached for his buttons, but I wasn't in the mood to play games.

"I'm telling you this one time, and one time only. Get off our porch, get out of our driveway, and get off our land. Leave now, or I will first call the police, and then I will pick you up by the collar and toss you down the stairs. You know I can do it, and you know I won't be gentle."

I reached in my purse and held up my cell phone, flipping it open to make my point. Without another word, Elliot headed down the steps, climbed in his car, and screeched out of the drive. The minute his car disappeared down the road, I unlocked the door and headed inside, stopping to latch the screen door behind me. I paused to call Kyle and tell him that Elliot had been here.

Kyle made a suggestion I hadn't thought of. "Persia, do you think he might be the one trying to sabotage Venus Envy? He's mad as shit at you."

"Interesting. Hadn't thought of that, and it's certainly worth a look, although I'm pretty sure Bebe Wilcox is behind this. But I've got another problem now. My recipe journal for my fragrances is missing. I couldn't find it at the shop, and I'm going to search here at home, but if you want to know the truth, I think somebody stole it."

Kyle's sigh was audible. "Do you have a copy of it?"

I cast my gaze down to the floor as Pete came running into the room, tongue lolling out as he bumped against my legs in greeting.

"No . . . no I didn't. I'm stupid, okay? And did I tell you
about the computer?" I recapped what Andy had told me.
"Auntie and I didn't have copies of our records that were
on there, either. We won't make that mistake again, but
there's nothing we can do now."

"Didn't you think ahead? Honestly, Miss Florence is
too bright to forget something like that." He sounded irri-
tated, which exacerbated my own mood.

"Listen, we made a mistake. It happens. Auntie got the
computer installed shortly before I arrived, and neither one
of us knew jack shit about using it. Jared was going to give
us a quick rundown, but we never had the time to get together. So give us a break."

After a pause, Kyle said, "I'm sorry. I didn't realize I
sounded so harsh. You're right. Mistakes happen to the
best of us." I knew he was thinking about his wife Katy,
who had misjudged the weather when she ran afoul of a
logging truck on a back road and lost her life. "If you can't
find your journal by tonight, come in and fill out a report.
By itself, the loss could be coincidence. But with everything else that's happened . . . you may be right. Everything sounds tied together."

I thanked him and then began hunting through the
house. We kept the place in fairly clean shape, though we
really needed a housekeeper. As I dug through the desks
and sideboards, I had no more luck than I had at the shop.
My journal had a velvet burgundy cover and would have
been easy to spot amidst all the green and yellow ledgers
that Auntie had strewn around the house.

Beast, Beauty, and Delilah decided to join in the hunt.
Beast and Beauty wanted to go for a walk and kept bringing me their leashes, while Delilah decided that *the* place
to be was the inside of every drawer I was searching. I'd

pull one open, pile everything on the floor, and she'd hop in the drawer. I'd take her out, replace the books and ledgers, and we'd move on to the next.

By the time I worked my way up to the third floor, Beauty and Beast had given up, off in search of more interesting diversions. Delilah, however, seemed to be having the time of her life. I ruffled her fur and gave her a sound smack on the head. She liked to be kissed.

"You're a phony, you old biddy. You pretend to be so nasty, and then I turn around and there you are, in all your fuzzy, furry, glory." We reached my bedroom, and I began searching. My vanity and dresser came up empty, but when I scrunched my head under the bed, I was in for a little surprise.

Over the past few months, I'd noticed little items disappearing. A bracelet, a string of sandalwood beads strung by Buddhist monks, a fuzzy glove. And now I knew where they'd gone: beneath my bed, along with a small treasure trove that included a dried-out, half-eaten piece of French bread and a couple of catnip mice. Delilah noticed me poking around and squeezed under the bed, hurrying up to the pile while chirping anxiously.

I laughed. "Are these yours, girl? Did you make yourself a nest of toys under here?" She looked so worried that I left everything except the bread. I didn't need the bracelet or beads or glove for awhile, and I knew where they were if need should arise. Delilah scanned my face, then, seeing I wasn't going to take them away from her, curled up next to her treasures and promptly fell asleep.

The journal wasn't in my perfumery, nor was it in my study. I leaned back in my leather chair, realizing that my initial fears were playing out. The journal was gone, and I was certain that somebody had stolen it. When Kyle had mentioned Elliot as a possible suspect, I'd been doubtful, but now I wondered. Could he be exacting revenge on me? He certainly hadn't forgiven me for abandoning him when he was arrested, but would he go to these lengths?

Or was it somebody else? How could Bebe Wilcox have gotten into the shop and stolen my notebook? Or had she delegated that responsibility to one of her cronies? I thought back to the last time I'd seen my journal . . . and then I knew. *Sharon Wellstone.* I'd pushed my journal to the side when she was trying to persuade me to join them. She must have seen it; she knew what it was since she'd been one of my clients. But she'd left empty-handed, so I really couldn't be positive it was her. I fully believed her capable of pulling such a stunt, but when had she found the opportunity?

Killian Reed had accused her of being a thief and a liar. What had she stolen from him? It seemed a good idea to find out—and to talk to him more about the corporate espionage he'd hinted at during our talks. Not to mention, I just wanted to see the man again. As I stood up and dusted off my jeans, I decided it was time to pay a visit to Sharon. Which meant going back to the convention.

Chapter Eight

As I sped along, weaving in and out of traffic, I called Tawny on my cell phone to let her know I was on the way. I also gave Auntie a quick buzz to let her know what I was planning. She agreed to my plan. We had to find some answers as to what the hell was going on. Venus Envy would sink like a stone if crap like this continued.

The conference seemed even more frantic, if that was possible, as I marched down the rows of vendors, pointedly ignoring the Belles, who seemed caught up in some more motivational cheerleading. They were huddled in a circle, chanting away. Maybe they'd morphed into some demon fan club who worshiped Bebe as their fiendish leader, I thought, then shook off the idea when I realized I was half-serious. I steered clear of their booth, taking an alternative route to reach Venus Envy's stall.

Tawny waved when she saw me, and after a quick hello, I asked, "Did you move my recipe journal? Do you even remember seeing it?"

Her eyes wide, she quickly shook her head. "Nope . . .

I never touch your stuff. I'm too nervous about messing something up. Maybe the cleaning lady?"

I hadn't realized I was so intimidating. "God, am I that much of an ogre? I called Clarisse a little while ago and she basically said the same thing you just did, in the same tone of voice." I glanced around. "Then let me ask you this. You remember when Sharon was in the store a few days ago? Did she come back later the same day?"

Tawny thought about it for a moment, then perked up. "Oh, yeah, she said she forgot something over by your station. But I had my hands full, so I told her to go take a look. She must have found it, whatever it was, because when I went over to help her, she was gone."

I groaned. "Have you seen her today?"

With a pop of her gum, Tawny shook her head. "Not that I remember, but then again, I haven't really been looking for her." She brightened. "I've passed out most of the samples, though." The table was nearly empty, and it looked like there'd been a big run on the Lazy Lilac line and the Juniper Girl products.

"Good job. Keep it up." I decided to make a run past Killian's stand before gathering my courage to stroll by Bebe's Cosmetics.

I found myself a little anxious as I headed toward the Donna Prima booth and realized that for the first time in ages, I was worried about how I looked. Shaking off my fears—insecurity wasn't pretty—I peeked in the booth, but Killian was nowhere to be seen. Trish, however, was minding the shop.

She gave me a knowing smile. "Killian's in a meeting right now. He'll be back later." She paused, then said, "Do you want to leave a message?"

I might have taken offense except for the glint in her

eye. I leaned across the table, returning her smile. "Hey
Trish, yeah, I do want to leave him a note." I jotted down
my phone number, the words "Call me," and handed her
the paper. "Say, would you mind terribly if I asked you a
couple questions?"

"That depends on what you want to know." She was ar-
ranging a basket of what looked like rouge and lipstick
samples.

"Have you seen Sharon Wellstone today?"

The smile on her face froze, then disappeared entirely
as a cold edge entered her voice. "No, and I have no desire
to see her." She set the basket on the corner of the table. "If
she's smart, she'll make herself scarce around here."

So Trish didn't like her either. Maybe I could dig up a
little information on just what Sharon had done at Donna
Prima. "I overheard Killian confront her the other day. He
really doesn't like her, does he?"

Trish clammed up. "I'm sure Killian will tell you what
you want to know about that," she said, but her voice was
simmering, and I had the feeling Killian wasn't the only
one who had a bad opinion of Sharon.

I shrugged. "No problem. I just need to get in touch
with her. Not that I want to," I added, sighing, not sure
how I was going to even speak to Sharon without losing
my cool.

Trish gazed at me for a moment. "You look so delighted
by the prospect," she said, her lips curling into a faint
smile. "I'll make sure Killian gets your note."

"Thanks, Trish. I appreciate it." As I headed off, she
gave me a little wave.

I was almost to Bebe's booth when I stopped short.
They had a new display—perfume oils. It hadn't been

there the day before. A warning bell went off in my head, and I glanced at the names.

Narcissus Nights. Tiaras and Roses. Dreamweaver. The sample cards were simply paper impregnated with scents, but a sinking feeling lodged in the pit of my gut, and I hurried back to Venus Envy's booth. Tawny was talking to Allison Montgomery, a brilliant player in Gull Harbor's social elite youth crowd. Allison had been a big help to me when I'd investigated Lydia Wang's death. I tapped her on the shoulder.

"Persia, hello—" she started to say, but I held my finger to my lips.

"Hi Allison. Listen, I have a *huge* favor to ask you, and I need it done soon, if you would." She blinked but waited for me to continue. "Listen, if you could go over to the Bebe booth and snag me several of their fragrance sampler cards, I'd appreciate it more than you could know. For reasons I'd rather not get into, I don't want to be seen picking them up."

Tawny raised her eyebrows and gave me a questioning look. I shook my head at her. Allison stared at me like I was nuts, but then shrugged.

"Sure, I don't have a problem with that. I take it that I'm not to mention you at all?" Allison actually smiled, a rare occurrence outside her social set.

"Right. I appreciate this," I said. "Get samples—two of each if possible—of Narcissus Nights, Tiaras and Roses, and Dreamweaver. Remember, don't tell them I asked you to do this."

Allison slipped off into the crowd.

Tawny leaned her elbows on the table. "Trouble?" she asked.

"Yeah, I think so. If it's what I'm afraid it might be, then you'd better call Kyle, because I don't think I'll be able to stop myself. I've had it with Bebe and Sharon, and I'm just about ready to deck the both of them."

Tawny put a hand on my wrist. "Persia, keep your cool. If it's as bad as you seem to think it is, you don't want to make it worse by acting first and thinking later. At least, that's what your aunt would say."

Just then, Allison returned. She dropped the samples on the counter. "I know why you wanted me to do this," she said in a whisper. "I hope you're wrong, for both your sake and theirs. Because if I were them, I would not want you on my bad side." With a glance at her watch, she added, "I'm late for a luncheon." And with that, she dashed for the door.

I picked up the sack and motioned for Tawny to slide over. As I took a seat next to her on the bench, I peeked in the bag and took out the sample cards. Slowly, one at a time, I opened one of each and held them to my nose. After a few seconds, I silently handed the trio to Tawny, who followed suit. It took her a little longer, but then realization dawned, and she let out a little "Oh" of surprise.

"Persia, those are your blends."

I sucked in a sharp breath. "Those bastards ripped me off . . . and Sharon Wellstone is behind it. My journal disappeared after she showed up at the shop. Now I know where it went." Dreamweaver was a replica of my Lite Dreams oil. Tiaras and Roses—Beauty Queen. And Narcissus Nights was my Narcissus Dreaming blend. Bebe's Cosmetics Company had not only stolen my journal, but they'd replicated my recipes, changing the names. They were probably banking on getting them out to the public at large before I ever noticed, changing them just enough to void any claim I might have that they stole my creations.

Tawny watched me, a nervous look on her face. "You better go outside and walk it off before you do something stupid."

I glanced up at her, my voice perfectly even. "Stupid? Now, would *I* go and do something stupid? I'm just going to go have a little talk with the Belles and casually drop the hint that perhaps they should reconsider stealing from me."

Tawny shook her head. "Oh, Persia, I don't like that look on your face."

"Why? Just what on earth do you think I'm going to do? Break Sharon's neck?" But she didn't have to answer. She knew exactly what I was thinking—that I was going to march over there and wipe the plastic smiles off of Bebe, Sharon, and anybody else who got in my way.

As I stood, Tawny shoved her cell phone into my hand. "Call your aunt! Do it, or you'll regret it later. I don't blame you, but I'm telling you, Persia—you do not want to land in jail over this."

I wavered. As much as I hated to admit it, Tawny was right. If I gave in to my instincts, Kyle would have to drag me out of the hall in handcuffs. I woodenly picked up the phone and started to dial Auntie, but then stopped. I was too angry to talk coherently.

"I'm headed to the beach. I have to calm down before I do anything." Before Tawny could reply, I was out the door. As I headed toward my car, I did make one call—to Bran. I asked him to meet me at Cove Egret in fifteen minutes, then hung up before he could say more than an "Okay."

With one leap, I cleared the door of the car, jumping into my Sebring. Now, if I could manage to keep my speed in check, I might make it to the ocean without an accident. I just prayed that Sharon Wellstone didn't meet me on the

road, because I'd have no hesitation in chasing her down
and settling the score.

↻

Cove Egret was a secluded inlet on the northern side of
Port Samanish. It was open to the winds that came sweep-
ing down Puget Sound and seldom used by tourists because of the dangerous undertow. Riptides were common,
dragging the unwary out as the waters rushed away from
the shore. A number of deaths had occurred before the Port
Samanish Council had voted to ban swimming in the area.
Since the grass and shrubs were sparse, and the wind never
seemed to fade in the inlet even on the warmest of days,
most of the tourists and a good share of the locals avoided
the area. I came here when I needed to think.

Bran was waiting for me, leaning against his truck. At
six three, he stood taller than me by five inches, and his
long dark hair was swept into a neat ponytail. He wore a
pair of olive-colored cargo shorts and a black mesh tank
top, an Aussie bush hat, and he looked absolutely gorgeous. My hormones surged. He was gorgeous, all right,
and sometimes a good hunk of man was just what the doctor ordered.

His leg was scarred where he'd had several pins in-
serted during a bad break earlier in the year. He'd caught
himself on a rope on his boat and almost ended up over-
board during a bad storm. If he'd gone over the side, he
would have died. As it was, he just suffered some seriously
nasty broken bones.

He waited silently as I screeched to a halt and slammed
the car door. I swung in beside him, and we headed toward
a large driftwood log that had buried itself half in the rocky
beach. At times, the waves tossed driftwood around like

Lincoln Logs; getting caught on the beach during a wild storm could result in getting crushed. Driftwood logs could kill . . . but most of the time, they sat, silent witnesses to the waves, bleached by the sun, sandblasted smooth by the wind and sand.

I dropped onto the log that had become our favorite place to picnic and leaned forward, elbows on knees, resting my chin on my hands. Bran settled himself in the sand, leaning back as he pulled his hat low to protect his eyes.

After a moment, I said, "Sharon Wellstone stole my journal. My fragrance journal. And now Bebe's Cosmetics is gearing up to sell replicas of my work under different names."

Bran glanced up at me. "That's pretty stupid. You can take them to court, can't you? Have them arrested for theft?"

The sound of waves crashing against the shore comforted me for a moment, but then I shook my head. "They'll change them enough to claim coincidence. And I'm a fucking idiot, Bran. I didn't even keep a copy of my recipes. How could I prove my charges? I don't know how many times I told Auntie I was going to do it—and I really meant to—but I never got around to it. Oh, I have some of my earlier recipes, but none from the past few months. I don't know how I could be so dense."

He put his hand on my knee and said nothing, staring out at the water. After a moment, I spilled my guts, telling him everything that had happened over the past few weeks.

"They're out to ruin us, Bran. And they may very well do so. We have a lot of circumstantial evidence, but nothing that will stand up in court. I'm not sure what to do. Without reasonable proof, Kyle isn't going to search their headquarters. Not to mention, they might have already destroyed my journal after copying the instructions. It's my word against theirs."

"Do you want my advice?" he asked.

I nodded. I liked to think of myself as an intelligent woman, but right now, I felt like a fool. "Whatever you've got, I want to hear."

He pushed himself up on the log next to me and put his arm around my shoulders. "Babe, go talk to Kyle again."

I nodded. "Shit . . . even if he wants to help, what can he do? But you're right. I guess that's my only choice."

"He's going to be the one to know what avenues are open to you. He'll believe you—even if he can't do much about it. And I think you need to talk to your aunt about better security in the shop. Miss Florence is a brilliant woman—as are you. But you both trust fate a little too much for comfort."

I glanced at him and laughed. "That seems pretty strange coming from your lips." Somehow, the idea that he didn't trust in fate seemed odd to me.

He snorted. "One of the first things you learn when you begin working with the paranormal is that you can't rely on magic unless you take care of the practical. All the luck in the world won't help somebody who doesn't keep their house in order."

I nodded. "Makes sense. Okay, so I'll go talk to Kyle. For whatever good that will do."

Bran pulled me close and nuzzled the top of my head. "Just don't ask him for any other kind of help, okay?"

I squashed a grin. "Well, he is rather handsome . . ."

"Hey!" Bran tightened his grip around my waist. "I thought you said he wasn't your type?"

Reaching out, I ran my fingers under his tank top. "He isn't, but that doesn't mean I can't tease." I glanced around. "Hey, Stanton, there's nobody here today. You want to take a little break before I go visit Kyle? I could seriously use a good—"

"Tension release?" he said, a secretive smile sliding over his face. He cupped my breast. "I love a woman who isn't afraid to ask for what she wants."

And with that, we landed in the sand, taking advantage of the privacy of the cove. As Bran slipped my top up, I closed my eyes and listened to the sound of water cresting on the beach. The feel of his body against mine pushed all thoughts of thieves and perfume and corporate intrigue out of my mind, and for a little while, I was able to forget about my worries.

❦

Kyle looked up as I came waltzing through the door. Though I was still mad as hell, my encounter with Bran had relaxed me, and I wasn't feeling quite so ready to gun down Bebe's Belles.

I slid into the chair opposite him and leaned forward. "I know who took my journal," I said, and laid it all out for him.

When I was done, Kyle blinked. "So, do you have any proof, anything at all, that would give you prior claim?"

"Here are the products we have on the shelves—the ones I made. And here are Bebe's sample cards. The fragrance is the same, and we've been carrying them for months, but there's no way to analyze these. By the time they market them, you can bet they'll change the formula just enough to keep themselves out of hot water." I handed him my bottles of fragrance, then the samples.

He sniffed each carefully. "Anything else? This is a

good start, but I know I can't get a search warrant on the basis of what you've shown me."

While I was racking my brain, trying to think of anything I'd overlooked, the phone rang. Kyle answered it, and by the look on his face, I could tell whatever the news was, it wasn't good. He turned away, lowering his voice. After a few minutes, he finished his conversation and dropped the receiver back in the cradle, then stared at me for a moment, a look of deliberation on his face.

Feeling suddenly ill at ease, I asked, "What is it? Something's happened. What's wrong?"

He cocked his head, giving a noncommittal shrug. "Where were you last night, Persia?"

I frowned, "At home for the most part. Why?"

Kyle sighed. "This is an official question, Persia. Where were you last night?"

Narrowing my eyes, I glared at him. "I want to know why you're asking me. Official business usually spells trouble."

Abruptly shifting into all-business-no-nonsense mode, Kyle said, "Fine, you want to know why I'm asking? Sharon Wellstone was just found outside the hotel, in the garden. She's seriously injured, and they're not sure if she's going to make it. Somebody shot her in the shoulder, which by itself wouldn't be critical, but when she fell, she hit her head. She's in a coma."

I stared at him, at first thinking he was pulling my leg. "If that's a joke, it's extremely bad taste, Kyle."

He shook his head. "I assure you, it's no joke. She's fighting for her life in the ICU right now. She's lucky it was so warm last night. As far as the doctor can tell, she was shot sometime between midnight and morning."

A gamut of feelings ran through me. While I was horri-

fied that someone might actually have taken a gun to her,
I couldn't help but feel a twinge of empathy. Only two
hours ago, I wanted to punch her lights out myself. Then it
dawned on me why Kyle had asked. Precisely because of
those sentiments. I'd left nothing to the imagination as far
as what I felt for the conniving thief.

"Oh wait—you can't think I did it? Come on, Kyle. You
know me better than that."

He shrugged. "We all like to think we know what our
friends are capable of, but I seem to remember you trying
to take a bite out of my finger when you were mad at me a
few months ago."

"That's ancient history, and you deserved it." I sighed
impatiently. "Listen, you want to know where I was? At
home, in bed with Bran. We spent a quiet evening alone
while Auntie was out at a Gull Harbor Business Women's
Meeting. He left around 1:00 AM, after we went for a walk
around the house to make sure nobody was prowling in the
gardens trying to destroy more of our flowers. I was alone
for the rest of the night, and Auntie saw me at breakfast."

Only the slightest blink told me that my statement had
had any impact on Kyle. He simply wrote down what I
said. "I take it Bran will confirm this?"

"Yeah, he'll confirm it." I pushed myself out of the
chair. "So, am I free to go? Or are you going to hold me on
suspicion of attempted murder?"

"Persia, you're a spitfire," he said. "You always were.
And I sincerely hope you'll always be one. You're free to
go, but don't leave town until I've had a chance to talk to
Bran and your aunt." He frowned. "Meanwhile, about your
journal . . . I'm sorry. There's nothing I can do legally at
the moment." He held up his hand to forestall my protests.

"I believe it was stolen, so don't start in on that. But my hands are tied. The law is specific."

I took a deep breath and pushed myself to my feet. "Kyle, I've got to get that journal back. My life's work with fragrances is in there. I was stupid, but do I deserve to see somebody wipe out everything I've accomplished over the years just because I didn't make a copy?"

He stood and circled the desk, placing a brotherly hand on my shoulder. "No, Persia, you don't deserve that. I promise you, we'll do everything we can."

Flashing him a subdued smile, I returned to my car, wondering who'd shot Sharon. As much as I wanted to feel sorry for her, I couldn't help but think that she'd probably brought it on herself.

⁀

Winthrop Winchester settled into a chair at the table, his black leather briefcase solid against the walnut tabletop. He removed a sheaf of papers, carefully placing them in front of me.

"I stopped by the hospital on the way and talked to the chief," he said. Auntie's lawyer, Winthrop, was the best money could hire in Gull Harbor. He was also charming, crafty, and won most of his cases by his sheer ability to cow the competition into submission.

"How's Sharon doing?" Even though I was pissed at her, I didn't want her to die. We couldn't lock her up for stealing my journal if she kicked the bucket. I bit my lip, realizing that my thoughts were sounding pretty callous, and tried to let go of some of the anger.

He gave me a speculative look. "She's still in danger. The doctor doesn't know if she's going to come out of the coma or not, and they won't be able to tell if there's been any permanent brain damage for awhile. She was shot in the shoulder, but it looks like they were aiming for her heart. That's not what did the most damage, however. When she fell, she hit her head on one of the concrete benches. All we can do is hope that she wakes up." *If she wakes up.* The words hung heavy between us.

I decided to get my fears out in the open. "Does Kyle seriously consider me a suspect?"

Winthrop shook his head. "I don't think so. There's certainly not enough evidence to run you in, although he wants a complete listing of any firearms in your possession, and your aunt's possession. That one's easy, considering neither one of you own a gun. But you do have the rest of last night to account for after Bran left. The latest report places Sharon's injury as happening around four in the morning—give or take a few hours. There's enough wiggle room that you're on the list of suspects, but not at the top."

"In other words, be grateful for small favors?"

He chuckled. "Something like that, yes. I don't think you have anything to worry about, though. Kyle didn't bite when I brought up your name."

I glanced over at Auntie. When I'd called her at the store to tell her about Sharon and my journal, she'd closed the shop and dropped by Winthrop's office. They'd returned to the house together, which was why we were having this powwow session.

Winthrop looked at his list of notes. "Let me get this straight. Sharon approached Persia, trying to convince her to leave Venus Envy. Your roses were doctored with organophosphates, at a level that could have been dangerous for your customers if you hadn't caught the mistake in time. Your computer was hacked into and your files de-

stroyed. Persia's journal of fragrance blends was stolen,
and Bebe's Cosmetics suddenly comes up with what seem
to be replicas. And Sharon Wellstone ends up on the wrong
end of a gun."

"That's about it," I said, looking at Auntie for confirmation.

She nodded. "A real mess, is what it is."

Winthrop glanced at me. "You said there were other
people mad at Sharon?"

I closed my eyes, struggling with my conscience. I
didn't want to tell Winthrop about Killian, but since I was
on the suspect list, I figured the truth was the best choice.

"I saw Killian Reed, of Donna Prima Cosmetics, get in
a screaming match with her. He accused her of being a
thief. According to him, she stole something from him or
his company. And Sharon was is some skirmish the other
day with a blonde whom I don't know. I think she's another
Belle, but I have no idea what they were arguing
about."

"What else?" Winthrop said, taking detailed notes.

"Nancy Louis and her animal rights activists. You heard
about the paint incident?" When he nodded, I continued.
"Sharon might have been one of their targets. The truth is,
I can't remember if Sharon was wearing a fur at lunch or
not, but it's worth a shot. But I'll bet you anything she has
one of Bebe's coats hanging in her closet.

Winthrop snorted. "Fur coats in August? Absurd."

Auntie laughed outright.

"Winthrop," she said, "you have not lived until you've
met a Belle in full regalia. They wear those cheap furs
everywhere. The minks are made from leftover scraps.
Anybody who knows fur, knows that. But a number of the
Belles are from . . . shall we say . . . poorer families who

don't really know what quality mink should look like. It boosts their self-confidence to wear them. You'll see a number of furs in the summer at luncheons and teas."

Winthrop grinned at Auntie, a bemused smile flickering across his lips. "Do tell, Florence. All right then, so we have three potential triggers right here, then. This Reed fellow, a mysterious blonde, and Nancy Louis. Did you tell Kyle any of this?" he asked, turning to me.

"Kyle and his men showed up when the Animal Freedom Association pulled their little stunt and carted away the perpetrators. I forgot to tell him about the rest, I was so pissed off about my journal."

"I'll have a talk with him after I leave here and mention the possibilities. They could be important leads."

I swallowed my pride. "Don't implicate Killian, please. Just tell Kyle what I said, but don't make it sound like I think Killian shot her."

Winthrop raised one eyebrow. "Do I detect a little interest here?"

I blushed, then shrugged. "He just seems like a really nice guy." Auntie gave me a questioning look but said nothing as Winthrop finished with his notes.

He sat back, frowning. "I've done some research on Bebe Wilcox. What I've found isn't pretty. Makeup may cover a multitude of sins, but it won't cover up fraud."

"Fraud?" Auntie asked. "Are you saying Bebe's Cosmetics isn't a legitimate company?"

"No, it seems this time Bebe has gone to the trouble of backing up her claims with an actual business, but it appears that in the past, things weren't so hunky-dory. As a matter of fact, Bebe Wilcox used to be Eudora Gallagher, who spent several years in and out of trouble with one at-

torney general after another, in at least five states. Somehow, she always managed to avoid prosecution."

Auntie and I both perked up. This was starting to sound
interesting.

Auntie leaned forward. "Do tell."

Winthrop gave her a long smile. "Do you remember the
Worthwright Scholarship fiasco? Several hundred people
were conned into donating close to twenty thousand dollars to phony school fund-raisers."

"Bebe?"

"It seems that she managed to avoid prosecution by settling out of court and returning the money. The charges
were mysteriously dropped. I think that the prosecutor at
the time was on the take, but we could never prove such a
charge. And there was the Scofield Retirement Fund . . . a
pyramid scheme in which a lot of older folks lost their life
savings. But Eudora managed to skip out on charges for
that, too. I could list half a dozen other fraudulent companies she was behind. And each time, she bought—or
lied—her way free. A few years ago, she changed her
name to Bebe Wilcox and founded Bebe's Cosmetics."

"So what's she up to this time?" Auntie asked.

Winthrop shrugged. "I have no idea, but my guess is
that, while the company and its products actually exist,
there's probably a lot of lying, spying, and outright theft
going on over there. Eudora isn't a straight shooter, and I
sincerely doubt that she changed her tactics along with her
name."

I considered the information. "She's built an army of
Belles who are rabidly loyal. . . . It's going to be hard getting in to find out where the hell my journal is."

Winthrop just smiled. "Oh, we'll think of something,
my dear, and we'll find your journal. I have no doubt of it.

It's just going to take some planning and diplomatic maneuvering. Now, how about a glass of iced tea?"

As I retired to the kitchen, I couldn't help but be thankful that Winthrop was on our side. He was a shark, and I was infinitely grateful that I wasn't on the menu.

Chapter Nine

While I arranged cookies on a plate and poured our drinks, I could hear Winthrop and Auntie discussing the paperwork that would legalize my partnership in the business, but my mind was running in a different direction.

Our roses were tainted. . . . Sharon screwed over Killian. . . . Bebe was a well-known scam artist. . . . My journal had been stolen, and my work ripped off. . . . And now, Sharon, was lying in a hospital bed, comatose from a gunshot.

How did the pieces all fit together? I was fairly certain that Bebe was the culprit behind our roses and my journal; that was a no-brainer, even though we couldn't prove it. But somebody had shot Sharon, and that was an entirely different ball of wax.

Who hated her enough to kill her? I knew that's how Kyle was looking at it, just as I knew he had to put me on his list, considering the accusations I'd made against the woman. But the truth was, as angry as I was at Sharon, I'd never make an attempt on her life over the theft of my work. It just wasn't in my nature. Revenge? Yes, but not of the bodily harm type. But *somebody* had shot her. She didn't hold that gun herself.

What about Killian? As much as I didn't want to think of him as a suspect, the fact remained that he had accused Sharon of being a thief, and his hatred for the woman was obvious. Could his feelings have led him to hurt her? Or was he in the same camp I was—guilty of anger but not of action?

Of course, there was also the chance that Sharon played a part in riling up the Animal Freedom Association. Could one of their fanatics have taken symbolic attack into actual violence? And there were a gaggle of competive Belles, no doubt some of whom might have had it in for her. A bevy of thoughts buzzing in my head, I loaded up a tray and headed back to the table.

Winthrop and Auntie looked up as I returned to the dining room. A packet of papers sat on my placemat and, after setting down the tray, I glanced over them. The partnership forms. They looked impressively legalistic, and I dreaded reading through every line.

"Give me a pen—" I started to say, but Auntie shook her head.

"You know better than that. Even with relatives, you read everything in there. Would you like a second legal opinion? I don't mind, and Winthrop will understand."

I stared at her. "It's not like I'm buying into the shop— this is a gift, one I very gratefully accept. Whatever terms you want, I'm fine with, as long as my creations are free to go with me if I ever have to leave."

Auntie glanced at Winthrop. "What do you think?"

He harrumphed. "As long as she signs a paper saying she's voluntarily waived a second opinion, then yes, it's fine." He turned to me. "Though, young woman, I highly recommend you avoid ever using this tactic with anyone except your aunt. Not everybody is as honest as Florence here."

I perked up. Nobody else in Gull Harbor ever called Auntie by her name without *Miss* attached. Nobody but Winthrop. Wondering if they had some sort of a past together, but not about to ask, I read quickly over the contract, saw that everything looked to be in order, then signed the waiver and initialed over a dozen pieces of paper that went into the formation of the partnership. By the time I was done, I had an eerie feeling that I'd just indentured myself for life.

Auntie shook my hand with look of mock solemnity on her face, then burst into a sunbeam grin and pulled me close for a hug. "We're partners, Imp. And I think we make a good team."

"Tell that to Sharon Wellstone," I said, thinking about the offer she'd tendered. "Apparently Bebe is under the assumption that I'd be better off working for them than you. I don't know just what rumors are going around, but I told Sharon to forget it."

Auntie stared at me, a glint in her eye. "You know, I pushed that incident to the side, but it does bring to mind a possible plan to find your missing journal."

Winthrop gazed at Auntie, and I could see the emotions churning on his face. "Florence Iris Vanderbilt, you're cooking up a scheme, aren't you?"

She winked at him. "Oh, Winthrop, you know me too well."

"Well, somebody let me in on the plan!" I snatched a cookie up and began to nibble on it, suddenly feeling very much the third wheel. I prided myself on being an intelligent woman, but now and then, Auntie got the better of me, and I'd be shocked back into remembering just how cagey and clever she was. Auntie was no slouch in the brains department, that was for sure.

She turned to me, a mischievous smile playing about her lips. "Persia, I think that it's time you left the employ of Venus Envy."

Stunned, I waved the partnership papers. "But you just made me a partner," I started to say, then saw the laughter on both of their faces. As I thought over our conversation, it hit me just what Auntie was thinking. "Oh, no, you can't ask me to go over to Bebe and beg her for a job! Besides, Sharon probably told them I wasn't interested."

Auntie shook her head. "Ten to one, it hasn't gotten back to Bebe yet. And even if it has, you could easily change your mind for one reason or another."

"But that's insane. I don't want to work for Bebe," I sputtered, looking for a way out. Now her idea was all too clear—I go over to Bebe's factory, ask for a job, infiltrate my way in, find proof that they stole my journal, and we nab them. "Besides, Kyle probably wouldn't approve."

"Since when have you ever chosen to listen to Kyle?" Auntie snorted. "I seem to remember a few months ago when you deliberately walked into danger to prove something Kyle couldn't act on."

I grimaced. She had me there, that was for certain. More often than not, I dismissed what he had to say. He was a good cop, smart, honest, but he went by the book, and sometimes life demanded that you step outside the box.

"What do you suggest I do? Sashay over there and say I've changed my mind? Won't they be a little suspicious?"

Winthrop leaned forward, folding his hands together. "If I might offer a suggestion?" Auntie nodded, and he continued, "Suppose you and Persia have a falling out? What happens if you have a huge fight? That would provide motivation for her to go bang on Bebe's door, asking about the job Sharon had mentioned. Hell, Florence, fire the girl and throw her out of this house to make it convincing. Persia can take a cheap apartment for a week or two to make it look like she's out on her ass."

I sat there, my mind whirling. Fire me? Throw me out of the house? Even though I knew we were talking temporary measures, my pulse started to race, and I realized just how much I loved living here at Moss Rose Cottage and working with Aunt Florence. If we'd been talking for real, I'd be totally trashed by now. As it was, even the *thought* of people thinking Auntie had disowned me hurt like hell. She was, after all, the only real mother I'd ever had.

Auntie latched onto his plan. "That's very good—and that would forestall any questions of loyalty to me. If they think she's mad at me, then they'll snap her up and try to nail the lid on Venus Envy's coffin."

It was about that time that she noticed my distress. With a quick arm around my shoulder, she pulled me close to her. "Oh, Imp, please don't look like that! You know I adore you, that I love you to pieces, but this is the only way we'll ever find your journal. It's also a chance for you to snoop around and see if you can find any evidence that they're the ones behind tainting our roses and crashing our computer."

I knew she was right, but I didn't want to face it. Inhaling deeply, I leaned on her shoulder. "I just can't stand people thinking you hate me, Auntie. I love you too much. I'll be the pariah of the town."

"Only as long as it takes to find your journal," Winthrop said. "And afterward, we can let people know it was all a plan to stop the demise of Venus Envy. Because, Persia, if things go on as they have, there won't be a store for you to take over when Florence wants to retire. Bebe Wilcox will win if you don't do something to stop her. I've looked at this from all angles, and Bebe has a definite advantage. She's not afraid to play dirty."

He had a point. Auntie and Winthrop were pretty darn sharp. I sighed. Sometimes sacrifice was necessary to achieve the desired end. I only wished the sacrifice in question wouldn't leave me stranded out of house and home, turning me into persona non grata. Even if it was only for a week or two, my ego was going to take a bruising.

"All right," I said, "I'm in, but I don't know how long I can keep it up."

"Then you'd better work fast," Winthrop said. "What can we stage between you two that will look believable?"

Whatever we came up with had to be probable enough to convince Bebe that we were on the outs. It wasn't as easy as it sounded; everybody knew we were tight. As we were discussing possibilities, the phone rang, and Auntie excused herself to answer it.

When she came back, her face was ashen. "That was Trevor with the estimate on how much it will take to replace the roses. We're talking over fifteen thousand dollars to renovate the gardens, including digging out all that soil and replacing it with new fill. Even if the tests come back clean, I don't want to take any chances. And it will take a good two years before we're able to harvest anything off of new plants. Some of the heritage roses we were using are terribly pricy, and he's not sure we can even *find* replacements for some of them." She sat down, burying her face in her hands.

I grimaced. Auntie was wealthy, yes, but fifteen thousand dollars was fifteen thousand dollars, any which way you looked at it. "We shouldn't have to put out one cent! This never should have happened in the first place. And it's not like it's our fault."

"At least you can write off the losses at the end of the year," Winthrop said, but even as he spoke, I jumped up, snapping my fingers.

"I've got it! I know just what we can do that might convince people Auntie and I are on the outs." I laid out my ideas. Both Auntie and Winthrop began to nod, and I could tell that they approved.

"The only question that remains is, how do we stage this?" Even as I spoke, my enthusiasm began to wane. My leave-taking would be all too public knowledge once the town gossip, Heddy Latherton, got wind of the news, and I'd be scum in a lot of people's eyes. But for the good of the shop and my own peace of mind, I knew I had to go through with it. As it was, luck—or rather, bad luck—was about to play right into our hands.

The next morning brought more unwelcome news. Trevor rang the bell at seven thirty. Still in my workout gear, I led him into the kitchen, where Auntie was finishing up making our breakfast. She'd scrambled eggs and fried up some ham, and motioned for me to add another plate to the table.

Trevor shook his head. "I already ate, but thanks." He held up several sheets of paper. "I stopped by to get the test results from Dave. I thought you'd want to know the results as soon as possible."

"Hold on. I have a feeling I'm going to want to sit down for this, by the look on your face." Auntie dished up our plates, and we carried them into the dining room, but neither one of us took a bite as we settled around the table.

"How bad is it?" she asked. I held my breath as he handed her the reports.

"Not good. Not only were the rose petals tainted, but the soil around the roses has high concentrations of insecticide in it. We have to confine the damage before it leaches through the soil any farther than it already has." His face clouded over; I had the sense that he'd taken the vandalism as a personal insult.

"We won't be using the word *organic* for awhile," Auntie said, flipping through the report. "What about the rest of the gardens? Give it to me in a nutshell."

"They checked out as clean. Either the SOB was scared off or didn't think to bring enough of the pesticide to go around. But one thing's for sure, we're going to have to go ahead with the plans to dig out and replace all the soil in the rose gardens. Even then, it's going to take several years to make sure that everything's clean again." He sighed. "Like I told you on the phone last night, this is going to cost you a pretty penny."

Auntie and I looked at one another.

"This cinches it," I said. "Like it or not, we have to do something."

With a nod, she turned to Trevor. "Who have you told about the contamination?"

When he said, "Nobody but Dave, Sarah, you, and Kyle," I knew we were home free.

❧

The next morning, I packed a bag before I left and tossed it in the trunk. On my way to the shop, I debated whether to tell Barbara about our plans before we put them into effect. On one hand, her surprise could be useful in spreading the word. On the other hand, she was my best friend,

and I didn't want her feeling pulled between me and my
aunt. Not to mention, she could seriously interfere with our
plans, albeit unwittingly. She'd do anything in her power
to avert rumors that we were on the outs, and right now, rumors were what we were aiming for.

After a moment, I pulled over to the side of the road and
fished my cell phone out of my purse. I hit number three
on speed dial and waited. Luck was with me. Barbara was
the one who answered.

"Listen, I need to talk to you about something now, but
it's private. Can you make sure you're not being overheard?" I paused while she secreted herself away from the
front of the bakery, then spilled the beans. "You have to
keep quiet about this, though. You can't even tell Dorian.
The only thing you can say is that you know Auntie and
I've had a falling out, once we stage our argument."

Barbara was speechless for a good ten seconds, an eternity for her. Then she sputtered to life. "I can't *believe* you
guys are going through with this! Oh my God, this is going
to be priceless."

"Priceless my ass. My head's going to be on the chopping block as far as a lot of people are concerned. But
Venus Envy means too much to us to just walk away and
watch everything sink. Since Kyle can't do anything, then
we'll take matters into our own hands. If I have to play bad
cop for awhile, then I'll be the bad cop.

Barb agreed to be one of our coconspirators, and I hung
up. So far, so good. Now, for the actual confrontation.

Auntie had gone in early. We'd debated telling Tawny,
but as much as we liked the girl, we couldn't be sure of her
ability to keep a secret. Since she was still at the convention,
we had some leeway. Trevor knew, of course, and I'd called
Bran. Both agreed to do what they could to further our plan.

As I walked in the front door, I noticed that Heddy was in the shop. Usually I ran the other way when I saw her, but today, the woman had perfect timing. She was standing by the counter, chatting with Auntie. The gossip maven of the town, Heddy was a pain in the neck, and Auntie despised her quick and easy tongue. She gave me a long look, and I knew Operation Infiltrate Bebe's was about to begin.

"Heddy was just telling me about Sharon's condition," Auntie said. Why was I not surprised? I had the feeling that Sharon's assault had been the center of Heddy's conversation since the news first hit the streets. Before Heddy could say a word, however, Auntie changed the subject. "So, what are you doing this afternoon, Heddy?"

"I'm due over at the Sherwood Forest Shopping Center by one PM," Heddy said. "We're wrapping gifts as part of a charity project that the Women's Association is sponsoring. Tell everybody to do their shopping over at Sherwood today!"

"How wonderful," Auntie murmured as I nodded and hurried past, into the back, where I quickly buzzed Trevor. He was waiting at the bakery for his cue.

"Get over here now. Heddy's here, and it's the perfect time to get this show on the road."

Trevor signed off, and I returned to my station where I started setting out my oils, after giving Auntie a quick nod. As I dusted off the counter, Trevor burst through the doors, panting heavily.

"Miss Florence, I have to talk to you. We have trouble—"

Florence glanced at Heddy, then quickly shushed him. "Persia, please watch the front? Trevor, come into my office. If you'll excuse me, Heddy?"

She bustled Trevor off to the back. As I'd expected, Heddy sidled over, hoping to catch a few tidbits of gossip.

I nervously glanced at the back of the store. At least I didn't have much of an acting job; once this news broke, I was as good as gone.

"I wonder what could have happened?" Heddy said, eyeing me like I had the key to the cookie jar.

I let out a long breath, then shrugged. "I'm not sure," I said, forcing doubt into my voice. Might as well let her think I was worried.

"Trevor seems in a bit of a fuss."

"Things haven't been easy lately," I said, sighing. "Everybody in town seems stressed. Even Auntie and I've had our share of squabbles. It must be the heat."

Heddy gave me a sage nod. "The weather can make a mess of things, all right. I was telling my niece just yester-day that we need a good rain."

Half listening, I arranged my oils, wishing that I'd been smarter and kept better tabs on my journal. If Bebe and her cronies hadn't swiped it, Auntie and I wouldn't have to participate in this charade.

Just then, Trevor came striding out. He stopped in the middle of the store and stared at me. "Miss Florence knows what you did. I can't believe you'd stab us in the back like that!" he said. Then, before I could answer, he stomped out the door, slamming it behind him.

"Wha—?" I glanced over at Heddy. "What's he talking about?"

She was about to say something when Auntie appeared, a storm cloud covering her face. "Persia, I need to see you. Now."

I cleared my throat. "Can it wait—"

"No! I said, now." She turned and stomped back to her office, and I followed, leaving Heddy to absorb the scene like a sponge. Once I shut the door behind me, Auntie and

I looked at one another and broke into low, hushed laughter. She dropped into her chair.

"Lordy, this is hard for me, Persia. I can't stand the thought of people thinking I've disowned you." She wiped the corners of her eyes and gave me a careworn smile.

I let myself down into the opposite chair, my knees quivering. "I know; I hate this, too. But if we want to save the store, and my work, we've got to do something."

Auntie sniffled. "I know, my dear. I know. All right. I suppose we'd better get this over with. After we're done . . ." Her voice trailed off, and I could see just how hard this was for her.

"I'll go find a studio. It's worth the cost, and it won't be for long. I'll keep in touch via phone, but I'd better not go back to the house."

"When we have Bebe by the balls, we're going to celebrate," she said, giving me a long hug. "I love you, my dear. And I love that you're willing to play the part. All right, if you're ready?"

"Hold on a second," I said, pulling out my blush to give myself an overly flushed look. "Okay." I took a deep breath. "Go for it."

Auntie moved closer to the door and opened it just a smidgen. Our voices would carry to the front. "How could you do this, Persia? Do you realize how much damage you've caused? I can't believe you didn't consult me—now look at the mess you've made! Do you know how much it's going to cost me to replace those gardens?"

Raising my voice, I shouted back. "It's not my fault! I didn't do anything to the damned roses!"

Auntie leaned against the doorframe. "Then who else could it have been? Trevor? Sarah? They've worked for me for years. You knew that I didn't want any pesticides

used, and yet you deliberately hired somebody to dust the
roses. Not only have we lost the crop, but I'm going to
have to replace all the flowers and the soil they're planted
in, thanks to contamination! You were in charge; it's your
responsibility. I can't believe how stupid you were!"

She gave me a painful look that said she couldn't believe she was saying what she was saying.

I mouthed, "It's okay; I love you." As she regrouped, I
launched in again.

"You don't believe me? You think I'm lying? How
could you? I've been like a daughter to you, and now you
think I betrayed you? That tears it. Call me when you come
to your senses." I gave her a quick peck on the cheek and
whispered, "I'll call you later today. Be strong. This won't
be for long." *I hope,* I added to myself.

I splashed my eyes with a few drops from my water bottle and roughly wiped it away to give myself that "trying
not to cry" look. Then I stomped out of the office, slamming the door behind me. As I marched to my station, I
studiously avoided looking at Heddy.

A few other people were in the shop, and I winced,
knowing they'd also heard the fracas. I grabbed my hobo
bag and headed for the door. As I shoved it open, I noticed
Barbara was standing near the front of the shop. She gave
me a quiet thumbs-up. Without a word, I hit the streets.

⟡

I drove to the only place in town where I knew I could rent
an apartment for a week or two without any strings attached. People had to think I was both broke and desperate, and living in the Deacon Street Apartments would give
me an air of authenticity. Bebe *had* to think Auntie had cut
me off from the cash flow.

Located across from the Delacorte Plaza, the apartment building was run down, hideously outdated, and had three solid strikes against it. One, I'd caught a murderer there, and the place brought back painful memories. Painful as in actual pain, not emotional. Thanks to that little escapade, I knew what it felt like to be pumped full of electricity.

The second strike was that our late cleaning lady, Marta, had lived—and died—there, and I felt rather sad every time I thought about her untimely death. And third, and perhaps the most relevant at this point, good old Andy Andrews lived there. If he caught wind that I'd moved in, he'd be pounding at my door.

However, the one major plus was that the Deacon Street Apartments offered a weekly option on furnished studios, which meant I wouldn't have to rent the place for an entire month should our plan work. Cheaper than a hotel, it made more sense for me to settle in there, if I was supposed to be broke and out of work.

I gingerly knocked on the manager's door. My expectations were not disappointed. A balding, middle-aged man in a ripped undershirt and dirty jeans answered the door. He had a beer belly that peeked out from the overly tight shirt, and a sleazy looking handlebar mustache that was waxed to a high sheen.

I forced a smile to my lips. "I'm interested in renting a studio for a week or two."

He stared at me for a minute, then shrugged. "Yeah, come on in. You want a beer?"

"No, thank you." I stepped into his apartment and looked around. From his demeanor I expected to see pin-ups everywhere, but instead, assorted paintings of elks and ducks decorated the walls. A box of old *Field & Stream* magazines clued me into what this guy's passion was . . .

or at least one of them. And instead of the requisite leopard and bear rugs, I found myself staring at rustic leather furniture that had long seen better days.

"Name?" He pulled a one-page application out of the desk drawer and handed it to me.

"Persia Vanderbilt." I accepted the paper and sat down on one of the cleaner looking chairs.

"I'm Carlos. Fill that out, and I'll show you the place. I got one studio vacant right now."

"How much is it?" I asked.

"Two hundred security deposit, two hundred a week. Cash, no checks. Furnished, includes basic utilities and cable. No pets, no loud parties. No refund if you leave before the week's up." He stared at the TV, which was muted. I glanced at the screen just in time to see a group of bikini-clad girls posing for a photographer. *Sports Illustrated* shoot, no doubt. Without a word, I filled out the application.

It didn't ask for much, just name, employer, income, previous residence. I filled them out, listing Venus Envy and my aunt as references. Even Bebe wouldn't go so far as to bribe the landlord for information. Or at least, I hoped she wouldn't. When I handed it back to him, he glanced over the information and shrugged.

"Looks okay to me," he said. "You want to see the place now?"

I followed him to the cranky old elevator and stepped in behind him. Once I was settled, I'd use the stairs. Safer that way. We stopped on the fifth floor, and I fought back a grimace. Great, Andy's floor. Carlos led me down the hall, the opposite direction. Thank heaven for small favors. He stopped in front of 501-A and unlocked the door, pushing it open. I sidled by, taking pains not to brush against him. Carlos had been a gentleman—in the rough—until now, and I planned on encouraging the behavior.

The apartment was small, of course. The bath had a shower instead of a tub, and the main room was fairly large, with a studio kitchenette. The paint on the walls was coming off in flakes, dirty yellow that had once passed for gold. The solitary window in the room looked across the street to the Delacorte Plaza. This was worth two hundred a week? I prayed that I wouldn't be here longer than that.

I turned around and forced another smile. "This will do just fine," I said, lying through my teeth.

Carlos grunted. "Good. When do you want to move in?"

"Don't you have to check my references?" I asked. I'd expected to spend at least one night in a hotel.

He grinned, and I saw that his teeth were stained. "Lady, you see this place. You can guess the type of tenants I usually get. The money's up front, they leave, no skin off my nose. They cause trouble, they know they're out the door. So you gonna take it or not?"

As I repressed a shudder and reached for my wallet, my stomach knotted. I already regretted our little charade.

Chapter Ten

❧❦

My first order of business was to pick up a few things for my new apartment. It would have been much easier to bring them from Moss Rose Cottage, but I wanted to be seen shelling out my precious shekels by the general public. If this sham was going to work, we had to play it up to the fullest.

I calculated when and where I'd have the most chance of being seen by my intended audience. As with most towns in western Washington, there was a mini-mall every few blocks. Even luckier, the one near the Red Door was the Sherwood Forest Shopping Center, the very place where Heddy would be wrapping gifts for her charity function. I could easily stage a well-timed accidental meeting and give her the gossip she was always on the lookout for.

The hot weather was still hanging heavy over the area, and I squinted as I slid behind the wheel. A quick fumble in the glove compartment produced my sunglasses, and I slid them on, blinking as my eyes adjusted to the change in light. As much as I loved the sun, this interminable heat was beginning to tax even my nerves. A steady parade of days in the mid to upper eighties wasn't normal around here, and tempers seemed to climb with the thermometer. As a gust of wind lightly sprang up, I pulled out from the apartment building and headed toward the Sherwood Forest Shopping Center.

The parking lot was jammed. It was near lunchtime, and a number of convention attendees looked like they were seeking their lunch outside of the Red Door, which had marvelous food and the price tags to go along with it. As I slung my purse over my shoulder and headed for the mall entrance, I glanced at the clock over the doors. A quarter of one. Perfect. Heddy would be around. All I had to do was meander by her booth, and she'd be all over me like a cat on catnip.

I stopped at the customer service desk. "I'm looking for the Gull Harbor Women's Association gift wrapping booth?"

The pertly dressed young woman pointed me in the right direction. "They're between the Bargain Bin and Hightown Department Store."

I thanked her, then shouldered through the shoppers until I hit the Bargain Bin. Normally I never shopped in dollar stores, but it would lend credibility to my claims of being short on cash. As I looked around the store at the hundreds of items, all under a dollar, I tried to think of what I would need. Linens and towels I'd sneak from the house. I wasn't about to use harshly woven washcloths on my face or sleep on sheets so thin they were itchy. But I could get away with a few plastic bowls and cups, and while I was at it, I loaded up on cheap kitchen gadgets that might actually come in handy. I added a palm-sized alarm clock and a bag of potato chips, then checked out. As I left

the store, bags prominently held for all to see, I turned so
that I'd have to make a beeline right by Heddy's table.

And there she was, just finishing up with a woman who
from the look of the wrapping paper had bought a gift for
a child's birthday. As soon as the woman moved off, I slid
out from the pillar behind which I'd been waiting and
walked across Heddy's line of sight. Within seconds, her
familiar voice rang out.

"Oh, Persia! Persia!"

Rather surprised that she sounded so friendly—I'd been
prepared for a hostile assault—I glanced over and did an
about-face.

"Heddy! Oh that's right. You're on gift patrol today,
aren't you?" I tried to sound flustered, stumbling over my
words as quickly as I could.

She motioned me over. "My dear, I'm about to take a
break. Let's go have a cup of tea. You must be totally frazz-
led." Her look of sympathy confused me. Heddy used
shameful secrets as her weapon of choice, but here she was
being nice as apple pie.

I glanced around, not wanting to be caught at length in
a restaurant with her. Orange Julius promised an easy com-
promise. "How about over there? I haven't had an OJ in
ages, and I'm so exhausted that I need the sugar."

We moved over to the counter, placed our orders, then
found a table out in the food court. I sat down, eyeing her
cautiously. She was friendly. Too friendly. What was up?

Heddy answered my question without being asked.
"I'm so sorry about what happened with your aunt. She
was out of line. I can't believe she blames you for what
happened in the gardens." Her keen glance took in every
nuance, so I decided I'd better watch myself. A slipup
could be costly.

"I told her I didn't do it, but I guess at this point, it doesn't matter. Since I was in charge of the gardens, I suppose that ultimately, it's my fault. But the fact remains that I'm out on my ass." I held up the bags. "I had to scramble and find an apartment until I can decide what to do, but I can't afford to stay there long unless I land another job."

"Then you're certain it's permanent? That your aunt won't relent?"

I shook my head. "She made it clear—she wants me out. I guess some mistakes you just can't rectify. The damage is enormous, and even though I didn't give the order to spray the roses, I'm taking the heat."

Heddy's eyes glittered. "Are you going to stay in Gull Harbor? You won't move back to Seattle?"

"No, at least not for awhile. I can't afford to move back to the city."

She looked shocked. "You're broke? But I thought you were sharing in the profits of the shop?"

I shrugged and stared at my drink. "The truth is, Heddy, that I haven't built up any savings. I'm afraid that I've been living on Auntie's good graces while plunging my salary back into the business. I guess that was a mistake. And the shop, to be honest, hasn't been doing very well lately. Bebe's Boutique has been pulling our business away."

Heddy chewed on her lip, marring the brilliant crimson lipstick she wore. She finally glanced up at me. "Venus Envy's prices are too high. Now, Bebe knows what she's doing. She keeps her prices low for her makeup and beauty supplies, and she's making a lot of money." She paused, and I could tell she was thinking about something.

Rather than push her—Heddy never responded to pushing—I glanced around the mall at the shoppers. The Sherwood Forest Shopping Center wasn't the largest mini-mall in town, but it had a loyal and faithful following. Soccer moms abounded, teens swarmed the food court and the Gap, and for the bookish crowd, there was a brand-new Barnes & Noble.

Heddy sucked on her straw, then after a moment, said, "You're looking for a new job?"

I nodded. "I have to pay rent. Auntie threw me out, so I just rented a weekly studio over at Deacon Street Apartments until I can figure out what to do." I repressed a grin as she winced. Even Heddy Latherton had her standards. "I just wish I'd taken Sharon up on her offer of a job with Bebe, but I can't very well ask her to reconsider, with everything that's happened."

"What offer? What are you talking about?" Her eyes narrowed as she studied my face. I played it for everything I was worth.

"Sharon offered me a chance to work for Bebe, and I turned her down. I never dreamed my aunt would betray me like this." I blinked furiously, and—sure enough—managed to come up with a solitary tear that traced its way down my cheek.

A soft light stole into Heddy's gaze as she leaned back. "Persia, what if I talk to Bebe for you? She's a friend of mine. I think that, Sharon's condition notwithstanding, Bebe might be willing to talk to you. I'll call her this afternoon. I know she took the day off from the convention."

Bingo! This was better than I'd expected. I forced a sad smile, wrote down my cell number—making a mental memo to change it after this was all over and done with—and picked up my bags.

"Thank you. But, why are you doing this? I thought

you'd be on my aunt's side." I couldn't pull off the lost-waif look, so I settled for a sad shrug.

She patted me on the arm. "Persia, you're a lot like me."

The hell I am, I thought but kept quiet.

"Your aunt doesn't understand you, but I do. And you've always been so pleasant to me. To be honest," she leaned closer, "sometimes I think your aunt doesn't even like me. I know I'm just oversensitive but . . ." With a little laugh, she was off, back to the gift wrapping tables, and I headed back to my apartment.

꙰

I'd no more than fastened my seatbelt when my cell phone rang. The number was unfamiliar, but the voice on the other end of the line was not.

"Persia? This is Killian. I need to talk to you!"

He sounded angry, and I had a feeling I knew what about. Might as well get it over with. "Sure, where do you want to meet? I'm at the Sherwood Forest Shopping Center right now."

"What about the Neko-Gecko?" He sounded surprised that I acceded so quickly.

The Neko-Gecko was a bistro near the Red Door. They were far more trendy than the BookWich, but Hollis—the owner—offered a decent burger after you plowed through the California cuisine offerings. I stopped in there every week or so for a bowl of his New England clam chowder.

"Fifteen minutes okay?" That would give me time to swipe on some fresh lipstick and rebraid my hair.

"See you then." Without another word, he hung up. I stared at the silent phone. Ten to one, Kyle told him that I'd mentioned Killian's blowup at Sharon. Dreading a confrontation, I performed a quick repair job on my hair and face, then headed out of the parking lot, taking care to skirt the shopaholics and tourists who were out in droves.

⁂

I could smell the goat cheese pizza from outside the door, but when I entered, I saw that the Neko-Gecko was fully into theme week. Apparently, lobster was on the menu this week. All the waiters were wearing little red hats with pincers on them, along with crimson aprons. I looked around for Killian and spotted him in the back, in a side booth. I hurried over, wanting to clear up whatever misunderstandings there might be between us.

Killian glanced up as I slid into the booth opposite him. He wasn't smiling. I took a deep breath, wondering whether to say something first, but he beat me to the punch.

"So, you told Kyle I might have tried to kill Sharon Wellstone. Thanks, Persia. I thought we were getting along better than that." His voice was cool, but beneath the bitterness, I could hear hurt.

Feeling vaguely guilty, I sighed and leaned forward. "I did *not* tell him that I thought you shot her. I told him that I'd witnessed an argument between the two of you. I also told him that I'd seen her arguing with several other Belles. And you're not the only suspect—I'm on the short list, too, you know."

He blinked. "Really? I didn't know that."

"Well, I am, and I know perfectly well how unsettling it is. Trust me, Kyle won't give our names to the paper unless he arrests one of us." I played with the water glass as the waitress came over to take our orders. Killian asked for a burger and fries, and I ordered the meat loaf and mashed potatoes.

"So, why are you a suspect?" he asked after the waitress left.

Should I tell him? Could I trust him? As I gazed into his eyes, I became aware of a creeping flush up my chest, into my neck and face. Killian had it going on, that was for sure, and even though I enjoyed my time with Bran, the spark wasn't anything like this. Killian's deep-set eyes mesmerized me, pulling me in. He wasn't an easy person to read, and I thought that if I had any psychic powers, now would be a good time for them to show themselves. Nada. I'd have to trust my intuition. And my intuition told me that Killian wouldn't sell me out.

"Sharon lifted my perfume journal. I'm sure of it."

Killian shook his head. "Wonderful, just wonderful. So she's still practicing her five-fingered discounts." He rested against the back of the booth and gave me a tired smile. "I'm sorry she got your journal. I don't have to ask what that means."

It was as good a time as any to find out just what he'd tell me. "What did Sharon do to make you so mad? You accused her of stealing. Was it money?"

The smile disappeared. "If only it had been money. No, she stole a formula from Donna Prima. Something that could make us a lot of money and give us an excellent standing in the cosmetics industry. We're frantically trying to duplicate the product, but she not only took the formula, she destroyed all our research files. We have to start from square one so we can back up our claims."

Destroyed their files? That had all too familiar a ring to it. "I assume you kept them on a computer?" I asked.

He nodded. "Yes . . . the files, the backups, every hard copy paper we'd printed out. All gone."

Corporate espionage. I expected to hear about this in

larger companies, but that it was so prevalent in small, unknown firms shocked me.

"How did she gain access to your files and the product?"

With a long sigh, he said, "Sharon was working for us. Or, at least we thought she was. But in truth, she was really spying for Bebe."

And then I saw it—a glimmer in his eye that told me Sharon had stolen more than a formula. "You and she had a thing going on, didn't you?"

His lips set firm, after a moment he said, "She's married. I don't mess around with married women. I'm not into causing breakups."

I stared at him for a moment, wondering how he felt about women who had boyfriends, as casual as they might be. "Sorry. I was just being nosy."

He caught my gaze, and we sat there, locked in a silent exchange that was broken only by the arrival of our meals. As I bit into my meat loaf, Killian toyed with his hamburger and fries. Finally, he said, "You were right. We were involved. It was over pretty fast. I didn't know she was married, and when she told me, I fired her. Unethical, maybe, but I don't like deceit."

"Why did she tell you, then?" Knowing Sharon, she could have kept it a secret for awhile.

Killian shrugged. "The more I've thought about it, the more I think she wanted to provoke me. By then, she had the formula. She knew I wouldn't want to have anything to do with her once I knew she was married, so she tricked me into dumping her. We were out at dinner when she dropped the bomb, and I never thought to check the office that night. I never thought she'd do something that underhanded."

I toyed with my drink. "What happened?"

"When I got to work the next morning, Trish was in tears. The paper files were all messed up, and the computer's hard drive had been wiped. I called the cops, but they couldn't find anything and even then, I didn't think Sharon might be guilty. It took us a week to sort through everything, and it was only then that we realized that every paper file was still there except for one formula. By then it was too late. Sharon had officially joined Bebe's employ, and I couldn't prove a damned thing. I hadn't even asked her to sign a noncompete agreement. Believe me, I require that now. But there was no concrete way to prove Sharon had done it. We're a small company; we don't keep security cameras around."

I set down my fork and stared at him. So Sharon's happy housewife demeanor had been a sham. "Did you tell Kyle all of this?"

He grimaced. "It's not like I had any choice. Yes, I told him, and now I'm on his list of most likely suspects." With a wry grin, he added, "I guess we both ended up on the short end of Sharon's stick."

"I'd like to show her just where to shove that stick—" I started, but then stopped. "Sorry, not appropriate, especially considering her condition. I'm just so angry, but I feel guilty over being angry now that she's fighting for her life."

Killian grunted. "You and me both. I don't have any feelings left for her—not in any positive way—but it's hard to admit my grudge. It's almost like I feel that if I say it aloud, then maybe I had something to do with her assault. Maybe I contributed somehow."

"I know exactly what you mean," I said. I wanted to throttle the woman, but those feelings were now intermingled with guilt. I knew that I should be more forgiving, more compassionate, but it just wasn't in me. "You want to know the truth?"

He nodded. "Sure, if you're not going to confess to me. I don't really want to play the role of Father Flannigan."

I wrinkled my nose. "Funny man. Oh so funny. Okay, the truth is that I don't want to forgive her. I don't want to feel sorry for her. She screwed me over big time. But I think I'm angriest at myself, because I was careless. I let my guard down; I didn't think. I was stupid for not making a backup copy of my recipes. I was stupid for trusting that if I left something at my station, it would be safe. I feel like an idiot, and I hate that." I slammed my hand down on the table, finally putting into words what had been nagging at me for the past two days.

Killian reached across the table and took my hand. I lifted my head, staring into his eyes, and a shudder ran up my thighs, through my stomach, making me catch my breath. He leaned down and pressed my fingers to his lips, and right then and there, I wanted him.

Confident in himself, Killian was sure of his place in the world, and his ego didn't require constant strokes. All of this I knew from that one touch. I ran my index finger along his palm, then gently let go.

"I hope I wasn't acting out of place," he said.

"No, no . . ." I searched for the right words. "Sharon's in the hospital. We're both suspects in her attack, and right now, I'm trying to save my aunt's business from going down the drain. Killian, listen to me. I'm going to have to do something that I hate the thought of."

I stopped, wondering what he'd think if he found out I was trying to join Bebe's company. "There are things I can't tell you right now, but please—trust me. I'm doing what I need to in order to help Venus Envy." I paused, then figured I might as well tell him about Bran. "And you should know that I've been seeing someone. We aren't exclusive, we aren't serious, but I want you to know that up front. Before anything happens."

"Thank you for telling me," he said. "But . . . do you think . . . ?" His expression filled in what he left unspoken.

"Yeah," I said, holding his gaze. "I think . . . yes. I want to find out."

"Good," he said, pulling out his wallet. "Because I can't get you out of my mind." He placed a twenty on the bill and waited for me to stand up before sliding out of his side of the booth. "So, will you keep me in the loop?"

I stared at the floor. "I can't tell you everything right now—you have to understand that. But I promise, at some point you'll know."

He slid a card into my hand. A number was written across the back. "Call me if you need me," he said. "You can trust me, Persia. I won't let you down." As he headed out the door, I knew he was telling the truth. I slipped the card in my purse, wondering just how much more complicated my life was going to become.

～

I stopped by the grocery store to pick up some bagels, cream cheese, lunch meat, soup, and frozen veggies before heading back to the dreary little apartment to sneak past Carlos's door, hoping to make it to the stairs before he heard me. Luck was on my side; he was nowhere in sight. I took the stairs two at a time, bags weighing me down. I already missed my workout room, and my body ached for movement. Exercise always helped me de-stress myself.

No sooner had I put the food away, when there came a

knock on the door. As I peeked through the peephole, I groaned. Andy Andrews! Somehow, he'd gotten word that I was living here. I debated simply not answering, but avoiding problems never made them go away for long.

As I opened the door, the look on his face shifted from disbelief to delight. Oh joy. I rested my hand on my hip, the other on the door.

"Andy, what do you want?"

"Shit man, I heard you moved into the building but didn't believe it. And yet, here you are!" He flashed me a goofy grin, and it was at that point that I saw the six-pack in his hand. "I brought you a welcome wagon gift. Want to hang out for awhile?"

I had no desire to hang out with Andy Andrews, but it occurred to me that continually turning him down might simply act as an incentive. And it wasn't like he was Elliot, who was beginning to scare me. No, Andy was basically harmless. He probably tried to put the make on every girl or woman who crossed his path who he found remotely attractive, and I doubted that I was special in that regard. However, maybe if I turned him into a buddy, he'd back off a little. With that thought in mind, I sighed, took a step back, and motioned for him to come in.

"Sure, we can hang out for a little while, but you keep your hands to yourself and your tongue in your mouth. Got it?" I laughed to take the edge off my words.

He flushed for a moment, then the embarrassment died out of his face. "Ah hell, and here I thought I'd win you over with my suave and charming ways."

As I accepted a beer and flopped down in the rocking chair, it occurred to me that I was in the most improbable situation that I could have thought up a day or so ago. Sitting in a slum, drinking beer with Andy, effectively out of work. Hey, I was turning into a slacker! Woohoo, and all that crap.

"So, you like working at the computer shop?"

He shrugged, wiping the foam off his lips. "Yeah, In-A-Fix is pretty cool. My boss is a good guy; he even lets me take off early if there's a skateboard competition or meet. I ride professionally, you know."

He said it the same way someone might talk about riding horses or driving a truck. I fought back a smile, not wanting him to think I was mocking him. "No, I didn't know," I said. "Won any trophies?"

He shifted until one foot was crossed under him, the other dangled over the edge of the sofa. "Yeah, a few. I'm pretty good. You ride?"

Actually, I did, but I wasn't sure what he'd make of the information. "Some. I ski, snowboard, surf, rock climb . . . you name it, I've probably done it."

His eyes lit up. "You don't find many chicks who can do all that. You sure you're over thirty?"

I attempted a frown but ended up laughing. "Yes, I'm thirty-one. And before you ask—no, I'm not interested. But it never hurts to make a new friend."

Andy let out an exaggerated sigh. "Well, it never hurts to see how far you can get. But that's cool. Say," he said, glancing around the place. "Why are you living here? Don't you live in that huge old house with your aunt?"

I was scrambling to think up something that wouldn't need a fifty-mile explanation to go along with it when my cell phone rang. "Just a moment, please," I said, fishing it out of my purse. As I flipped it open, pressed Talk, and held it to my ear, I heard a voice that seemed familiar. And then I placed it—I'd been waiting for the call.

"Persia? This is Bebe Wilcox. I talked to Heddy Lath-

erton today, and she said you might be looking for a new
position. If so, we need to talk."

My lighthearted mood slipping away like water off
duck's down, I motioned to Andy that I'd be a moment and
slipped into the bathroom. As I summoned an answer, my
stomach flipped, and I knew that this was it—the chance
I'd been both dreading and hoping for. "Thank you, Bebe.
I'd like very much to meet you and to discuss options."

As she named the place, my mind was racing. Here it
was—the chance to recover my journal, to prove that Bebe
was behind the attempts to destroy Venus Envy. We'd only
have one shot. I had to play it just right, or we'd lose the
shop for good, and my aunt would be heartbroken.

Chapter Eleven

I agreed to meet Bebe the next morning at ten, at her company. Promptly after hanging up, I said good night to Andy, then phoned my aunt and told her the news. "Word gets around fast," I said.

Auntie sighed. "I don't like people thinking I'd kick you out or that you'd betray me." Her voice was trembling, and I realized just how hard this whole mess had been on her. Venus Envy had been the cream of Gull Harbor—beloved and trusted, and within less than three months, Bebe Wilcox had managed to undermine all that.

"I won't let you down, Auntie. Or the shop." As I said good-bye and hung up, a sense a loss hit my heart. Over the past months since I'd returned to Gull Harbor, Auntie had once again moved into a central place in my life. My sense of family had returned, and now something was threatening that bond.

Sleep that night didn't come easy. For one thing, it was just too hot and muggy. For another, the bed in my new apartment was about as comfortable as a slab of granite. I missed Moss Rose Cottage more than I had anticipated.

The minute my alarm went off, I jumped out of bed. After my three-minute exercise, I worked my way through a simplified yoga routine, spent ten minutes in a headstand, then gulped down a glass of juice and a couple of protein bars. After a quick shower in the cramped bathroom, I sorted through the clothes I'd brought with me.

I finally pulled out a pair of black jeans and an olive green tank top that would go with my stiletto Candies. I wanted to feel at my strongest today when facing Bebe, and anything that increased my height to towering proportions was a good thing. A glance in the mirror told me that I looked pretty good, if not professional. I'd just use my outfit to my advantage by telling Bebe I'd had to move quickly, and hadn't had time to retrieve the rest of my clothes yet.

As I headed out to my car, I noticed that the air was thick. Thunderstorm weather. Sure enough, when I looked to the sky, I saw the beginnings of a thick formation of cumulonimbus clouds. Not a good sign. We'd be seeing lightning by nightfall at the latest.

I sped along, mulling over my best approach. I didn't dare lay it on too thick, or she'd never believe me. However, it wouldn't do to be blasé, either, or I'd arouse suspicion. I pulled into one of the empty parking spaces labeled Visitor's Parking in front of the building. As I slipped out of my car, my nerves jangled. I was heading into enemy territory without backup.

Bebe's Cosmetics was housed in a small suite of offices on the north side of Port Samanish Island, about a mile outside the Gull Harbor city limits. The building was old, obviously built long before Bebe came along. I caught a glimpse of a faded sign that told me this had once been a medical park. A muggy breeze sprang up as I pushed open the door and entered the heart of Bebe's Cosmetics.

As I headed toward the stairs—Bebe had told me to meet her in her office—the acrid smell of chemicals singed my nose. They permeated the building, and I wondered just what the hell they were using here.

The corridor was long and narrow, with offices on either side. Several of them were filled with boxes, apparently being used as storage rooms, but as I turned right, I came face-to-face with a door bearing a large plaque that read "Bebe Wilcox, President." Taking a deep breath, I opened the door.

The office was subdivided into two sections, with the outer office manned by a secretary. She was perky, that much was apparent from just a glance. And she was yellow and cream—very yellow. Yellow as in it looked like one of her kids had dumped a box of crayons into her washing machine. Her jacket, headband, and medium-heel pumps were all the color of lemon pudding. Her skirt was a muted cream and did nothing to offset the blinding effect from the rest of her ensemble. She blinked once behind bright, big leopard print glasses, and then a brilliant smile spread across her face and stayed there.

"Welcome to Bebe's Cosmetics. My name is Debra. May I help you?" she asked, and I could see every brilliantly polished tooth in her mouth. I wondered if her cheeks hurt from smiling so wide.

I cleared my throat. "I'm Persia Vanderbilt, and I have an appointment with Bebe this morning."

She pointed to a low settee. "Please have a seat. Ms. Wilcox will be with you in a moment. After I obediently sat down, she picked up the phone and whispered into it, eying me as she spoke. I tried to hear what she was saying, but no dice. She replaced the receiver. "Would you like a cup of coffee? A cappuccino? Mocha? Latte? Tea?"

A hint of the old paranoia crept up, but I pushed it aside. For some reason, just hearing Bebe's name rang alarm bells in my head. I forced a smile and said, "Iced tea would be lovely. With lemon, please. No sugar."

Debra picked up the phone again and, once more, spoke so softly that I couldn't catch it. "Your tea will be here in a moment. Meanwhile, there are magazines on the table, if you'd like to read while you wait."

I nodded, not trusting myself to say too much at this point. As Debra went back to her work, I glanced around the office. It was spacious, I'd give it that much. Bebe had obviously chosen the best suite for herself. The furniture looked tasteful enough on the surface, but when I examined the weave, the craftsmanship proved shoddy and the detail of the floral print was muddy. The tables and desk were covered with veneer, and the art on the walls was random, a floral arrangement here, a waterscape there, with no cohesive theme throughout the room. I had the sense that the place had been thrown together without any planning. Slipshod, just like her products. A pretty package on the outside, but little substance or thought when you opened it up and took a closer look.

As I waited, I visualized the way I wanted things to go when I met Bebe. I'd spent a week at an evening workshop at the end of June, which was led by one of my students at the Grays Harbor Community College, where I taught a four-week self-defense course for women four times a year.

Summer quarter had recently ended, but I'd made friends with a woman named Sareena, and she led workshops in visualization, meditation, and goal-setting. Bran had vouched for her, and I'd found the workshop of great help in clarifying to myself just who I was and what I wanted.

The outer door opened, and another woman—again clad in brilliant yellow—entered the room, carrying a tray. On the tray were two Styrofoam cups. Nonrecyclable. That figured, considering Bebe seemed to take the cheapest route on things. The girl handed me my tea. One whiff told me they'd forgot the lemon, but I wasn't going to complain.

I took a sip and grimaced. Bitter, almost as if it had been burnt. As I set down the cup on a plastic coaster, the door to the inner office opened, and Bebe stepped out. She glanced around, frowned, then motioned for me to come in the office.

Bebe Wilcox, aka Eudora Gallagher, was a formidable woman from a distance, and even more intimidating up close. She was my height, although my stilettos gave me the advantage, but her entire demeanor enveloped the room. Close up, I could tell that Bebe was in her late fifties, and she had a hardened edge below all the makeup plastered on her face. Her eyes were stony, her smile cold, and when she shook my hand, I had the feeling I had just walked into a rattlesnake's den.

"Persia, so glad you could make it. Sit down," she said, shutting the door behind her. I murmured a polite hello and took my seat, expecting the cat-and-mouse dance to go on for awhile. Bebe surprised me.

She sat on the corner of her desk looking down at me. "Let's cut the crap, Persia. I don't have time for niceties, and I'm pretty sure you're a lot like me, from what I hear. Sharon offered you a job. You turned her down. You've changed your mind, and the job's still open. Do you want to work for me or not?"

Well, she cut right to the chase, that was for sure. "That's about the size of it," I said. "I thought about moving back to Seattle, but—"

"But it takes money to set up house there, and you don't have any, now that your aunt has slapped your hand out of the cookie jar." Bebe abruptly stood and returned to her chair behind her desk, where she opened her purse and pulled out a pack of cigarettes, tapping one out. As she lit it and exhaled a ring of smoke, I tried not to cough.

"So, let's get right to the point. We still want you. You start tomorrow, working in research and development. But, you must be willing to do whatever it takes to make sure Bebe's Cosmetics end up in every state, in every purse, in every cosmetics bag, of every woman in this country."

Her eyes were too bright, her shoulders too straight. Unsettled, the thought occurred to me that Bebe had the makings of a dictator, and she wouldn't be satisfied with penny ante followers. I dreaded thinking what working under her would be like, but I was about to find out.

"What exactly will I be doing?" I asked.

She smiled knowingly. "Close to the same thing you've been doing for Venus Envy. You'll just be working at a faster pace, and you won't be playing gardener. We buy all of our ingredients."

And their ingredients sucked, I thought, but kept my mouth shut. "I seem to have lost my journal with all my recipes in it," I said, watching her face.

She gazed at me, impassive, and I couldn't tell whether or not I'd struck a mark. "What a shame. I'm sure that must hurt, but don't worry, you'll be creating a new one. So it's settled, you'll be here at nine tomorrow morning?"

I took my cue and stood. "Nine sharp."

As I started to stand, Bebe stopped me. "A couple more

things, just so there aren't any miscommunications. You do realize that everything you create here at Bebe's belongs to the company? You won't be working on any formulas away from the office, you won't be creating any custom blends for friends on the side. You won't be claiming any creations as your own. Do I make myself clear?"

As she spoke, I could see the triumph glowing in her eyes. I wanted to backhand her one, bring her to her knees for all the crap she'd pulled. But I knew that any such action would not only ruin all our plans but land me in jail. I kept calm and collected.

"Clear as crystal," I said. I managed to keep my temper in check long enough to negotiate my salary, then, both relieved and anxious, I slipped out the door.

⁂

The first thing I did when I left Bebe's was to head for a McDonald's where I wouldn't be noticed. As I edged into a parking space, I called Auntie on my cell phone and filled her in on what had happened.

"I don't know how much of Bebe I can take. She's a first-class bitch. Frankly, I think the woman is nuts. She's got the weirdest stare." For me to admit that I was nervous around somebody was a sore spot, and Auntie knew it. I could almost always hold my own, and when I couldn't, I did a pretty good job of bluffing, but when it came to intimidation, Bebe had years of practice under her belt. I'd hate to see what she was like around some of the more timid women who worked for her.

Auntie sighed. "I'm sorry, Persia." She paused, then added, "If you want to forget this, just say so. We'll struggle to keep the shop going. Surely we can figure out a way to pull it off."

I thought about it for a moment. "How bad were our losses last month?"

"Discounting the roses? We were down fifteen percent. That may not seem like a lot, but it's the second month in a row since Bebe's Boutique opened that we've taken a hit. I'm not sure if we can weather it out until people figure out that she's selling them a shoddy bill of goods."

I stared at the dashboard. Auntie had put a lot of her money and heart into Venus Envy, and she'd taken me in when I had no place to go. We'd served the community, and now we were taking some direct hits. "No, I'll go through with it. We have to try. I want my journal back, and I want vindication. I love Venus Envy, and I don't want to go back to Seattle."

"Oh honey, you'll always have a home with me, Venus Envy or not. Never worry about that."

The love in her voice made me bite my lip. "Auntie, we'll fumble through somehow. Give me a few days to see what I find. And won't Bebe Wilcox rue the day she ever set out to ruin Venus Envy when we get done with her!"

Auntie laughed then, and it felt good to hear the spark of hope in her voice. "We'll turn the tables on her, Imp. I'll talk to you later. Love you."

I clicked the Off button and pocketed my phone. Auntie and I had built a bridge from the past into the present, and I wasn't about to let anyone or anything knock a chink into it. I eased through the drive-through. Might as well take something home to eat, considering that my refrigerator was the size of a two-drawer filing cabinet.

❧

The thunderstorm was still building by the time I got back to the apartment, but it looked ready to break. I flipped the top up on my Sebring and raced for the door, beating the big fat raindrops that showered down by less than a minute. A crack of thunder split the air as a flash of blue ripped across the sky, and the rain came streaming down. So much for the dry spell, although the heat hadn't dissipated. It was muggy as hell, and I was sweating, even in my tank top.

Carlos wasn't anywhere to be seen, and I took the stairs two at a time, balancing on my stilettos as I bypassed dust bunnies and smears of old gum and—much to my disgust—a used condom. I peeked into the hall. No sign of Andy, thank God. He was probably at work, and with any luck, by the time he got home, I'd be out of the apartment.

I had barely started in on my second hamburger when there was knock on the door. Frowning, I peeked through the peephole. Kyle! What the heck was he doing here? I opened the door.

"Come on in." I moved so he could enter the apartment and watched as his look of disbelief grew as he saw my suitcase and scattered clothes on the bed. "What brings you to my neck of the woods?" I hadn't decided whether to play it straight with him or not.

He stood next to the table, planting his feet wide in what I thought of as the typical cop's stance. I repressed a smile as he sniffed and glanced at my lunch the way Beauty and Beast stared at the dinner table. "What's this I hear about you moving out of your aunt's place? What happened? Somebody told me Miss Florence threw you out, but I know better than that."

Although his voice held only a mild curiosity, I knew he was fishing for information. I shrugged. "Would you believe me if I told you she blames me for the roses being tampered with?"

He snorted. "Try again."

I smiled. "I wanted a change of pace?" The jig was up, but I wondered how long he'd let me go on. A harmless game of cat and mouse before I gave in and told him what was going on.

"Lies, all lies. Tell me the truth, Persia. I don't have all day to stand here and play guessing games."

"And just who invited you to play? Why do you care?" I sat down and bit into my burger again.

He turned one of the dinette chairs around and straddled it. "Okay, okay, you made your point. I'm nosy. But since you're on my suspects list, I can't help but wonder just what you're up to. Truce?"

I raised an eyebrow. "Truce in the same breath as 'on your suspects list'? That's a good one." But I knew I wasn't going to get out of this without coming clean. "Okay, fine," I said, setting my hamburger down on the wrapper. "You want the truth? I'll tell you, but only if you promise to keep your mouth shut. Swear, or I don't dish."

Kyle grinned. "You're cocky, just like Hoffman. You should have been born a man, Persia."

"I take offense at that," I said, sticking out my tongue. "Since when do women have to be compliant and grovel at your uniformed feet? I play life on my own terms, not on how people think I should."

He raised one eyebrow. "At least your tongue isn't pierced. Okay, okay . . . I promise—unless it's against the law, and then I'll run you in and slap you behind bars. Because I have the feeling you're up to something dangerous, stubborn woman that you are."

"I'm a Capricorn. What do you expect?" I retorted. "We goats butt our heads against anybody standing in our way, and we have to keep climbing those mountains, regardless of how steep the peak is." I dipped a fry in ketchup.

"Okay, you want to know what I'm up to? Here's the deal: I've gone to work at Bebe's in order to find out the truth about my journal. You said you can't do anything, but I'll be damned if I'm going to take this lying down. While I'm at it, I'm also keeping my eyes peeled to find out just how Bebe plans on finishing her demolition of Venus Envy. She's the one behind contaminating our roses. I know it, and I intend to find enough evidence so that you have to step in."

Kyle stared at me, mouth open, as he slumped against the back of the seat. "You're spying on them?"

"Call it what you like. They stole my journal. They've been systematically trying to put us out of business. Consider it 'gathering evidence,' and it sounds better." The look on his face perked up my appetite, and I happily polished off the rest of my burger, then washed my hands at the kitchenette sink.

"So this is all an elaborate plan that you and your aunt cooked up?"

"And Winthrop as well, actually," I said. "I think he enjoys walking on the edge a little. He's pretty cool for a good ol' boy lawyer." I leaned against the counter and waited to see what Kyle would have to say next.

He stared at me for a moment, then sighed and picked up one of my leftover fries, popping it in his mouth. "Well, you're not exactly doing anything illegal, even if it does seem a little shady. But you better be careful. Bebe Wilcox has a rap sheet, if you didn't know—"

"Yeah, we know all about her scams when she was Eudora Gallagher. So you finally decided she's a suspect in the case of our roses?" Surprised that he'd checked her out,

I thought maybe Kyle was a little more interested in our case than he'd let on, but he blew that idea out of the water.

"I checked her out because of Sharon. Bebe and Sharon are reported to have had words shortly before Sharon was hurt."

I frowned. So Bebe was on the suspect list, too. Killian and I were keeping nefarious company. "If I might ask, what's the status of your investigation? Do you have any leads at all, besides Killian, me, and Bebe?"

He shrugged. "You know I can't discuss the case with you, especially since your alibi isn't airtight. But we may be on to something. I just want you to promise me to be careful. You're walking into a viper's den, Persia, and I don't want to see you get bit."

The look on his face was so serious that I didn't bother trying to make a joke. Obviously, Kyle knew more than I did, but it was clear that he wasn't going to tell me just what he knew. I nodded. "I give you my word. I'll be as careful as I can. But you understand why I have to do this? If you can't go in for us . . . well . . . we have no choice."

"Damn it, I wish you had more proof than just those sample cards. There's no way to really analyze them. We can't prove a thing." He slammed his hand on the table. "For what it's worth, off the record, I think they stole your journal. But don't you repeat that."

I sighed. Auntie and I were on the right track. I knew it. Kyle knew it. But we only had one chance to kick the bastards in the balls. "So what else is going down? I haven't seen hide nor hair of your cousin Jared in several weeks." Another sore subject between us, but at this point, I wasn't interested in censoring myself.

Kyle cleared his throat. "Jared and I've been talking a little more than usual," he said.

I perked up. If the two were on speaking terms, they'd made progress. Kyle and his cousin didn't get along at all, and that made it difficult for me, since Jared and I were good friends, despite some glaringly bad decisions he'd made in his life.

"Really? That's a shock, but not an unwelcome one."

"Don't hold your breath. We aren't friends yet. But I do know that he's going through a rough patch with his relationship right now. His ma told me last time I saw her. Of course, he can't go home to talk about it."

Jared's father hated the fact that Jared was gay more than he loved his son, so Jared talked to his mother whenever he got the chance. She visited him at his place but, according to Jared, he hadn't set foot in his parents' house since he'd divorced his wife. She'd come home early one day and caught him in bed with a man.

"Really? What's going on? I thought he and Rod were doing fine." I liked Rod; he never made me feel like a fag hag, and he wasn't jealous of my friendship with Jared.

Kyle shrugged. "Seven year itch, maybe? Or however many years they've been together. I guess Rod is starting to feel antsy. I'm thinking my cousin may be facing what he put his wife through so many years ago. What goes around, comes around, though I really don't wish him unhappiness." I knew that Kyle wasn't entirely comfortable with the gay thing either, but he made an effort. I also knew that he would never wish pain on his cousin, having been wounded in his own heart so deeply.

With so many shake-ups this summer; I was beginning to look forward to autumn. Maybe the cool rains would chill down tempers and libidos and backstabbers and rivals. Meanwhile, we'd muddle through the best we could. I'd have to give Jared a call and try to catch him for a long talk. He needed somebody to listen to him and, while life in Gull Harbor was pretty liberal, I was still one of his best friends.

"Thanks for the news," I said. Impulsively, I rested my hand lightly on Kyle's shoulder. "I know you're still mad at your cousin for what he did, but there are so many horrible things that go on in this world. Maybe it's time to let it go? Jared should never have married Allison, I agree. But he did, and it was a mistake. There's nothing he can do to make up for that, but is it enough to keep you at arm's length for the rest of your life?"

Kyle caught his breath. "Persia, we've talked about this before. You know how I feel. I talked to him—that's the best I can do for now."

I shook my head, matching him almost inch for inch in my Candies. "Okay, I'll back off," I said.

He sighed, then headed toward the door. "I'd better get back to work. Please, again, be careful, and call me if you need anything. I don't want you to end up like Sharon." Before he could leave, his cell phone beeped. He stopped to look at the number, then immediately hit Redial. After a few low whispers, he flipped it shut. "Sharon's taken a turn for the worse. They're going to call in a priest. Just in case."

I swallowed. Sharon's assault was bad enough, but the thought that it might turn into murder was far, far worse. I scuffed the floor. "I just don't understand. I know how to kill somebody using my martial arts; but to think of actually using my knowledge, except in self-defense, boggles my mind. That's why Elliot's still alive."

"I know, Persia." Kyle gave me a tight smile. "And that's what separates you from whoever it is that shot Sharon."

I glanced up. "So you're taking me off your list of suspects?"

"No," he said. "I can't do that, but I know you didn't do it. I know you better than you give me credit for. It was somebody out for revenge on a big scale. That's why I want you to be careful when you're at work."

And then it dawned on me. "You think somebody at the company did it? Or you think that whoever shot her was out to wreak revenge on the company."

Again, Killian's face popped up in my mind, and I shuddered. I didn't want him to be guilty, but he had better reason than me to shoot Sharon. I could re-create some of my recipes—at least come up with acceptable substitutes. But Donna Prima had been on the verge of a big discovery, and Sharon had not only stolen the formula to it, she'd also set them back years in research. That was strong motivation.

Then again, Sharon had made a lot of enemies. Hell, she'd cheated on her husband, it could even be that he was out for revenge. "What about her husband?" I asked suddenly.

Kyle blinked. "We're checking into his alibi. Trust me, we aren't overlooking anybody," he said, as I shut the door behind him.

There were too many possibilities, and none of them gave me any sense of security. What had Auntie and I gotten ourselves into? But we had to follow through. It was either that or fold up shop. And Venus Envy was too dear to us to let it go.

Chapter Twelve

The storm lasted through the evening, forks of light splitting the sky every few minutes, followed by crescendos of rolling thunder. I longed to be at Moss Rose Cottage, watching from the living room window as the waves swelled in Puget Sound, but since that was out of the question, and since I had no intention of spending another evening captive with Andy, or worse yet—Carlos—I headed out to meet Barb for a drink. We'd agreed to meet at Tony's Bar & Grill.

I caught my hair back into a chignon—the humidity had made it frizz like crazy—and slipped into a khaki skirt and a loose cotton weave top. A glance out the window told me the rain hadn't let up; in fact, it was sluicing down like water over a burst dam.

Ducking as I exited the building, I dashed for the car, grateful I'd remembered to put up the top before coming in. Otherwise, I'd have a very expensive wading pool by now. I inched through the streets, barely able to see, despite the windshield wipers working at full speed. Tony's was only a couple of miles away, but it took me twice as long to get there as it normally would. Better safe than sorry, I thought. My aunt might be a speed demon, but my driving was one place I preferred to exercise caution.

I parked as close to the building as I could, but it wasn't close enough. On the way through the lot, a rap-spewing lowrider sped by, splashing me as it bounced through a large puddle. Wonderful! Drenched with muddy water, I yanked open the door and entered the restaurant, looking for Barb. She was waiting for me in the front. I noticed she'd seized the opportunity to hide her haircut with a jaunty beret. I gave her a weak wave as her gaze ran over my outfit.

"How did you get here? Swim?" She giggled.

"Very funny. Apparently somebody driving through the parking lot decided I needed a bath."

We followed the waitress to a booth near the back. Barb ordered a glass of red wine and a plate of nachos, and I ordered scalding hot tea with lemon and an order of calamari. After the waitress disappeared, I pulled the chopsticks out of my hair and shook it loose, relaxing for the first time that day.

"I start my new job tomorrow," I said.

Barb shook her head. "I think you're nuts. But if this is what you and your aunt want to do, then I hope it works out. Just be careful. Those Belles at the convention looked like they could beat a sumo into submission."

"There's more reason than that to be cautious." I leaned forward. "Kyle won't tell me what, but something's going on there. Something underhanded. He came by my new digs to try to talk me out of going through with our plan, but as I told him, we have no other choice."

Barb sucked in a quick breath of air. "Are you certain

you want to do this, Persia? Surely once people realize that Bebe's Boutique is a sham and a rip-off, they'll come back to Venus Envy."

"By then there may not be a shop. We've lost money the past couple of months. Now we have to replace fifteen thousand dollars' worth of roses. Auntie can't do that unless she knows Venus Envy has a future. If the shop closes, all we'll have is one very expensive, very pretty, and very unnecessary new rose garden."

Barb was about to say something when a shadow fell over our booth. I looked up to see Mae Johnson, from the service station, staring down at me with a scathing look on her face.

"How could you do that to your aunt? I was talking to Ana Winston, and she was in your store the other day when you flounced out. While it isn't my place to interfere, I just can't walk by you and keep my mouth shut!" She looked as though I'd punched her in the stomach. "You should respect your aunt more—she's done so much for you."

I blinked. Heddy Latherton's helpful response had been unexpected; *this* was not. This was the reaction I expected Auntie's loyal friends to have, but that didn't make it any easier to hear. I steeled myself and looked her calmly in the face. "Listen, Mae, I didn't do anything—Auntie's got it all wrong."

"Didn't do anything? Didn't do anything? You just ruined her rose garden! How could you be such an ungrateful child?" She shook her head, turned, and stomped away.

Thoroughly chastised, I turned back to Barb, who had watched the whole interplay openmouthed. "I guess she told me," I said.

Barb gulped. "I guess so. Oh, Persia, I'm so sorry. Even though I know you and your aunt planned this, I didn't think

the outcry would be this bad. You must feel horrible." She
peeked down the aisle to where Mae was settling back in at
her table. "I didn't think she was capable of being so rude."

"People surprise you once they lose the calm veneer of
civilization. I'm no longer surprised by anything anybody
does." *Well, almost,* I thought. Sometimes it wasn't wise to
make blanket statements. Old Coyote, the trickster, was
out there, listening, just waiting to make life miserable for
people who thought they knew it all.

I told her about Heddy calling Bebe, and my interview
with the maven of bad makeup. "I have to make very sure
that anything I concoct while I'm there isn't worth re-
creating. Because, scam artist or not, she'll own the rights
to the formulas. So, what should I wear tomorrow?"

Barb frowned. "I don't know. What's the usual apparel
for a corporate spy?" She laughed, then abruptly stopped
as the waitress appeared with our orders. As soon as she
had deposited the food in front of us and left, we were off
and running, discussing what my camouflage outfit should
consist of.

On the way home, I relaxed at Barb's while she ran over
to Auntie's. I'd asked her to pack a suitcase of clothes for
me and to grab my boom box. Then, after one last brownie,
I headed for my depressing little apartment in my shabby
apartment building. I dropped into bed, exhausted, but not
quite tired enough to fall asleep right away. Finally, after
getting out of bed and running through a few gentle yoga
asanas, I was able to sleep.

I don't know why I expected it to be any different, but my
first day at Bebe's was an exercise in patience. Morning
arrived to shower me with a stream of golden sunlight

pouring through the window. The storm had passed. I slipped a CD into the boom box, and Beck blasted out from the speakers as I took a deep breath and dressed for battle.

In the back of my closet at Auntie's, I'd stuffed a few little suits from the days when I worked the counters at various department stores, and I'd had Barb pack a couple of them for me. I selected a skirt and jacket that—while not the brilliant yellow of the Belle mentality—still matched their basic style. As I slid into the skirt, I had to hold my breath while zipping it up the side.

The zipper didn't want to close. Great, I'd put on an inch or so on my waistline—mostly muscle—over the past few years. I sucked in my gut again, yanking the fastener. It caught at my waist, I let out my breath, cautious to avoid undoing my victory. The fabric stretched across my thighs, skintight, and wincing, I glanced in the mirror.

Damn, my butt looked good! The curves I'd put on were looking mighty fine, if I said so myself. Feeling more confident, despite having to hold my breath, I finished buttoning the silky cream shirt that complemented the vivid aqua of the suit, and then slid on the bolero jacket. It cupped my breasts snugly, barely able to fasten. As one of my favorite shows on TV kept saying, "Lock and load the girls."

Another look in the mirror told me that if I'd gained even two more pounds, the suit would be a goner. As it was, I was giving everybody and their brother a show—the skintight fabric accentuated every curve on my body. Feeling out of character but oddly confident, I caught my hair into a tight bun and then fixed my face, going for the full-face routine. I finished up with a vivid plum eye shadow, an eye-popping fuchsia lipstick, big earrings, and a pair of three and a half inch high silver pumps.

One thing was for sure, I wouldn't be eating lunch, not if I hoped to keep my skirt zipped. I might manage an energy bar, if lucky, and I dreaded facing the day without breakfast. I popped my chewable calcium tablets and vitamin C, hoping that they'd take off the edge of hunger until I could grab a candy bar or something.

As I headed toward the stairs, a familiar whistle echoed from down the hall. Andy Andrews was staring at me, a look of disbelief on his face.

"Damn, you look good." He shook his head, circling me like a vulture. "I've never seen you look so . . . so . . ."

"So corporate?"

"So Barbie doll. You fit the uniform, though."

I didn't know whether to feel flattered or insulted. "Gee, thanks?"

He glanced at his watch. "Shit, I've got to go. Say, want to get together tonight? We could go out, have a drink or two . . ." His trademark leer followed the comment, but I noticed he'd toned it down just a little.

"Thanks, Andy, but I've got a date," I said. I was lying, but at this point figured that it might be the easiest way to turn him down. He shrugged, then headed for the elevator while I made tracks down the stairs.

Bebe's Cosmetics was aflutter with women hustling through the halls, some in dresses, some in suits, all in full makeup. Nobody seemed to recognize me, though a few faces looked familiar from the convention. All the same, as I made my way toward Bebe's office, I had the distinct feeling that I was being watched. By who, I wasn't sure, but there were eyes trained on my back.

Bebe was nowhere to be seen, but Debra handed me a

packet of paperwork to fill out and steered me into a small
conference room containing several tables, walls covered
with dry erase boards, and one window that overlooked a
back parking lot and a few storage facilities in what looked
to be a barren field. As I gazed around the sterile room, I
realized how much I again missed my aunt and being at
Venus Envy.

Overcome with homesickness, it was all I could do to
force myself into a chair to look over the paperwork. The
application was standard, but the other papers—the nondis-
closure form and the contract granting all rights to anything
I created on their premises or while in their employ—
nagged at me. How could I sign something that a judge
might later use against me?

And then, the kicker. A noncompetition agreement. If I
signed it, I wouldn't be able to return to Venus Envy. Shit.

I peeked out the door at Debra. "I forgot to bring some
of the information. Mind if I take all this home with me to
fill out? I'll turn it in tomorrow?" I crossed my fingers.

Debra frowned. "Bebe usually likes to wrap up the paperwork on the first day. I'd ask her, but she's gone until
Monday."

Gone until Monday, huh? That gave me several days to
poke around without her knowing it. "Listen, I'd go home
now, but she wanted me to get right to work. One day can't
hurt, can it?" I gave her a wide smile. "I know you're busy,
and I'm so sorry I'm such a space cadet. That time of the
month, you know." I played the card almost every woman
could sympathize with.

Debra's eyes lit up, and she gave me an understanding
nod. "Oh, trust me, I'm a wreck four days out of every
month. I have to say, you're braver than I am, wearing a
pastel skirt." She glanced around, then motioned me over

to the desk. "Don't worry about the forms. I can change the date stamp before I clock them in tomorrow. Bebe . . . it's been awhile since she's had to deal with PMS." The look on her face told me Bebe Wilcox wouldn't let a thing like cramps put a dent in her day, and she probably had little sympathy for anyone so afflicted.

"Thanks," I said, filing away a note that Debra was probably unappreciated and overworked. "So what next?"

"Here's your temporary badge," she handed me a name tag. "Your permanent one will be ready next week."

I plastered it on my suit, wondering if the permanent passes were sturdier than this. "Okay. Next?"

Debra consulted a memo on her desk. "Why don't you have a seat while I call Ms. Doyle? She's the head of the research department, where you'll be working."

"What's she like?" I asked.

Debra quirked her mouth and snickered. "Ms. Doyle makes Ms. Wilcox look as friendly as a puppy. I do not envy you." She picked up the phone while I took a seat and waited.

It took another ten minutes before Leila Doyle appeared. She looked familiar, but I couldn't place her. Small in stature, Ms. Doyle managed to fill the room. Around fifty—maybe older or younger but somewhere in that range—she was petite and immaculate, with a stare straight out of a deep freeze, and she smelled like Le Jardin. With one sweep, she ran her gaze over me and gestured for me to follow her.

I glanced at Debra, who studiously kept her eyes on her desk. As I followed Leila down the hall, I wondered whether she'd be overseeing me the entire time. My guess was that not much escaped those birdlike eyes. Not a chance in hell of poking around with her in the room.

Leila led me to the elevator, which we took to the third floor. As we marched through the hall, I was struck by the muted energy of the place. Quiet, the floor felt empty, as if it had been unused for a long time. The walls were a pale shade of orange that seemed thirty years out of date, and the carpet, a worn purple with gold accents that may once have been fleurs-de-lis.

We stopped in front a set of double doors. Stenciled on the window were the words, Research & Development— 1A. Authorized Personnel Only.

Leila stopped abruptly, her voice brisk. "You'll need a lab coat. Standard dress for our section consists of trousers—pressed and clean, of course—and a short-sleeved shirt. No jeans, no short skirts, no long sleeves in my department. You don't want sleeves drooping into the products or something acidic dropping on your leg. Last year, one of my girls gave herself a third-degree burn on her thigh because she was wearing shorts." Without giving me a chance to say a word, she plowed right on. "Tomorrow you will be properly attired. In the meantime, you may use one of the spare coats we keep for visitors."

She opened the door a crack and stood back, forcing me to squeeze by her. I could feel her disapproving stare and wondered if she was this abrupt with everyone, or if she simply disapproved of Bebe's decision to hire me.

The lab bore no resemblance to anything I'd expected. I don't know what I thought I'd find—perhaps some mad scientist's laboratory out of a cheesy made-for-TV movie, but if beakers and Bunsen burners existed in the building, they weren't here. Instead, the room possessed the same sterility as the conference room I'd been in. Bleak mint green walls, counters covered in utilitarian Formica, a dry erase board stretching across one wall. Three closets held supplies, two on one side of the room, one on another. There were four workstations and a central meeting table with chairs around it.

One of the workstations looked like an artist's studio, with crayons and oil pastels and colored pencils scattered around the surface. Three sketchpads of varying sizes were stacked to one side, alongside a large pile of what looked like old beauty magazines. A half-eaten sandwich sat to the other side, next to a Diet Coke and an open magazine. From where I was standing, the magazine looked like *Modern Makeup*.

The second and third stations were more traditional, but still no gas jets or lab beakers. One consisted of a sink, a hand mirror, a basket full of wet wipes and soaps, and what seemed to be various makeup removers. The third held row after row of samplers—small cards with samples of various cosmetics on them, much like the cards that Bebe's booth had been offering with my fragrances on them. I craned my neck to read the top one. *Evelyn Vox*. Evelyn Vox was an up-and-coming young designer who had recently launched a new line of lipsticks.

The fourth station was obviously mine. A triple row of oils stretched across the work area, along with a box of empty bottles, eyedroppers, cotton swabs, and various other paraphernalia. Leila steered me toward the chair.

"Amy, Rhonda, and Janette are on coffee break. They start at seven AM, as you will, starting tomorrow." She pointed to the chair. "Sit."

I contemplated saying, *Say please,* but decided that would be counterproductive. I sat.

"What size are you?"

"Size?"

"So I can find you an appropriate lab coat. Here at

Bebe's Cosmetics, we do not subscribe to the one-size-fits-all theory. Do you wear a small, medium, or large?" She tipped her head, staring at me over the top of her glasses like I was dense.

It was obvious I took neither a small nor large, but I merely cleared my throat and said, "Medium."

She nodded, then marched to one of the closets and withdrew a bright yellow lab coat from within. I removed my own jacket, looking around for a place to hang it up. Leila let out a sigh of exasperation and grabbed it out of my hand, striding over to a coat rack that I'd somehow managed to miss. I slipped on the lab coat, thanking my lucky stars I didn't really *need* the job here.

She returned, shoving a steno pad in my direction, along with a pen. "Take notes; I'm busy and don't intend to repeat myself."

I repressed a grimace and opened the notebook, jotting down her instructions as quickly as I could.

"These are your fragrance oils, base oils, and equipment. If you run out, or need an oil you cannot find here, you are to ask Debra for a purchase order. Fill it out in triplicate, and turn it in to me. I'll make the final decision on whether the purchase is appropriate. We have a limited budget, so try to make do with what you've got."

I glanced at the oils. All synthetic, and all low grade. I'd have tossed them out if I found them in Venus Envy's inventory.

"You will find, in the bottom left drawer, notebooks, pencils, and other supplies. You can replenish them from the storeroom on the back wall. When you remove something from the storeroom, you are to make a notation on the clipboard you'll find just inside the door. We keep track of how many supplies are used by each employee."

Oh yeah, this was getting more fun with every minute! When the boss counted how many Post-it notes his employees used, there was either a severe theft problem or a control issue. And I had the feeling that Bebe's employees weren't using that many stickies.

Leila ticked off the next few points on her fingers, and I realized these were the big rules . . . the ones that could make you or break you, depending on how well you followed them.

"You will find a wireless laptop in that drawer. You will not remove the computer from this room. Every evening, before you leave this building, you will file a progress report. The forms are on the computer. You will use company e-mail to voice concerns. You will not use this computer for any personal business whatsoever. You will not discuss your work with your immediate coworkers, nor will you ask them about their work. You will keep your mouth shut about your progress outside this room, unless specifically asked to discuss it by either Ms. Wilcox or myself. You will not discuss your salary. Do you understand?"

I swallowed and nodded.

"Good. Now, to your job duties. You are here to develop new fragrance lines for company products. As you know, most cosmetics, shampoos, and other assorted beauty products possess a chemical scent in their natural state. It's your job to make them smell good—therefore you will be receiving samples of our products, on which you will experiment. You will not remove these samples from the building. Do you understand?"

She was talking so fast that it was all I could do to keep up with her. I scribbled frantically, deciding silence was the better part of valor.

"In addition, to maintain your position, you will be required to come up with three new fragrances a week for our fragrance lines. If you do not have a product to work on at the moment, you will create sample fragrances for future products. Very few of these will be acceptable, but we hope you'll come up with several successes. Your work has been noticed, you have what it takes to develop viable products. However, since you are in our employ now, you will never claim that you've created a Bebe fragrance. Do you understand?"

"One moment, please," I said, breaking in with the hope that I was misunderstanding her. "Are you saying that you actually create *perfumes* here?" Creating a perfume was far more complex in scope than what I did at Venus Envy, but even my perfumery at Moss Rose Cottage was better equipped than this place. There was no way in hell I could make anything resembling a modern perfume with what I had here.

Leila raised her eyebrows. "What seems to be eluding you?"

"Perfume making is an exacting art. I blend fragrances, I don't *make perfume*." I glanced at her. "Sometimes, I've added a cologne base, but that's only when my clients requested it, and again, it's not the same as perfumery."

She shot me down with a well-aimed look of derision. "You won't be making perfumes—not in that sense. You are a cog in a wheel here, *Ms. Vanderbilt*. Your job is to cover up unpleasant scents of our products with ones of a more fragrant nature. Do you need any further clarification?" She folded her arms, waiting.

Keep quiet, I thought. *Don't blow it.*

"So, do you have any more questions?" Leila asked, looking ready to pounce. It was obvious that she didn't like me, and I didn't want to give her any reason to fire me.

Though, considering I was here at Bebe's request, I rather doubted she'd do that without consulting the head honcho herself.

I shook my head. "No, I just didn't understand at first."

She held my gaze for a moment longer, then gave me an abrupt nod. "Good. I suggest you spend an hour getting familiar with your station. Make certain you know how to use the computer, and if you have any questions, knock on my door. I'm down the hall, to the right. I'll have one of the girls bring you some samples of a new rouge that needs a light fragrance. You'll come up with five options by the end of tomorrow. If you fail to perform satisfactorily after a week, we'll reevaluate your employment."

As she turned to swish her way out of the room, I could have sworn I saw little horns growing out of her head, but of course, it was a trick of the light. The real devil in this joint occupied the main office.

*

When my lab mates returned from their break, they stopped cold, staring at me. One of them introduced herself as Janette. I recognized her; she'd been the tall blonde having words with Sharon at the convention. It dawned on me Leila had been the one separating the two. That's where I'd seen her before.

Janette stood in front of the pile of sample cards from other companies. Tall she was, and very blonde, with a wasp waist that belied her use of a corsetiere. She winked at me. "We know who you are," she said. "Persia, from Venus Envy. I heard they were trying to recruit you, but I'm surprised they managed. Rumor has it you liked your work there."

Amy, petite and wide-eyed in that Japanese manga way,

flashed me an infectious grin. "Janette's blunt. Don't mind her," she said, picking up her sketch pad.

I shrugged. "Blunt doesn't hurt my feelings. My aunt and I had words; she thinks I did something I didn't. One way or another, it led to me leaving."

The third member of our little quartet was Rhonda, a cagy brunette to whom I took an instant liking. She kept her eyes on my face as she introduced herself. "So, welcome to hell. They probably have this place bugged, but what the fuck? I'm good at my job; they aren't going to fire me. Our intrepid leader, Leila, is brilliant, if a bitch. Hear that, Lee?" she called out, a grin on her face. "I just gave you a compliment, you old biddy."

Janette and Amy giggled, though I detected a certain nervousness in their laughter. I had the feeling they were less confident in their staying powers at Bebe's than Rhonda was.

"So, we aren't supposed to talk about our work?" I asked.

Rhonda snorted. "Of course we aren't, but that doesn't stop us, unless Ms. L is in the room. You're working on the fragrances to scent this crap? Good. God knows we need it. Smell this." She shoved a small pot of what looked like rouge in my face, and an acrid smell wafted up, reminding me of ammonia.

I grimaced. "I'm supposed to cover that up?"

"Apparently so. Good luck. Whatever you come up with is going to have to nullify that mess. God knows what it does to the skin." She tossed the pot on my counter.

I rested my elbows on the counter. "Why are you working here? You don't seem too confident of the products." I'd expected carbon copies of the Belles, but instead I'd found living, breathing people.

Rhonda and Janette burst into laughter.

Rhonda shook her head. "Rent. And it's a stepping-stone to a bigger and better job. All I do is figure out the best way to remove the products from skin, which means I have to try the damned things on first. I've had more breakouts in the past six months than I had during puberty. I swear, this stuff is pure crap. I'm just biding my time till I can move on to another company and get out of this hell-hole."

"What about the noncompetition agreement? Didn't you have to sign one?" Just how did they plan on getting around that little matter? I wondered.

Amy shrugged. "What are you talking about? We didn't have to sign anything like that."

Interesting. So I was hired with restrictions. I hoped for their sake that the room wasn't bugged, but decided to ask anyway. I turned to Amy and Janette. "So I'm working on fragrances. Rhonda's trying out cleansing routines. What about you two?"

Janette grinned. "I'm going through these samples, try-ing to find something that I think would be good for Bebe to replicate. Amy's sketching out sample bottles and pack-aging—she's a commercial artist."

Just then, the phone rang and she dashed over to the table to answer it. As the other girls got to work, I opened my lower left drawer and pulled out the beat-up laptop that I found inside. I had just plugged it in and turned it on when I overheard Janette laugh.

"Yeah, thanks Auntie T. No, I haven't found it yet, but when I do, I'll let you know. I know, you need it right away, but I've only got so much leeway. Yes, I promise. Yes. I love you, too." She hung up. When she saw me watching her, she shrugged. "I lost one of my aunt's earrings. I've been looking for it, but so far, no luck."

Though her explanation made perfect sense, I had the feeling she was lying to me. And something else about her conversation on the phone rang a bell, but I couldn't place it. I returned to the laptop and started poking around. During lunchtime, I'd start investigating the building. Until then, I'd better look busy, just in case the big bad Ms. L dropped in to see how I was doing.

Chapter Thirteen

I spent the morning playing with the laptop and double-checking all of my supplies. The selection of oils was worse than I thought. I wouldn't have to worry about creating something I might lose to Bebe while I was here—I wouldn't want my name on anything made out of this schlock.

By lunchtime I was starving, and the band on my skirt was beginning to cut into my waist. I thought about running home to change clothes, but when I peeked out the window and saw Leila leaving the building with another woman who looked like a Belle in full uniform—bright yellow coat and cream skirt—I decided to have a look around while I had the opportunity. I'd still have to be cautious, but at least the dragon lady wouldn't be around to smack my hands if she caught me getting into anything.

I begged off lunch with my coworkers, pleading a headache, and waited until they'd cleared out of the room. A quick glance in the supply closets told me there wasn't much to be found beyond the barest-bones supplies.

Hurrying into the hall, I was relieved to find it empty. It seemed the third floor was in the unpopular section of the camp. With a glance over my shoulder, I strode the length of the hall.

One set of double doors marked Testing, and Authorized Personnel Only caught my eye. The glass on the front was glazed, but I squinted through the frosty pane and, after detecting no motion or sound from within, cautiously pushed on the door. At first, it seemed to be locked, but then I realized it was just stuck. I shoved harder, and it popped open.

The lights were on, but the room had a musty odor to it, one of dust and mildew and faded urine. Wrinkling my nose against the assault, I glanced around. There were animal cages lining the back wall, but they were devoid of anything resembling food, fur, or feathers. A thick layer of dust coated the counters and furniture, and the sinks were bone dry. Now, this was more like what I'd been expecting, but the room had obviously gone unused for some time.

Puzzled, I shook my head. Maybe their testing facility had been moved to another room? The Animal Freedom Association had been adamant that Bebe's tested on animals. Could they be wrong? Or had Bebe merely gone underground to prevent a backlash?

The filing cabinets in the room were empty, too, and I decided not to waste any more time here. I made sure the doors were fully shut behind me, and headed for Leila's office.

Though I made sure my temporary badge was affixed to my lab coat, I didn't have to worry. The halls remained empty, and nobody was around to ask me what I was doing. Since I'd seen Leila carrying her purse as she left the building, I felt confident that she was going out for lunch. I knocked on her office door, and when there was no answer, carefully cracked it and peeked in. Nobody in sight.

I slipped inside the room and closed the door. I had the urge to leave it ajar, so I could hear if anybody was coming, but it seemed that Leila preferred her privacy, and an open door might attract suspicion.

Two doors on the other side of the room caught my attention, and I opened the first, holding my breath. A half bath. So Leila rated her own restroom? She must be fairly high up in the company. I noted with interest that none of Bebe's cosmetics or toiletries graced the counter. In fact, a bottle of Venus Envy's Lilac Bliss hand lotion sat on the faux marble top. My blood began to boil.

They were trying to put us out of business, but they used our products? No doubt they were just frothing at the mouth to re-create everything that had our name on it. Forcing myself to remain calm, I closed the door and peeked in the next one, which proved to be a supply closet that was almost empty.

Keeping one ear cocked for the sound of any movement, I headed toward Leila's desk. Fastidiously neat, the heavy oak bench was old; I'd place it at fifty years, at the very least. Nothing I'd seen in this joint was even halfway as nice as this desk. I slipped into her chair and glanced over the papers on the desktop. There was a memo from Bebe about me starting work, but nothing of importance on it. A file of employee time sheets. A long list that I guessed were either current Bebe's cosmetics or proposed names.

Carefully replacing everything, I opened her desk drawers. Nada. Except for the lower right-hand drawer, which was locked. I glanced at the clock. I didn't have time to try to pick it, and if I did manage to wrangle it open, chances were good that I wouldn't be able to shut it properly.

Moving to the file cabinet, I opened the first drawer at random. There, staring up at me, were three huge files. One bore the name Urban Gurlz, another was titled Donna Prima, and the third—Venus Envy.

Bingo! I'd hit the jackpot. I reached for the file on Venus Envy when I heard laughter in the hall. Shit! I couldn't get caught now! And then, I caught a whiff of Le Jardin filtering in from the other side of the door. Leila, all right. I glanced around, frantically searching for a place to hide. The bathroom was too risky; no doubt she'd go in there to freshen up after lunch. My one chance was the supply closet.

I had barely secreted myself inside when I heard the outer door open. Thinking quickly, I slipped off my shoes and held them in my hands before pressing my ear against the wood. I heard a soft sigh, then a noise that I imagined was Leila setting down her bag. After another moment, her heels clicked by into the bathroom, followed by the sound of a door shutting firmly. I had no time to waste. Biting my lip, I carefully opened the supply closet door and shut it gently behind me, then silently tiptoed out of her office. I managed to close her door, slip on my shoes, and hurry back to the laboratory before anybody saw me.

As I entered the lab, I saw Janette, Rhonda, and Amy coming down the hall from the elevator. I waited for them to catch up.

"How's your headache?" Janette asked. "Are you sure you don't want any Tylenol?" She lifted her purse.

I shook my head. "Thanks, but it's better." In truth, I really did have a headache now. A hunger headache, and a stress headache all mishmashed into one thumping head-pounder. Amy was holding a McDonald's bag, and I glanced at it, not realizing I was staring.

She grinned. "You didn't manage any lunch, did you?"

Ruefully, I shook my head. "No, I tried to rest for a bit to get rid of the headache and forgot to eat."

Rhonda snorted. "I've done that way too many times. Here, I've got a candy bar, if you'd like that?" She pulled out a Milky Way, and I accepted it gratefully. Amy handed me the rest of her fries, and Janette dug through her purse and came up with a small package of beef jerky. As I settled in at my station, I gulped down lunch and, for just a moment, felt sorry that I was pulling one over on them. They seemed nice enough, even though they worked for the enemy.

The afternoon passed slowly. I mixed up a couple of batches of fragrance that I didn't particularly like, but that—when blended with the products I'd been given—covered their chemical scent. While I jotted down the proportions for the samples on the report forms, I thought about those three files in Leila's office.

What was in them? What could take up so much room in the drawer? Each file had been a good inch thick, and the drawer had been empty save for a few other folders in the back that I hadn't had a chance to look at. I had to get back in there and see what was hiding in those dossiers.

As I thought about the three companies listed, I looked for something they had in common. Urban Gurlz I knew of by reputation. They were an up-and-coming riot grrrl enterprise, and their products bore distinctly unpalatable names, but they were popular among the teen set and the Goth kids, and they were actually rather pretty. Somehow, the gentle silver-gray eye shadow seemed much nicer if you didn't think about it as Zombie Surprise.

At Venus Envy, we didn't make cosmetics, but we did specialize in toiletries and fragrances. And Donna Prima, of course, belonged to Killian, and was more like a micro-brew setup of a full-scale cosmetics firm.

According to Killian, the formula Sharon had stolen from Donna Prima had the potential to earn big bucks. I wondered whether it was Julian or Trish who had come up with it.

It occurred to me that if the product was indeed that good, maybe one of my coworkers had put in some time on it. Or maybe, they knew something about it. Wondering how to go about finding out, I puttered around with my work for another hour or so, looking busy, then on afternoon break, I followed the girls to the lounge. Thankfully, it was smoke-free. While Amy stretched out with her head down on the table, resting on her arms, Rhonda busied herself with coffee.

I sidled up to Janette, who was gulping a small can of apple juice, along with a small bag of chocolate-covered peanuts. She looked a little pale.

"Are you okay?" I asked.

She shook her head. "Will be in a few minutes. I go through food fast, and need to eat every few hours. I'm on a starch-free diet, and it works great, but I can't skip meals or snacks."

I nodded. "Me either, and I eat as much as a horse."

"You don't look it," she said, appraising my figure.

"I work out a lot—Pilates, yoga, weights, martial arts. I'm a real exercise nut. Love it, and always have."

She glanced around the room, and I noticed she lowered her voice. "So, how do you like it here so far?"

I smiled. "Oh, it's not so bad. I've worked in worse places than this." Again, true. Xander Potpourri Company had been a hellhole. "Say, I'm feeling a little out of my element. You wouldn't be interested in catching some dinner after work? My treat. I was thinking you could give me the lowdown on what it's like to work here."

Janette laughed. "But if I do that, you'll run screaming and never come back." Pouring the last of the peanuts into her mouth, she followed them with another swig of juice. After swallowing, she glanced at the clock. "Sure, why not? I don't have any plans. Where do you want to eat?"

"What kind of food do you like?" I asked.

"I'm a steak-and-salad type of girl," Janette said.

"Steak it is," I said. "We can go to the Keg. It's nearby, and they're pretty good."

"They are indeed," Janette said, grinning at me. "For now, though, we'd better get back to work. Leila likes to make surprise visits to see if we're *lollygagging*, as she puts it. Tonight, I'll make sure you get the lowdown on everything. You can't be too careful around here," she added, lowering her voice. "There are spies everywhere. But then again, I imagine you know what that's like, having worked for Venus Envy. The industry's rife with backstabbers."

I longed to assure her that not every place was like that, that Auntie wouldn't dream of running her business on fear, but I didn't dare. Maybe, once this business was taken care of, if Janette and I found some basis for a friendship, I might be able to convince her that there were good employers out there, employers who valued their workers.

❧

Dinner provided a few surprises. After we ordered, I briefly told Janette my cover story about the roses and how Auntie blamed me, even though I hadn't done anything.

"What hurts the most is that she didn't trust me. She pushed me out like some bum, and now I'm scrounging to make ends meet."

"That's harsh. Let me get the check," Janette said. "You must be scrimping until payday, and I'm doing just fine."

"Oh, no." I hastily backtracked. "My credit cards are clear, and I want to buy dinner because you're being so kind. I will admit," I said conspiratorially, "I'm rather nervous. After all, Bebe's is in direct competition with my aunt, and I know that Aunt Florence is going to blow a gasket once she hears I've started working at Bebe's. I can pretty much kiss that relationship good-bye. But I think it was already damaged beyond repair. I guess this is a new start, all the way around."

"That has to be difficult. I know how I'd feel if my family believed I was doing something underhanded," Janette said. She seemed to mean it, and I wondered if that meant her aunt knew where she was working and approved.

"Are you from Gull Harbor?" I asked.

"No," she said, shaking her head. "I live near my aunt. My parents are still alive, though, they just live back east. I came out here to attend the University of Washington." Janette played with her glass of Chardonnay.

"What's your aunt's name?" The thought crossed my mind that it might be one of Bebe's coworkers. Surely nepotism held sway here when it came to employment.

"Patricia," she said, hesitating a moment.

Something about the way she said it rang alarm bells, but I didn't want to be too forward. I just nodded and said,

"So tell me, what should I be on the lookout for at Bebe's? I'm not used to working in a corporate atmosphere."

Janette laughed. "I can tell. Frankly, I'm surprised that you accepted a job there, but I guess work is work."

"That's the truth," I said, playing along. "It wasn't my first choice."

"You should keep clear of anybody who has a private office. I'm serious. All of the corporate bigwigs are absolutely vile. I'm surprised Leila left you in one piece today. She was furious when Bebe announced you were being hired for the position."

"Why? Was someone fired to make room for me?" That could account for Leila's attitude toward me, all right.

"Not exactly. Leila wanted one of her friends for the job—a woman named Sharon Wellstone—but Bebe wanted you." She stopped, contemplating me with wide eyes, as if wondering just how much to say. "You walked into a hornet's nest, you know."

Now we were getting somewhere. I glanced down at my mai tai, swirling the fruity drink with my swizzle. "So they had an argument over who was going to get the job?"

"That's about right. Leila's the only one who's ever stood up to Bebe as far as I can tell. From what I've heard through the grapevine, Bebe ordered Sharon to recruit you—she knew Sharon wanted the job, and she does things like that to make employees prove their loyalty. Apparently, you refused, so Sharon begged for a chance to prove herself, and Bebe finally let her submit a few sample fragrances. They were actually quite lovely," she said, surprise filling her voice. "Nobody thought she'd come up with anything so good."

Thanks to me and my journal, I thought but kept my mouth shut.

"So Bebe agreed to give her a chance. That same day, Sharon was shot."

"Oh my God, you mean that's the Sharon Wellstone in the newspaper?" I looked up at her with wide eyes.

"One and the same. Leila wanted to hold the job open for Sharon, even though she's in critical condition. I was in the lounge, and they were having a huge argument right outside the door a couple days ago. Bebe told Leila that while she felt sorry for Sharon, the company had to move on. Then, I guess you changed your mind, and she hired you."

Oh, Jeez. Sharon was Leila's pet. No wonder she'd given me the evil eye. Sharon must have been secretly relieved when I refused the job offer, and she saw her chance to take over the fragrance line with the help of my journal. But then she was shot, and I happened to need a job. Bebe thought she'd lucked out thanks to my change of heart.

Which meant—my mind ran aground on a new possibility—*Bebe might not know about my missing journal.* It might not even be at the company! If Sharon hadn't bothered to tell them about the theft, but kept it secret, she might have been hoping to sneak into the job using replicas of my work. I struggled to maintain my equilibrium while putting on a properly horrified face over the whole mess.

I buttered a dinner roll. "I'll walk softly around Leila."

"Good idea." Janette dug into her salad.

We ate silently for a few minutes, then I asked, "So you've only been there a few months?"

"Yeah . . . going on two. I just graduated with my BS in chemistry. This is my first job outside of college."

"Where do you want to end up, career-wise?"

She patted her lips with her napkin; a thin stain of red spreading across the cloth. She followed my gaze. "No, it's not Bebe's. I use M.A.C."

I grinned at her. "So you aren't planning on becoming a Belle?"

"Oh good Lord, no. I'm only working at Bebe's until I can make enough money to go back to school and get my PhD. I'd like to eventually get into biochemical research. That's what my aunt does. This is pocket change while I figure out how to pay for my master's degree."

By the end of dessert—we both had the white chocolate cheesecake—I figured I'd gotten everything out of her I was going to get. I thanked her for a lovely evening and took off for my apartment.

As I pulled up in front of the building, my stomach sank. A police cruiser was parked in the visitor parking. I stepped out of my car and saw that Kyle was inside the prowl car. He noticed me, motioned for me to wait, and then unfolded himself from the sedan.

"Hey, Kyle, what's up?"

He glanced over me with a curious look on his face but only said, "I need to talk to you, and the parking lot isn't a good place for it."

I immediately panicked. "Aunt Florence—is she okay?"

He nodded. "She's fine, as far as I know. This is about something else. Let's go up to your apartment."

"Come on, then," I said, curious. He was being exceptionally furtive, even more than usual. I led him to the stairs, but he balked and thumbed toward the elevator.

"I've walked enough for one day."

The ride up was loud and noisy, as always, but even though I tried to stare him down, Kyle remained impassive. We hit the fifth floor, and I unlocked my door, ushering him in.

"Hold on, I have to get out of this outfit before I scream," I said, grabbing my jeans and a tank top and heading for the bathroom.

He snorted. "I thought that jacket looked a little confining. You're about ready to spill out of it, and while that wouldn't distress me in the least, I don't think you'd be so pleased."

Slamming the door behind me, I wiggled my way out of the skirt and top, staring at the fabric marks that crisscrossed my legs and stomach. Joy, just what I needed: texturizing.

Kyle was poking through the refrigerator when I emerged from the bathroom. "You have anything cold to drink besides water?"

" 'Fraid water will have to do," I said. "I haven't had time to do much shopping. So tell me, what's so important that you'd wait outside these delightfully ugly apartments for me?"

He shut the fridge and turned back to me, no longer smiling. "Sharon died today, Persia. There was no brain activity, and her husband gave orders to disconnect life support. The combination of the blow to her head and the gunshot wound proved deadly. This case is now officially a homicide."

Shit. I sighed and slumped in the recliner. "Damn it. I disliked the woman since she got involved with the Belles, but I didn't wish her any harm." I glanced up, suddenly apprehensive. I was still a suspect. I wondered if that's why he was here. "You come to arrest me? Or just to let me know?"

"I've already told you that I know you didn't kill her, Persia, so stop talking nonsense. I may not be able to remove you from the suspect list, but this wouldn't be your style. Especially using a gun. No, I'm afraid that my conclusions are focusing more and more in one direction."

In the pit of my stomach, I knew what he was going to say. "Killian? You think that Killian killed her?"

He shrugged. "He doesn't have a good alibi. He has a good motive. I'm not ready to make an arrest yet, but yes, he's a serious contender." He stretched out on the sofa. "Damn, this thing is bumpy. So, how was your day?"

I gently folded myself into the lotus position, crossing my legs with ease. "Very strange. I found out that Sharon was supposed to start the job that I was hired for, but she was shot before she could take it."

Kyle straightened up. "What?"

"Sharon was bucking for a promotion. She presented samples of fragrance blends to them that they loved—and my guess is that's where my stolen journal comes into play. I'm not so sure Bebe has the journal now. Once I turned Sharon's job offer down, she came back in the store, stole my journal, and used it to land herself a new job. The job Bebe wanted me to take."

"Anything else I should know about this matter?" Kyle was looking more and more interested.

I shrugged. "Bebe didn't want Sharon to have the job; she wanted me. She only relented after Sharon informed her that I refused. My supervisor, Leila Doyle, was championing her, and Leila and Bebe had a big argument about it, but that's hearsay, and I don't want to tell you who told me because I don't want her getting in deep shit with the old bats who run the company. And there are three large files in Leila's office that I want a look at, one on Venus Envy, one on Donna Prima, and one on Urban Gurlz."

He made a note of it in his pocket-sized notebook. "Great, now you're rifling through file cabinets. Are you *sure* you're safe there? If this Doyle woman doesn't want you there, do you think she's safe for you to be around?"

"Kyle, this is a business, not a Mafia family."

"And Sharon's dead," he said. "Murders happen over far less than somebody swiping someone else's job. Not to mention the espionage you've been talking about—that's enough for some people to dump their rivals in the drink. There's a lot to puzzle through, but while we're in the process, I want you to take care of yourself."

A knock on the door interrupted us. I unfolded myself, rose, and answered. There stood Bran, a bottle of wine in his hand. He peeked over my shoulder at Kyle. "You need some privacy?" he asked, a grin lurking in his eyes.

Grateful to see him, I nodded for him to come in. Kyle gave him a curt nod, then stood up. "I suppose I should mosey out of here. Persia, think about what we discussed, and whether it's really worth what you stand to gain. We aren't playing penny ante poker. The stakes are real, and dangerous. I think we're up to no-limit Texas hold 'em."

I let out a long breath. "I know you're concerned. I'm concerned, too. But a lot rests on what I might be able to find out. It's gone beyond a missing journal and stealing customers. There's something going on there, Kyle, and I want to know what it is. I have to get a look at those files."

"Just stay out of the official investigation. You're still on my list. And let me know what you find out." He nodded to Bran. "Evening Stanton."

Bran flashed him a broad smile, which Kyle did not

return. "Good to see you, Chief," he said, as Kyle swept past.

As I shut the door, I couldn't help but wonder about Killian. He had a lot to lose—and more was wrapped up in failure for him than for my aunt. If Venus Envy went under, then yes, it was the end of one dream and a lot of money down the drain. But Auntie would survive and most likely thrive. She was smart, and she had more than enough to handle the loss, even though it would be a blow in the pocketbook.

But Killian . . . what else did he have except for his company? He wasn't married. I had no idea whether he had money beyond Donna Prima. His whole life was wrapped up in that company. Had he killed Sharon? But something whispered *No*, and it wasn't my aching loins doing the talking.

If Sharon had stolen my journal and kept it for herself, then where could she have put it? Her apartment? Kyle and his men had been all over the place, looking for clues to her assailant. If the journal had been secreted there, they would have found it. Which meant she probably took it to work with her. But considering that Bebe didn't want her to have the job, would Sharon have shared the contents? Or would she have kept it private, planning on using it to further her career, one fragrance of mine at a time?

If that was the case, then the journal was probably hidden somewhere on the premises of the company. The question was—where?

These and other thoughts filling my mind, I turned to Bran, who seemed uncertain. "What do you need?" he asked.

I stared at him, my body aching. I wanted Killian, but

he wasn't mine to have. And I had Bran, who was a tall drink of water on his own. I closed my eyes, shaking as Bran reached for me, pulling me to him so my back rested against his chest. I slowly raised my arms, and he drew off my tank top, then unhooked my bra, his fingers sliding around my waist to cup my breasts. I caught my breath, leaning into him as his featherlight touch slid down my belly.

The room was spinning, and when he disrobed and entered me, there on the bed in the dusky heat of the impending night, I forgot about everything else and gave myself over to the sensation.

Chapter Fourteen

⋙ ⋘

B ran left around midnight, after I assured him I would be okay. I padded into the bathroom, then set the alarm and climbed back into bed. Five o'clock saw me up and dressed. I only had so much time before they caught on to why I was working at Bebe's, and if I was going to do any snooping, I'd better snoop now. With Sharon dead, things were heating up, and I didn't want to stick my neck in that arena any more than I had to.

I made sure to put on the casual trousers and short-sleeved shirt that Leila had requested, then patted my blue-bell faerie tattoo and whispered, "Bring me a little luck today, if you could." After eating a peanut butter sandwich and an apple, I grabbed my keys and headed out.

The building was still quiet—one light burned in a far corner on the first floor, but that could easily be a janitor. If the building was locked, I was in for trouble, but as I took hold of the door, it opened. Somebody had beat me in, but that didn't surprise me. Just as long as it wasn't Leila. On my way up to the third floor, I realized I'd forgotten to bring a camera, which seemed to be the quickest way to copy documents. No doubt, there would be information in Leila's files that I'd want to remember. Of course, if I had the guts, I could swipe a few pages, photocopy them, and then hustle them back into the cabinet before they were missed.

Leila's office was locked. I hadn't been prepared for that. I glanced around to make sure nobody was watching, then knelt down to examine the lock. Flimsy and old. Probably with an unguarded latch. A quick shuffle through my purse produced my library card, which was more flexible than a credit card and easier to replace. As I slid the plastic in the crack of the door and began jiggling it around, a soft click sounded, and the knob turned in my hand.

I slipped inside and locked the door again. At least I'd have a little warning if she showed up early. Pulling a compact flashlight out of my purse, I quickly headed for the file cabinet and opened the drawer. There they were— the three files. Though curious to see what the other two might have hidden away in their depths, I didn't have time to go through them. I carefully withdrew Venus Envy's file and closed the drawer, then took it into the supply room and sat on the floor.

My first surprise was to find an exact copy of our inventory sheets. How the hell had they gotten those? And letters Auntie had written to suppliers? As I flipped through the papers, it began to dawn on me just how they'd come across the information: our computer. Bebe had found a way to hack in; they'd gotten to our files, copied them, then unleashed a virus to wipe our computer, or something of that nature. After that, they printed out the info and filed it away. I wondered what it was doing in Leila's office, but then again, if she was going to supervise me, surely Bebe would give her a rundown on everything she knew about Venus Envy. Everything of importance that had been on our computer was in the file, instead of in our computer where it should have been.

What to do, though? I had to make copies of at least a few of the pages—ones that would prove, at least to Auntie and possibly Kyle, that Bebe had been skulking around. Maybe we could ask Andy if there was any way to prove that they'd hacked our computer, now that we knew in which direction to look.

I debated taking the entire file, but that would be both dangerous and stupid. The nearest copy machine was in the lounge, and I didn't want to chance being caught—too many people were due to show up for work over the next hour or so. Finally, I chose a few pages with the most incriminating evidence, then cautiously replaced the file just as I'd found it. As I started to slide the papers in my purse, I lost my hold on the hobo bag, and it fell to the floor. Dropping to my knees, I shone my flashlight around to make sure that nothing had scattered that Leila might later find.

Nope, nothing. As I scrambled to my feet, I glanced at the desk. From my vantage point, I could see a set of keys peeking out from behind a fluted vase. I took a closer look. The key chain said Maintenance. What was Leila doing with a janitor's key? And then I knew. This was quite possibly a set of master keys, and my bet was that every bigwig at Bebe's had a set. There was only one way to find out for certain. I palmed the keys, then quickly slipped out of the room, making sure everything was as it had been when I entered.

❧

An hour later, over an egg and sausage muffin at McDonald's, I thumbed through the photocopies, then dropped them off at my apartment before returning to work. Upon my arrival, I was pleasantly surprised to find that Leila was out of the office until the afternoon. I briefly thought about returning to photocopy the entire contents of the file, but there were too many people running around the halls, making the chance of discovery too great.

The second surprise wasn't nearly as welcome. Apparently Bebe had left word with Debra that they were to conduct a memorial for Sharon in the early afternoon. Attendance was required, even though Bebe couldn't make it. Janette and I walked ahead of Amy and Rhonda, who were engaged in a conversation about a movie.

"You okay?" I asked Janette.

She shook her head. "I'll let you know by the end of the day. I'm just worried about something."

When I tentatively tried to draw her out, she clammed up and switched the conversation to something less personal.

As we took our seats in the meeting hall, Debra slipped up next to me, but there was no place for her to sit down. She glowered. "I thought you were bringing in your paperwork today? Bebe will have my hide if I don't have it by the time she gets back."

I shook my head. "Oh hell. I'm sorry, I left it on the table at home. I had it all ready to go and walked out the door without it. Tell you what, I'll run home right after work and bring it back. Are you going to be here around six?"

She sighed. "No, I'm leaving early to catch the ferry to Seattle. Just leave it on my desk, and I'll come in a few minutes early and take care of it. But please don't forget again, or you'll get us both in trouble."

I reassured her that I would have it in bright and early on her desk, and she wandered off to find a seat near the front near the main entrance. I assumed that she'd either been one of Sharon's friends, or she was looking to make a hasty exit when this thing was over. Janette and I glanced around the rapidly filling room. All the Belles were in full bloom—with their yellow jackets and tight cream-colored skirts, and they all wore lilies pinned to their breast. I'd never seen so much big hair in my life. The B-52's had nothing on these women.

The meeting hall itself was shabby and smelled like a brothel, the combination of stale smoke and cheap perfume overwhelming. One hundred seats filled the back third of the room, rising on a gradual incline. Down front, a podium stood on a small stage, illuminated by a single light. A movie screen had been lowered behind the lectern, and I had the feeling we weren't getting through this without the requisite PowerPoint presentation. Though when I thought about it, I wouldn't put it past them to drag out an overhead projector.

The auditorium could hold a hundred people, but only about sixty chairs were taken, the majority of those by Belles. As I gazed around, I realized that the staff who actually produced the products was extremely limited. Either that or there was a lot of summer colds going around. The sea of yellow jackets told me that the sales department provided the motivating factor in this company—sales, hype, and forced enthusiasm.

The woman taking the podium looked like a queen bee herself. Her entire outfit was lemon yellow, and her hair fell in coppery waves, tumbling over her shoulders. I sighed, glanced at the clock, then over at Janette. She was sitting upright, her face a blank mask.

"Hello, hello, is this on?" The woman at the podium cleared her throat, tapped on the microphone, and then held up her hand for silence. We quieted down, though I noticed a few people shifted in their seats.

"As most of you know, I'm Rita Sanders, in charge of human resources and PR. I have a painful announcement to make," she said. "Sharon Wellstone, one of our brightest Belles, succumbed to her gunshot wounds yesterday, and died at around four o'clock. Her death has officially been labeled a homicide."

A buzz filled the room. Apparently some of Bebe's employees hadn't watched the news. I glanced around, looking for any reactions that seemed out of place, but it was hard to tell how many people felt from where I was sitting.

"Bebe called and asked that we gather to honor Sharon's memory, and that's what we're going to do." An image flashed on the screen in back of her, and Sharon stared down at us, magnified to a grainy resolution, every flaw on her skin glaringly obvious. Her eyes were dark and cunning. I wondered just what had driven her into the Belles.

The crowd shuffled in their seats, and I caught the scent of unease running through the auditorium. After a pause, Rita said, "The authorities don't know who killed Sharon, but we're confident they'll find out. And now, Ms. Leila Doyle, head of research and development, will offer a few words in her memory."

Leila appeared from the side of the stage. She looked haggard, the lines on her face deeper than they'd seemed the day before, and her suit was wrinkled. I even saw what looked like a little stain on the front of her blouse. I had the

feeling this was the most unkempt she'd been in her life
and was suddenly curious as to what could cause such a
quick transformation.

"Thank you for coming," she said, the jagged edge of
grief cutting through her voice, and it dawned on me that
she was struggling not to cry. Had she really liked Sharon
so much? Had they been good friends instead of just
coworkers?

"I've known Sharon since she was born," Leila began,
her voice raspy. "Her mother was my best friend, and I was
Sharon's godmother."

Godmother? So that was the connection between them.
I stared at my hands, feeling sorry for both Sharon and
Leila. I didn't like either woman, but Sharon didn't deserve to have her life snuffed out, and Leila was obviously
in pain from her loss.

"Sharon was a good wife, and though she and her husband never had the children they'd hoped for, she thought
they had a good marriage. John's decision last year to separate from Sharon hit her hard. I wanted to help pull her
out of her depression, and so I found her a position here, as
a Belle, one of the best remedies for low self-esteem I can
think of."

While Leila paused to clear her throat and dab at her
eyes with her handkerchief, I thought about what she'd
said. I hadn't known that Sharon and her husband were
splitting; that could easily account for the change in behavior and her fierce devotion to Bebe's Belles. If her ego
had been hit by the divorce, then she'd naturally be loyal
to those who helped her shore it back up, who gave her a
haven when she needed reassurance. Neither did it escape
me that Leila's words were a subtle jab at John and would
no doubt influence the way some of the Belles and their

families behaved toward him. Leila was sneaking one in below the belt, whether she realized it or not.

"Sharon was quickly working her way up to becoming one of our top Belles, and what most of you don't know is that she was about to start on a new endeavor in our research department. She proved herself adept at discovering new products, and we all had such high hopes for her. And even though she was struck down in her prime, she'll never be forgotten. To keep her memory alive, we are naming our newest product in her honor."

People were starting to shuffle, and I got the impression not everybody cared as much about Sharon's death as did Leila. She stared into the audience with that glacial stare of hers, and the room quieted down.

"Sharon was working with our skin care research and development team. They had just finished developing a new product when Sharon was attacked. Unfortunately, she didn't live to see it unveiled. And so it is with both sadness and pride that I announce our newest product to hit the markets—Sharonique, the first in our antiaging line!"

Sharon's face disappeared from the screen as the image of a gigantic tube of cream sporting a nimbus of pink burned itself into our gaze. The name was, indeed, Sharonique, though it looked like the text had been added after the picture was taken. No doubt Sharonique wasn't their initial choice of names, but circumstances demanded homage, and homage there would be. It also occurred to me that this was the tackiest use of somebody's death to promote sales that I'd seen in a long time. The Belles would outdo themselves trying to hawk the cream, and they'd do so in Sharon's name.

Beside me, Janette jerked. I whispered, "What's wrong?" but she didn't answer.

Leila continued her pitch with more enthusiasm than I'd thought her capable of. "Sharonique is our newest defense against wrinkles and age-related lines. We think this will be a winner, so we want you Belles to push it. The product will be available for shipment within two weeks. We're asking every Belle to begin using the product so you can claim 'scout's honor' when your customers ask you if you like it."

Throughout her little monologue, her demeanor had shifted from tragic loss to rah-rah team. My sympathy for her dried up. So much for grief. I glanced at Janette. Her face was a blank slate, and she let out a loud sigh but refused to meet my gaze. After a few more comments along the vein of "Sell, sell, sell," Leila released us to go back to work.

As we filed out of the auditorium, I tried to catch up with Janette, but she hurried ahead of me, and by the time I got to the laboratory, she was on the phone, talking in hushed whispers.

Amy and Rhonda were both subdued. Amy shrugged when I asked if she was okay. "I didn't know Sharon," she said, "but it's always a bummer when somebody gets killed." She took off for the storeroom.

Rhonda was more direct and to the point. "It's going to be glum city around here for awhile. Sharon didn't have a lot of friends among the Belles—she wasn't good at teamwork. With her, it was always about looking out for number one, but Leila loved her, of course. And everybody's going to have to pretend they did, too, so we don't rock the boat."

"Leila wasn't acting then?" I asked.

"Nope, the two were like this." Rhonda held up two

fingers, crossed. "Leila's going to be a real bitch for awhile, so watch your step."

I nodded, letting my mind wander to my journal. Where should I start looking for it? Tonight, a few hours after closing, I planned on using those keys I'd palmed to sneak back into the building. Chances are, her grief so overt, Leila wouldn't even notice they were gone.

My first order of business—even before I left for the day—should be to find Sharon's office so I wouldn't waste valuable time in a wild-goose chase.

Janette finished up with her phone call and stomped back over to her desk. As I watched, half paying attention, she began piling her things in a box. Curious, I was about to ask what she was doing, when Leila entered the room, a vague look of distaste on her face.

"Janette, you wanted to talk to me?" Her voice echoed in the room as she stood there, arms folded across her chest. The silence that followed her statement was deafening.

Janette stared at her, eyes cold. "Yeah, you two-bit, con-niving bitch. I quit. You make me sick, you and Bebe. You're nothing but a bunch of thieves and liars, and you'd better watch your back, because one of these days, you're going to get what's coming to you." She stripped off her lab coat and tossed it on the floor at Leila's feet.

"Ms. Jensen, you will remove yourself from the prem-ises immediately. I don't know what this is all about, but I'll get to the bottom of it." Leila took a step forward, and we all pulled back. All except Janette, who grabbed her bag and stormed out the door.

Jensen . . . where had I heard that name before? And then, the pieces clicked. Of course! Janette Jensen, who lived near her aunt Patricia. Patricia Jensen. Janette's aunt was Trish Jensen from Donna Prima, and the antiaging cream must have been the product that Sharon had swiped. Killian and his crew had been working like crazy to re-create and market it again before Bebe pushed through production, but he'd failed. Janette must have been doing the same thing I was—infiltrating the enemy.

Staring after her, Leila said, "Don't just stand there like a group of cows chewing their cud. Get back to work, and I don't want to be bothered. If you have a problem, figure it out yourself." She marched out of the room.

I inhaled and let it out slowly, trying to keep my face impassive. I wasn't about to complicate matters by saying anything. Apparently, both Rhonda and Amy were of the same mind-set, and we worked through the afternoon without so much as a "How are you doing?"

❧

After work, I was so antsy that I called Barb and asked if she wanted to meet me at the BookWich for a quick bite. Dorian was going bowling with his buddies, so she said she'd meet me there in twenty minutes.

I hurried back to the apartment—which I was coming to hate—and slipped into black jeans and a black tank top. I tossed my tote bag, containing my wallet, a flashlight, a camera and film, my cell phone, and a pair of gloves, into the backseat of my Sebring and headed downtown.

A twinge of loneliness ran through me as I pulled up behind the BookWich. The back entry to Venus Envy was only a few doors over, and a wave of homesickness hit me, even though I'd only been gone a couple of days. And even more than the shop, I missed being home. Moss Rose Cottage was my haven now, and Auntie, my family, and I couldn't imagine living anywhere else.

Barb was holding a booth for us when I entered the

café. The smells of pot roast and gravy and chicken soup
filled the air, and even in the quiet heat of the early
evening, I found myself craving a good, hot meal. I slid in
opposite to her and eagerly sipped at my iced tea, which
she'd already ordered.

"Thanks," I said. "Hey, nice outfit. I love it!"

Barb grinned. Her mangled cut was covered with a
flowered Hermes scarf, which looked very much like a
cloche. She had paired it with a pair of sky-blue hip-
hugging jeans and a white eyelet button blouse and, alto-
gether, looked like a regular fashionista.

"So, how goes life on the dark side?" she asked.

I shook my head. "Makes me miss the daily grind at
Venus Envy more than you can imagine. It's scary over
there. I feel like I've stumbled into my own private twi-
light zone, only Rod Serling isn't anywhere around to nar-
rate my way out of it. The place is surreal. Especially when
the Belles are wandering around in their bright yellow
jackets like a group of Stepford wasps."

Tilda made her way to our table. "Ready to order,
girls?"

I looked at Barb, who nodded. "Yes, thanks," I said.
"I'll have a bowl of chicken noodle soup and a double
order of cheese bread."

Barb grinned. "I see the stress hasn't affected your appetite." She glanced over the menu one last time. "Why
don't you bring me a fishwich with coleslaw, and a side of
mozzarella sticks?" Tilda nodded, then moved off.

"So, did you hear Sharon died?"

Barb leaned back against her seat. "Yeah. I did. Bad
news there. Do you know if Kyle is any closer to finding
the murderer?"

I shrugged. "Haven't talked to him much. I've been so

focused on trying to find out just how they've been under-
cutting us. I did make two discoveries, however, that confirm my suspicions." I told her about the files in Leila's
office, as well as my suspicions about Sharon and my
journal.

"Then it could still be hidden there somewhere?"

"That's my guess." I dangled the keys in front of her.
"And these babies are going to help me find out." Leaning
forward so no one could overhear, I whispered, "I think
I've got the master key on here."

"Don't they have a security system?"

"You'd think they would, wouldn't you? But nope . . . I
had a look on my way out of the building. Nada. Of course,
Venus Envy doesn't either. I think if our shop grows any
more, we'll install one, but they're expensive, and moni-
toring doesn't come cheap." I played with the straw on my
iced tea.

Barb flashed me a look that I knew only too well. "Can
I come with you? I'm good at snooping!"

"No," I said, wondering how I was going to get out of
this one. Barbara was hard to dissuade when she put her
mind to something. "I can get away with it, but if you were
caught in there, you could be charged with breaking and
entering—you don't have a reason to be there."

"Neither do you," she argued.

"No, but I do work there. I can probably talk my way
out of a scene if I get caught. I'm sorry, Barb, but this time
you can't go."

Barb sighed. "You have to take those files to Kyle. Do
you think he could get a search warrant with them? Would
it be enough?"

I shrugged. "I don't know. But something big is going
down. One of my coworkers stormed out today, and I'm

certain she was there for the same reason I am." I gave her a rundown on what had gone down between Janette and Leila. "It wasn't pretty, I'll tell you that."

"So, it sounds like Killian was right, if they have files on Donna Prima and Urban Gurlz," Barb said, her eyes widening. "Bebe is stealing from a lot of companies, including his. How can she get away with all of this crap? Surely there's some way to put a stop to her."

"This is par for the course when you're dealing with corporations. It happens all the time, and they get away with it. Bebe has just applied it on a smaller scale than we usually hear about. And so much relies on proof. Killian told me that Sharon had destroyed all their files on that particular formula, which *has* to be the antiaging cream. That would account for how agitated Janette was during the meeting."

"So if Donna Prima has no proof they actually developed it, then it's their word against Bebe's, and she has the finished product, right?"

"Right. Frankly, at this point, I just want out of the mess. All I want is to protect Venus Envy and to get my journal back."

As Tilda brought our orders, I thought about the papers sitting on my dinette table. Barbara was right—something ought to be done, but I didn't know enough about the law pertaining to these matters to know where I should take them, given the circumstances. Maybe it was time for another talk with Winthrop. I'd lay everything out that I'd learned and see what he had to say. I was about to tell Barb my plan when my cell phone rang. I fished it out of my purse and glanced at the caller ID. Auntie! Eagerly, I flipped it open and answered.

"Persia? I'm so glad I got hold of you."

"I miss you," I blurted out. "I miss being home. But I've got some interesting news to tell you. And after tonight, I'll hopefully know a lot more." She caught her breath, and I could sense her hesitation through the phone line. "Something's wrong, isn't it? Are you okay?"

"I'm fine, Imp. Don't you worry about me. Listen, I want you to come home. You're not going back to Bebe's. We'll find another way to keep them from ruining our shop. I'm a damned good businesswoman, and you've got more brains than you know what to do with. I want you to pack your bags and give your notice at the apartment tonight."

I stared at Barb, who was looking at me expectantly. Auntie sounded so worried, and she seldom ever directly told me what to do. "Are you sure you're okay? Is Trevor okay? Sarah?"

"Yes, yes, Imp. We're fine. It's you I'm worried about."

"Then you heard Sharon died?" That had to be it. Auntie would automatically assume that whoever killed Sharon would be out for me. It wasn't logical, but my aunt loved me like a mother, and that was the way mothers acted.

Her voice shaky, Auntie said, "Imp, Kyle found out more about Bebe's background. She's apparently a widow. Six times over—from Seattle down to Portland. You can't tell me that anybody can lose six husbands without having a hand in it somehow. From the way he talked, I have the feeling they may be reopening the investigation into those deaths."

"And he thinks she had something to do with Sharon's murder?" My heart leapt. If Bebe had killed Sharon, it meant Killian was off the hook.

"I don't think so. He also said he was headed out to

arrest a suspect in her murder. It should be on the news tonight," she said.

"Who?" My breath caught in my throat, but she put my fears to rest.

"Breathe easy. Kyle wanted you to know that both you and Killian are off the hook. But he wouldn't give me a name."

"Then if Bebe didn't shoot Sharon, and Kyle's on his way to arrest the killer, I should be able to get in and out with the evidence we need without a problem. You have nothing to worry about! The receptionist told me that Bebe won't be in until Monday morning. I have to finish this through, Auntie. I can't just walk away."

"I don't like it. Even if Bebe had nothing to do with Sharon's death, she's still a very dangerous woman. You aren't safe."

"Life isn't safe, but I give you my word that I'll be as careful as I can. I've found a way into the building, and all I need to do is search Sharon's office. Then I grab the files on Venus Envy and I'm done. I'll get my butt out of there, and we'll take everything to Winthrop and let him handle it."

"Please, Imp, I'm begging you. Don't go back."

I sighed. "Would it make you feel better if I took somebody with me? Someone who has as much—if not more— at stake than we do?"

She hesitated. "You're dead set on this, aren't you?"

I took a deep breath. "Auntie, you brought me up to treat people ethically. You taught me to be honest and to be true to myself. How can I walk away when we're being run out of business? How can I turn my head when I know Bebe Wilcox is trying to destroy the other small beauty businesses around here by running them into the ground?

I'm no bleeding heart or do-gooder, but I am your niece. I am the way I am because you brought me up to be this way."

Auntie sighed. Loudly. "Persia, I wish to hell that you weren't such a good girl. What are you going to do?"

"I don't want to tell you over the phone, but if I'm wrong, then I'll come home and let it drop. If I'm right, then Venus Envy will pull out of the mire, and we'll squash Bebe like the bug she is."

"Be careful, Imp. If you don't phone me by midnight, I'm contacting Kyle and asking him to hunt you down."

"It's a deal," I said. "I love you."

"I love you, too. Promise me you won't take any unnecessary risks"

"Cross my heart," I said, folding my phone and dropping it back into my purse. I wasn't about to add *and hope to die.* There was such a thing as tempting the universe, and I wasn't interested in trying my luck.

Chapter Fifteen

━◦◎◦ ◦◎◦━

I persuaded Barb to go back to her place so I could relax for a moment without having to stare at the drab walls of my studio. "I want to see the news—I want to know who Kyle's arresting."

Dorian was gone, so we had the house to ourselves. We settled on the sofa in their family room, and Barb flipped on the TV. Channel Six's breaking news was on—they were talking to Kyle, all right.

"Chief Laughlin, you've arrested a woman in connection with Sharon Wellstone's murder?"

Kyle appeared on screen. He nodded, paused for a moment, then said, "We arrested Janette Jensen tonight, for the murder of Sharon Wellstone. We found the murder weapon in her car, and we have a motive."

I gasped. Janette? He really thought Janette had killed Sharon? But she had motive—he was right. She was Trish Jensen's niece, and I knew that she'd been undercover, searching for the truth about the stolen antiaging cream.

Barb looked over at me. "You know her?"

"I worked with her at Bebe's. She's Trish Jensen's niece, and I'm pretty sure she was spying for Donna Prima. Janette though . . . I don't believe for an instant she's guilty. At least, I don't think so." I glanced at the clock. "I need to make a phone call, if you'll excuse me." I punched in star-82 to unblock my number.

Killian picked up on the first ring. "Persia, I was wondering when I'd hear from you. Are you watching the news?"

"Not only that, but I was there this afternoon when Janette stormed out after calling Leila all sorts of names."

"You were there?" He perked up, and I could hear the curiosity in his voice.

"Yeah. I don't know if you heard, but Auntie and I staged a falling-out, and I went undercover at Bebe's, looking for evidence that they stole my journal. I found more than I bargained for."

He snorted. "No doubt. I've been so busy the past few days trying to figure out what Donna Prima is going to do now, that I hadn't heard about your supposed defection."

I paused, then said, "Do you think Janette did it? Do you think she shot Sharon?"

He paused for a moment, then said, "No. I might, if Sharon had threatened her or her aunt with bodily harm, but no, I don't believe it."

"Listen, I've got a proposition for you. I found a file in Leila's cabinet all about Donna Prima, as well as one on Venus Envy and Urban Gurlz."

"Urban Gurlz? I knew Bebe's spring lines looked too close to theirs for comfort. I take it you're going to swipe them?"

"Yeah. I've already found proof that Bebe hacked our computer. Her, or somebody in her employ. I want to know what's in the rest of that file, and I have to find my journal. With everything in chaos due to Janette's arrest, this might be our best chance to find out exactly what they've been up to."

"Sounds promising," he said, but I could still hear hesitation in his voice.

"Killian," I said, lowering my voice. "They unveiled a new antiaging cream today. One that seemed to upset Janette."

He paused, then slowly said, "I know."

"This was your cream, right?"

Another pause, then, "Yes. The one Sharon swiped. So where and when do we meet?"

My stomach flipped, and I realized how much I wanted to see him again. "Meet me in front of the Delacorte Plaza at ten thirty. That should be late enough. You can follow me over from there."

He agreed, then signed off. I stared at the phone.

"You really have a thing for him, don't you?" Barb's voice brought me back to earth. "I can see it in your face."

"Yes . . . no . . . I don't know." I couldn't tell whether the butterflies in my stomach were due to seeing Killian again or to the thought of breaking into Bebe's factory.

"What about Bran?"

I fidgeted. "Bran's wonderful, a really good man, but he and I will never be anything more than bed-friends." I shook my head. "Okay, I'm heading out. I'd better get home and get ready before Killian shows up." As I made my way to the door, she stopped me.

"Persia, do you really think Killian's safe? He was a suspect in Sharon's death, wasn't he?"

I sighed. "I know you're worried, but trust me, Kyle would never let him off the hook if he didn't believe Killian's innocent. And remember—Kyle found the murder weapon in Janette's car." I paused. "Listen, I'm far from naive. I've never blindly trusted anybody. And right now, my gut is telling me that Killian and I are alike. We both want revenge, but neither one of us will cross that invisible line."

"Just be cautious. Please?" She opened the door. I waved and stepped into the muggy evening. Another thunderstorm was on the way. I could smell it in the air.

⁂

Killian was waiting for me at the Delacorte Plaza as we agreed, and followed me to Bebe's. I motioned for him to get into my car for a moment so we could talk before heading into the building.

He was dressed in a pair of black leather pants and a black polo shirt, and his gingery hair had been sleeked back. With his dark shades, he could almost pass for Hispanic or Italian. My pulse quickened, and I had to force myself to quit staring as he slid into the seat.

"Nice car," he said. "You like it?"

I shrugged. "She's okay, but I think I might want to trade it in for an Acura." I said, listening to the silence that descended around us. Even in summer, Gull Harbor closed up shop around six or seven except for the mall, the movie theaters, and the restaurants. After a moment, I filled him in on what I'd found in the file. He nodded, taking it in but making no comment.

"Sharon stole the antiaging cream Trish was working on, didn't she?" I asked. He blinked, then nodded. "It's really good, isn't it?"

After a moment, he said, "Probably one of the best around. Trish is a genius when it comes to skin care. This could have put her at the top of her game. I would have lost her, though. Some bigger company would have head-hunted her away, no doubt about that."

"And now they think her niece killed Sharon. Maybe Sharon caught on to her, threatened to tell Bebe or Leila." I stared out the window, wondering if that could be the motive. If Janette had been at the convention with the Belles, and Sharon threatened to rat her out, she might have struck out in panic.

Killian frowned. "You might be right. I tried to call Trish tonight but couldn't get any answer. She must be devastated by this. I sure didn't put her niece up to spying at Bebe's, so it must have been Trish's idea."

"Oh God, that makes it worse. Trish is probably blaming herself."

The parking lot was devoid of other cars, and we'd parked well away from any streetlamps to avoid undue notice. I glanced at the clock. "Almost ten. I guess this is it," I said but made no move to open my door. The silence between us grew deafening.

Killian slowly leaned over the gearshift. I held my breath as his lips met mine, and sank into the kiss I'd been waiting for. Deep and resonant, filled with hints of dark passion and rolling ocean waves, it reverberated through my body from head to toe, setting me aflame. Gasping, I pulled away, wide-eyed. Killian had the same look, and we stared at one another, not saying a word. After a moment, I reluctantly pulled away.

As I grabbed my tote bag and slipped out of my seat, Killian emerged from the passenger seat and came around to my side, bracing me by the shoulders. I held his gaze, unblinking, then swallowed.

"We'd better get moving," I said, gesturing to the building. He nodded, and we jogged across the lot, up to the back entrance.

My hunch was correct—I held the master key in my hand. As I unlocked the door, a hush enveloped us. I couldn't help but think of Sharon, forever hushed, forever silenced. I may not have liked her, but death held such finality . . . no going back, no saying, "I've changed my mind" after you killed someone. No reprieve, for either victim or murderer.

The building was so quiet I could almost hear it breathe. Using my flashlight, I wound along through the darkened corridors toward the stairs. The elevator might be noticed in the silence, if anybody was still around.

Our first destination was Leila's office. Killian closed the door as I headed for the filing cabinet. I quickly pulled out the files and handed him the one for Donna Prima.

"Here, take this," I said, grabbing the file for Venus Envy. I paused, then grabbed the rest of them and shoved them in my bag. "No doubt Janette's already spilling the beans about how Bebe's company spies and steals. I'm pretty sure Leila will be in here to shred the evidence as soon as she figures out what's going on, so we might as well take it before she destroys it. I'm headed over to Sharon's office to look for my journal. They haven't cleaned out her office. I think they really expected her to recover."

He nodded. "You *will* be coming back?"

I gave him a long, hungering look. "I've got a good reason to come back. Sharon's office is near Bebe's office—it's on the bottom floor. Room 105. If you need me, come get me."

With luck, there wouldn't be anybody working late tonight, I thought as I jogged through the hall. Even so, the corridor seemed twice as long as it had during the daytime. As I jogged toward the stairs, it occurred to me that when I first returned to Gull Harbor I'd been seeking sanctuary— a safe haven where I could escape from the fear and worry that Elliot's unsavory coworkers might take it in their heads to come after me because they were mad at him. And now—just look at me. Visions of signing up with the CIA as a female James Bond ran through my head, but I nixed that as quickly as it flashed through my mind. Just because one *could* do something, didn't mean one *should*.

The stairwell was lit by a pale, cold bulb, and I took the stairs two at a time, watching my shadow follow me along the cold concrete wall. *Me and my shadow* . . . yep, an army of one, all right.

Sharon's office was two doors down from Bebe's and, as I'd hoped, the master key opened it without a single protest. I slipped inside, shining my light over the walls. Motivational posters abounded, as did a plethora of brilliant yellow silk flowers. Sharon's office was smaller than Leila's, with no private bath or storeroom. *All the easier to search, my dear* I thought.

Now where to start? I stared at the desk. If I was Sharon and I wanted to protect the source of what might well be my ticket to a new career, where would I hide it? I was now convinced Bebe knew nothing about my missing journal. This had been Sharon's little guarantee on the side. She would have known that Bebe, being who she was, would have demanded that she hand over the recipes.

So where would I hide a stolen journal? Not in a drawer. Too easy. Bebe's Belles were competitive, so I wouldn't trust a filing cabinet or any place easily accessible by my coworkers. Maybe under something?

I pushed her chair away from the desk and dropped to

my knees, peeking into the cubbyhole. And there it was—
held to the bottom of the desk by a piece of duct tape.

My journal. I slowly reached for it, pulling the duct tape
away from the cover. It stripped away some of the design.
Auntie had given me that journal years ago, and now I
stared at the torn cover, and tears welled up in my eyes.
Damn that bitch! How dare she steal my work? I'd put in
long hours over these blends—they were my creations, my
art, and she'd been planning on passing them off as her
own, with no thought to how I'd feel.

I'd be damned if anybody would ever do this to me
again. I slipped the journal into my tote bag and headed toward the door.

As I locked the door behind me, I found myself staring
at Bebe's office. What secrets was she hiding? Could I find
something more? I longed to take her down, to expose her
for what she truly was. I wanted to fully vindicate Venus
Envy and throw light on every dirty trick she'd played.
Sure, I had what I'd come for—my journal. But maybe . . .
even though it was a risk, I had to dig a little deeper. I fit
the master key in the lock and turned. *Click.*

I slipped past Debra's station into Bebe's inner office
and made a beeline for her desk. The lower left drawer was
locked and, in a fit of pique, I grabbed her letter opener and
slammed it between drawer and the frame, using the stiff
metal to pry the lock. The drawer slid open, splinters sticking in my gloves.

Inside, I found a half-empty flask of bourbon. So Bebe
had a secret friend? That figured, but it wasn't newswor-
thy. However, next to the bottle rested a pile of file folders.
I opened the first, flashing my light onto the pages. It
looked like a report of some sort. I glanced through, looking for the summary.

Five out of the ten products you submitted for evalua-
tion are contaminated and pose significant risk to the
consumer, should you release them to the public. Our
findings indicate the possibility of increased rates of
certain cancers and tumors, as well as significant risk to
those with allergies to metal, asthmatics, or those with
compromised immune systems. Our recommendations
are that you completely eliminate this line from consid-
eration, or that you start again from ground zero, using
ingredients of a quality consistent with regulatory standards.

Whoa! Now that was interesting. So not only were
Bebe's ingredients poor quality, they were downright dangerous. I flipped through the file and found a memo from
Bebe, written to Leila and a couple of other names I didn't
recognize. The date indicated it had been sent two days
after the Date Received stamp on the report. I skimmed
until I came to the end.

Since this was a private laboratory, we have the choice
whether to ignore the findings or to pursue them. It is
not in our financial interests to dispose of such a large
quantity of supplies. These reports are usually worst-
case scenarios, and I foresee no problem since there are
no clear regulations for the release of cosmetics pro-
viding we don't use ingredients that have already been
banned by the FDA. This memo and the report it dis-
cusses is to be held in strict confidentiality, and not to
be discussed with anyone except me. My decision is
final on this matter, and I am not open to other options
at this point.

Holy shit! Bebe had turned her back on an analysis showing that her products weren't just substandard but a definite health risk to the consumer. This was what I'd been looking for. These notes could blow her out of the water. No wonder she'd kept it under lock and key, and no wonder that Leila had insisted that we keep our mouths shut about the various projects we were working on.

Did I dare steal them? Should I make a copy instead? I hesitated for a moment, then slid the files into my tote bag. Of course, Bebe would know somebody had been rifling her things—after all, I'd busted up her desk drawer, and her files would be missing, but by the time she returned, the police would already have these. The police and the FDA and the attorney general and the newspaper.

As I closed the drawer and picked up my tote bag, I heard a noise in the outer office. Shit! Who the hell was that? Killian? Praying that it was him, I cautiously slid along the wall until I was next to the door. I peeked out. Nobody around. Debra's desk stood silent witness to an empty room.

My imagination must be working overtime. Either that, or Sharon's ghost had decided to drop in and hang out for awhile. I let out my breath and closed Bebe's door. As I cautiously approached the door leading into the hall, I noticed the faint scent of Enchantment in the air. A new perfume from D'Rosse, it had only been on the market for a few months. I hadn't smelled it when I first entered, and Killian hadn't been wearing it, so somebody had been in Debra's office while I was putting the reports away. Who? A night watchman? Didn't seem likely, unless he was a she.

I stared at the doorknob, willing myself to reach out and turn it. Was somebody waiting on the other side for me? Or had they peeked in, decided nothing was amiss, and gone on? One way or another, I couldn't stay here all night. I had to leave sometime.

Taking a deep breath, I turned the knob, then slowly stepped into the hallway and started to close the door.

"Hello, Persia. Nice to see you again." Bebe emerged from behind the door where she'd been hiding.

"Oh, hell, you aren't supposed to be here!" I backed up a step. Bebe didn't look all too pleased to see me, and I had the feeling she'd be even less pleased if she had a look in my tote bag.

"*Oh, hell,* is right. What were you doing in my office?" Bebe stood there, dressed in her impeccable power suit, matching me inch for inch. A faint smile on her face told me she already knew what I was up to.

"Looking for something," I said, figuring it was useless to try to bluff my way out of it. Try as she might, Auntie had never taught me to be a good poker player, and I was pretty sure that Bebe was one of the greats. "But I found what I was after in Sharon's office, so I'll be on my way, and I won't be back." Keeping my gaze fastened on her face, I started to back up. I had no delusions that she'd let me go so easily, but maybe I could gain the upper hand long enough to run for the exit.

But Bebe wasn't anybody's fool. She let out a little laugh, then withdrew her hand from her pocket, and in it, I saw a lady's revolver. A small pistol, but when it came to bullets, size really didn't matter.

"I think we should have a little talk first," she said, motioning for me to return to the office. "You might want to raise your hands. I'm known to have quick reflexes, and if I happen to see you move a little too fast, there's no telling what might happen."

I slid the tote bag over my shoulder and, keeping my breath steady, followed her instructions. Auntie had been right; I should never had come back. Freakin' A . . . What was I going to do now?

It wasn't like the movies, there was no cavalry waiting to charge in and save me. At least not until midnight, when Auntie would call Kyle if she hadn't heard from me. Even if Killian came to my aid, he wouldn't be expecting to see Bebe, and it was all too probable that he might end up on my side of the gun.

"Bebe, think about this. Sharon's dead. If they find me, they might turn their attention away from Janette and ask just who's still out there with a gun. Let me go, and I'll walk away with my journal. That's all I wanted, and I found it. Sharon stole it, you know."

I prayed that she wouldn't notice the damage to her drawer. If she did, my bluff was over. She probably wouldn't look too favorably on leaving me in one piece, capable of talking to the cops.

Bebe motioned for me to sit down near Debra's desk. "Just how did you get in here in the first place? How did you get in the building?"

I shrugged. "Just lucky?"

She sighed. "So many of you young women are smart-asses today. You think you're such hot shit, but let me tell you something, missy. You don't know jack. You weren't around when women were struggling for the freedom just to get out of the house so we could work. Or when we tried to figure out how to feed a family of growing children on a secretary's wages after our husbands ran off screwing younger women. And I imagine that you never once in your life worried that you might not be able to make a living wage just because you're a woman."

I shook my head. "Bebe, a lot of women went through that hell, but they didn't turn to scamming people in order to make it. A lot of women still go through hell, but they're honest." Maybe if I could get her in a conversation, she'd listen to reason. "I hear what you're saying—but frankly, with your background it just sounds like another bluff. I don't understand why you've resorted to lies and theft when you've got the charisma that could have taken you up the ranks in a corporation—legitimately."

She let out a sharp laugh. "Why move up the ranks when I can be at the top from the beginning? Anyway, none of that matters. You say you found your journal in Sharon's office, and that's all you wanted. So just what were you doing in *my* office?" And then, a look stole over her face that I didn't like. It was the look of realization, of understanding. "You were in my desk, weren't you? Come on, let's go have a look."

I didn't want to be in that small, enclosed room with her, so far from the hallway, and I didn't want her knowing I had the files. "Save yourself the trouble. I broke into your desk. I saw the reports."

She paused. I had the feeling that I'd just bet my last chip. Now the play was in her corner. If I could keep her from acting on impulse, I might be able to catch her off guard long enough to hit the door and get out of the building. Granted, she was as tall as me, but I would guarantee I was faster.

"I see. What were you planning to do with the information? And don't lie and tell me you were going to keep your mouth shut. You're talking to the mother of all bluffers." Bebe allowed a little smile to creep out of hiding.

I shrugged. "I don't know . . . hadn't decided yet." And then it hit me; she still didn't know that my fight with Auntie was a setup. "My job's okay, but I could use more money than you're offering."

"Blackmail? You were planning on climbing the ladder the easy way and you tell me *I'm* corrupt? Well, I have to admit you've got balls. The trouble is, how could I ever trust you again? Remember, no honor among thieves, my dear. A fact of life I learned the hard way, long ago." I could tell she was considering the idea. If I could just convince her that I was a worthy apprentice, I might have a chance.

"Give me a try, make me your right-hand woman. You'd be surprised how handy I can be in a pinch." I tried to keep from fidgeting; the last thing I needed was to reinforce how nervous I was.

Bebe cocked her head. "You remind me of me, when I was younger. Leila's getting on toward retirement age," she said, musing, "Maybe I should think about a fresh face for the department."

And then my luck caved in. My cell phone rang. I'd forgotten to turn off the ringer, and it echoed through the room. I glanced at the clock. Not midnight, but I knew, in my gut, that it was Auntie.

"Let me see your phone," Bebe said, training the gun on me. I dug it out of my tote bag and handed it to her. "Open it," she said.

I did, and she glanced at the caller ID. It was Auntie, all right. Florence Vanderbilt, the screen read. Bebe let out a slow chuckle. "You almost made it, my dear. Answer and tell her that everything's fine." Again, she raised her gun and aimed for my skull. I punched the Talk button.

Auntie's voice rang loud enough for Bebe to hear, even though I pressed the phone to my ear as hard as I could in order to mute her voice. "Persia, are you all right? I've been so worried that I couldn't wait to call you. Did you find what you were looking for? I don't care if you did or not, I want you to get your butt home, child."

Bebe smiled, cold as glacier ice, and pointed to the gun, then to me. I closed my eyes, wishing to hell that I'd left the damned phone in the car. How could I have been so stupid? But my cell phone was my security blanket. I could call for help with it. Only this time, help had called me and put me in danger.

"Everything's okay, *Florence*. I'm fine. I'll be home later on, though." If only she could catch the hint.

Auntie wasn't stupid. She immediately lowered her voice. "You never call me by my name. Are you in trouble?"

"Yes, that's right," I said, breathing a sigh of relief. "Just dandy." Bebe was motioning for me to get off the phone. "I have to go now, Florence. I'll see you later." *I hope,* I added silently.

"I'll call Kyle," Auntie said, almost whispering. I flipped the phone shut.

"That wasn't so bad, now, was it?" Bebe said. "You almost had me fooled, Persia. In another life, I would have helped you go so far. But alas, that's not your destiny. Okay, set the phone down on my desk and let's go."

"Go? Where?" I was fighting to remain calm, but I did as she asked, placing my cell phone on the corner of her desk.

"We're going to take a little drive. The night is growing long; nobody will bother us. And tomorrow, everything will return to normal. You just won't be around to see it. Hold out your hands. Now."

I hesitated, wondering if perhaps I could disarm her after all. My instinct was to fight it out, but the gun and bullets looked very real in my book. I wasn't Bruce Lee; I didn't trust myself to be able to dodge a moving projectile of that speed and size.

Apparently, Bebe wasn't in a patient mood. Before I knew what she was doing, she raised her other arm and I heard a hiss.

As a blast of pepper spray hit me in the eyes. I tried to scream but couldn't—my throat felt paralyzed. I dropped to my knees and covered my face against another attack while trying to wrap my mind around the searing pain that sparked through my eyes as they began to swell.

Panicked, I realized that my throat was also swelling. I gasped for air, but then reflex took over and I gagged, losing everything that had been in my stomach. Petrified, I wondered if I'd choke, but managed to spit out the residue. I clung to what short, ragged breaths I could suck into my lungs.

The burn wasn't dissipating. I knew enough about pepper spray to know that the effects could last up to an hour, giving Bebe ample opportunity to force my compliance. She grabbed my wrists, and I blindly tried to pull away, but when she said, "Do you want another blast?" I gave in, allowing her to bind my hands with duct tape.

She yanked me to my feet, and dizzy, barely able to see through the blurry haze of tears and pain, I staggered along as she pushed me in front of her. I started to fall again, but her rough strength jerked me upright by my braid.

As we headed out the door, I prayed that Killian would see what was happening and call the cops. For his sake, it would be safest if he didn't try to interfere.

As we exited the building and a blast of warm evening air hit my face, I tried to regain some semblance of control, but I might as well have been on a nightmare drinking binge. The pain was still too fresh, and my coordination was shot. At least I was breathing, but even that hurt—my lungs fried by the capsaicin.

"Here we are," Bebe said. "Are you ready to go for a little ride?"

And then panic set in as I wondered if this was going to be the last night of my life.

Chapter Sixteen

The sky echoed with the sounds of thunder not far away. Once again, I took a deep breath, trying to scream, but my larynx was still paralyzed. The moist and dusky heat of the summer night thickened as we stood there.

Did I stand a chance in hell of escaping? If I could see clearly, if I hadn't been in such racking pain, I might have gone for it—tried to make it behind another car. But contrary to all the popular TV shows, a speeding bullet is always faster than a running person. Bebe might not be a good shot, but I couldn't bank on that, especially when I was incapacitated.

I ran through my options but came up blank. Unable to speak, I couldn't try to persuade her to give it up, to let me go. Just then I heard something and—blinking in the dim flash of a lightning strike—saw the hazy outline of what I knew to be her big old Mercedes. She had popped the trunk and pushed me toward it, stepping back quickly to raise both gun and pepper spray again. "Get in."

"Bebe, don't do this—" I tried to say, but my voice only

croaked. She held up what looked like the pepper spray, and I shut up real fast.

"I'm getting impatient," she said.

I half crawled, half fell into the trunk, banging my head a couple times on the way. With my wrists bound, it was doubly hard, but as I maneuvered into the cargo space, I felt the tape give a little. She hadn't used enough to wrap them round twice! Maybe I could work it loose if I tried. I forced myself not to fidget so she wouldn't notice.

"Good girl. Have a nice rest, Persia. Although you'll have plenty of time for that in just a little while." The trunk swung shut and latched firmly.

My tote bag was still hanging over my shoulder, I realized. She hadn't looked in it, and both the files and a flashlight were in there. As the car dipped a little—Bebe must be getting in the front seat—I set to work on the tape around my wrists, twisting them back and forth as I used my teeth to gnaw at the raised corner.

The front door slammed, the engine turned, and we were moving. I worked frantically at the tape, focusing all my attention on it. The pain was still severe, but I was able to clear my throat. My breathing had lightened up and I gasped as the tension in my lungs began to ease.

Another moment, and I struck pay dirt. The loose corner of the tape ripped as I gave it a good yank with my teeth. Thank God I'd kept them clean, cavity free, and drank enough milk. I twisted my wrists in opposite directions, managing to split the section that I'd been working on. Yet another minute, and I was free, peeling the tape away from my skin, not even noticing as it ripped out the sparse hair on my arms.

Now to escape from the car. I tried pushing against the back of the trunk. Newer cars often had panels that opened into the backseat, but this wasn't one of them. I pounded on the roof, but it was firmly locked. Finally, I managed to slide my tote bag off my shoulder and fished in it, searching for the flashlight. As I flipped it on, the pale light gave me faint comfort. My vision was still blurred, but the pain wasn't quite so intense.

I knew now that Bebe was going to kill me. She had a lot to lose if I walked away free. I wanted to rationalize that she would place a higher value on my life than on her business, but when I looked at it coldly, I knew that she would aim that gun at my head and fire, no remorse, no regrets. She was in the process of trying to build an empire, and I was the dynamite that could destroy her plans.

So it made sense that she was taking me somewhere where I wouldn't be easily found. Which meant that I had a few minutes to plan.

Something kept nagging at the back of my mind—something I remembered telling somebody. I scrambled for the elusive memory, and then, when I heard the turn signal click, and felt the car swing to the left, it flooded back into my mind.

One of the survival tips from my self-defense classes taught that, if ever locked in a trunk by an assailant, break the taillight and try to stick your hand out the hole. The trick had saved several lives when the cops stopped the car because of the broken light or seeing somebody's hand dangling out the back of the trunk. I just never thought I'd be the one having to take my own advice. I shook everything out of my tote bag and wrapped the cloth around my hand, then pulled away the panel covering the left taillight.

Taking a deep breath, I smashed my fist into the light. The glow from the bulb popped and vanished as the glass

shattered. Now for the right. I broke the light and then tried
to smash the cover.

Abruptly, the car hit a bumpy patch and I had to with-
draw my hand to avoid both the bag and my skin from
being slashed on the jagged remains of the bulb. A moment later, the car pulled to a stop. Oh shit. No sirens, so
the cops weren't to thank.

Frantic, I felt around in the trunk, hoping for a crowbar
or anything else that might be usable as a weapon. Nada.
Didn't the woman even keep a jack in her trunk? I exhaled
and tried to calm my mind. She wouldn't shoot me while I
was still in the trunk, she wasn't that stupid. No, she'd kill
me away from her car so there wouldn't be any blood-
stains. I was going to have to take her down the hard way.

But a little thought nagged at me, that I might not come
out of this alive. Quickly, I yanked a few hairs from my
head and scattered them around, trying to slide a couple
under the taillight panel, then reached up to make sure that
the roof of the trunk was covered with fingerprints. If she
did manage to kill me, I wanted evidence pointing to her.

A rustling told me she was near the trunk, then a click,
and it opened. She was still holding the gun, and, under the
faint light from the clouds, I could see she was staring at
the taillights with an angry expression on her face.

"You're resourceful, I'll give you that," she said. "Get
out."

I unfolded myself and climbed out. Though my face
and my body hurt like hell, I hadn't cramped. Thank
heaven for small favors. I glanced around to see where we
were and smelled the water before I saw or heard it. The
breakers were coming in, and farther back on the beach
stood the blurry outline of a tall building. We were on

Lighthouse Spit, and chances were good that we were alone.

"Get your things from the trunk. Make sure you have everything." She noticed my flashlight. "Use that to double-check."

Removing evidence, I thought. But she couldn't find everything—every fiber, every hair, every print. I slung my bag over my shoulder.

"Now, I want you to walk along the pier, out to the very end," she said.

Lighthouse Spit was a long, narrow spit of land leading out into the inlet. It ended in a pier, and during the summer, boats would moor along it. A great place for walking out to watch the waves, it was usually deserted by night. But right now, I didn't feel like a nature walk, especially one I knew was intended to be my last.

I swung in front of her, all the while gauging where the best place to make my stand was. Could I just jump in the water? Swim for safety? August nights weren't that cold, and I was a good swimmer. But then, how long would she wait, and how far would I have to swim in the dark? The riptides were an ever-present danger, and I was still suffering the effects of the pepper spray. We were on the beach, nearing the path, and there were no trees here, no bushes, just open sand. If I ran, chances were I'd take a bullet. That didn't mean she'd hit me in a vital area, but it didn't mean she wouldn't.

The sound of a car pulling up broke into my thoughts, and as Bebe started, I grabbed the chance and whirled, my feet flying. My reflexes took over and I landed a haphazard kick in her stomach. She groaned, then fell backward. No time to waste! She had the gun and the pepper spray. I half jumped, half fell on top of her, sprawling with a bone-jarring thud. She tried to fight me off, and I saw that the gun was still in her hand, aimed directly at my shoulder.

I grabbed for her arm, trying to force it back so the muzzle was pointed away from me, but she was stronger than she looked. I was going to have to hurt her before she managed to pull the trigger. I raised my arm, then brought my left fist down center on her face. She screamed, and the coppery smell of blood filled the air as her arm went limp. Knocking the gun out of reach, I blinked, trying to see what damage I'd managed. Well, well, well. A broken nose, by the looks of it. Sticky drops of blood clung to my hand, and I hoped to God I didn't have any open cuts.

Killian raced up from where he'd parked behind Bebe. He slid to his knees and stared at the two of us. "Are you all right?" he asked, his voice echoing through the night.

"No, I'm hurt—pepper spray," I said. "She was going to shoot me."

"I know, I followed you, but I didn't want to spook her until she stopped the car and I could get close enough to help. I lost her at the last turn, and it took me a few minutes to backtrack."

Bebe moaned. "Get off of me, you little bitch."

I wanted nothing more than to comply, but there was no way I was letting her escape. "We need to get Kyle out here—"

"He's on his way. I saw her leading you out of the building and called him from my car. He should be here any minute. He was on the other side of town." Killian looked around. "I can check to see if I have any rope so we can tie her up. Can you hold her a little longer?"

I grimaced, my body seriously protesting any further movement at this point. "I don't think so. Help me, please."

"You—you hired someone to kill Sharon," Bebe managed to say, staring up at Killian. I suddenly worried that she might choke on the blood if I kept her on her back, so I slipped off but kept hold of her wrists and dragged her to a sitting position.

Killian took over, pulling her arms behind her and pinning them there. So he was stronger than I was—that was a new one for me, and I smiled quietly. Even Bran couldn't beat me at arm wrestling.

"What? I barely knew Janette, and I sure didn't hire her to kill anybody." he said. I patted Bebe down while he held her, confiscating her pepper spray. The gun lay a little ways away on the sand.

Bebe leaned forward. "I think I'm going to throw up," she said, and we moved to allow her room. As a stream of feathery liquid mingled with blood spilled out of her mouth, I looked away. Blood, I could stomach. Vomit, not so much.

"May I wipe my mouth?" Bebe gave me such a beseeching look that I relented. She was, after all, a lady. A would-be murderer, yes, but a proper one. I reached in my tote bag and found a tissue, handing it to her. She seemed to have given up any hope of getting away, because she sat there limply, wiping her mouth and nose as the blood continued to stream.

"I suppose we should call for an ambulance, too," I said. Killian flipped out his cell phone and put in a call to Kyle. When he hung up, he said, "On its way. The chief called them. His ETA is about three minutes."

I found another tissue for Bebe, who mutely accepted it, staring dully ahead. She nodded to me, quickly stopping to gently prod her nose. "I have to give it to you, girl, you know how to fight. I suppose this means the end to everything I've been working for."

I broke a faint grin. Bebe wasn't worth the paper her birth certificate was printed on, but at least she could concede defeat when the game was over. "Considering you had no qualms about walking over everybody else to get what you wanted, I don't feel sorry for you," I said. "You screwed Venus Envy over as best as you could, as well as Donna Prima and who knows how many other little businesses."

She gave me a speculative look. "Business, my dear. Simply business. I have nothing against you or your aunt. In fact, I still think that—had you a slightly different bent—you would have made an excellent addition to my company. You and I could have gone a long ways."

"Yeah, straight to prison, which is where you're headed. For numerous sins." I looked up at Killian, who was staring out at the water.

"Trish," he murmured.

"What?" I heard the wail of sirens in the near vicinity. "Kyle's almost here. The ambulance can't be far behind."

"Trish," Killian said. "I know who murdered Sharon. It was Trish." He blinked, then rubbed his hand across his eyes. "I should have known. She was so paranoid about her work—so protective."

I winced, trying not to rub my eyes. It made sense, it made too much sense. Was Janette in jail because of her aunt's crimes? "We have to stop her before she leaves town. If she was able to shoot Sharon in cold blood and leave her there to die, I wouldn't put it past her to skip town, leaving Janette to take the blame."

Just then, Kyle pulled in, lights and sirens going. The loneliest sound in the world, I thought—the sound of sirens in the night. He swung out of his cruiser and raced over.

"You okay?" he shot at me.

I shook my head. "Yeah, I'll be fine. I'll go see the doctor before I go home, but the effects are starting to wear off. Pepper spray," I added before he could say a word. We filled him in on what had gone down. Bebe kept her mouth shut, only acknowledging her rights had been read to her, asking to speak to her lawyer as the ambulance loaded her in the back and took off for the hospital. A second patrol car showed up to follow the ambulance.

Kyle, Killian, and I sat there, staring out at the ocean as it crashed against the breakers in front of the spit. I took a shaky breath. This was the second time in my life I'd come close to dying, and I didn't like it any more than I had the first. Killian quietly told Kyle what he thought about Trish.

"Let's go have a talk with her," Kyle said.

"She might talk more if I'm there," Killian said. "I'm her friend. I understand what that cream meant to her—both her career and her sense of self-worth. She created a masterpiece, she really did. It would have put Donna Prima in league with the big boys."

I sighed. After everything broke in the papers, chances were good that Donna Prima was done for. The company would never recover from the bad publicity. If they'd been big enough, they might have bought silence. But they were still a start-up, and who on earth would want to use a cream created by a murderer, no matter how good it was?

Kyle shook his head. "You really think she'd kill over a face cream?"

Killian smiled sadly. "People have killed over far less, haven't they?"

On that sobering thought, we headed back to the cars.

Kyle called for a tow truck to impound Bebe's car, and I told him I'd ride over with Killian. I needed to call Auntie and let her know I was safe.

As I opened the door to Killian's Jag, I looked up. Kyle was watching me, and in the shadows, I thought I saw resignation on his face. Resignation and the beginnings of understanding. It was better that way, I thought, as I slid into the low-slung seat. Maybe he could let go of a fantasy and find something real.

⋆

As soon as we were buckled in, I put in a call to Auntie. She burst into tears when she heard my voice. "I called Kyle after I talked to you, but I didn't know where you were," she said. "I was frantic with worry."

"I know, Auntie, and I'm sorry. But I'm safe now. There are a few things we have to take care of first, but I'll call you when I'm ready to come home. It's going to be a long night—you should get some rest. I'm okay."

She didn't want to hang up, but I convinced her that I'd love nothing more than a pot of hot chicken soup when I was done, the kind she made from scratch. It would give her something to do while waiting for me, and truth was, Auntie's chicken soup was quickly becoming a comfort food for me. I stared at the silent phone, counting my many blessings.

The ride over to Trish's house was tense, but when we hit the stoplight at Rhine and Mariner streets, Killian reached over and slid his hand onto my knee, very lightly. I ran my fingers over his skin. It was all we needed to say.

Trish lived in a suburb near the west side of Gull Harbor. Her lights were blazing as we pulled in behind Kyle, and I had the feeling that she knew we were on our way.

Kyle went first, while we waited at the edge of the sidewalk. Trish opened the door on the first ring and beckoned us in. She was fully dressed, even though it was well past midnight, and her handbag sat on the coffee table, along with a light wrap.

She offered us coffee, which we politely declined, and then motioned for us to be seated. I glanced around the room. Stark white with brilliant splashes of red and black. The room was chic, avant-garde almost, and cold as ice. The prints on the walls were geometric, the vases angular rather than round. I glanced at Killian, who in turn was watching Trish.

"I guess you know why we've come," Kyle said.

Trish let out a loud sigh. "I know. I'd like to tell you everything now. I can't let you hold my niece any longer. I was going to come down to the station tomorrow and confess. I'm the one who shot Sharon."

Kyle stared at her. "Would you like a lawyer present before you say anything more?"

With a smile, Trish stood up and peeked around the corner, whispering something. A short little man with beady eyes appeared from the other room. He was dressed in a dark suit and, while I didn't recognize him, it didn't take a genius to figure out that Trish had already made provisions in that direction.

"Paul Manning," the man said to Kyle. "I believe we've met in the past."

"Manning, I remember you." Inclining his head slightly, Kyle added, "I take it you're Ms. Jensen's attorney?"

"Yes. She's prepared to give a full statement after you've read her her rights." Manning glanced over at us. "You want them here?" he asked her.

Trish shrugged. "I hardly think it matters," she said,

then turned to Killian. "I'm so sorry, Killian. I never meant to do anything that would jeopardize Donna Prima. But I guess things don't always turn out like we want them to."

Kyle seemed taken aback but quickly took control of the situation. "Let's go down to the station to do this. I'd like to record her confession." Trish and her lawyer had no objections, so we headed out into the night again. Manning and Trish drove in front of Kyle, who kept watch to make sure they made it to their destination, while Killian and I brought up the rear.

"Did you ever suspect that she might be the one?" I asked.

"No, but then I would never have guessed that she'd let the cops think I was a suspect, either." Killian shook his head. "She'd better not count on me to be a character witness for her, that's all I have to say." His voice was hard, but I understood exactly what he was going through. When I found out what Elliot had been up to—even though it hadn't been as serious as murder—I'd felt totally betrayed.

"This is going to be rough on Janette," I said. "I like her."

"She's a good kid," he said. "At least she'll come out of this with her skin intact." He pulled into the parking lot, and we sat there for a moment, staring at the police station. "I'm closing down Donna Prima," he said, after a moment.

"I figured as much. I don't know what else you can do until this blows over. What will you do after you've shut down the company?" I asked, realizing that I needed to know. Killian was different than anybody I'd ever met. He set off alarm bells in the pit of my stomach. I could be vulnerable to this man, and it frightened me as much as it intrigued me.

He looked over at me. "I'm not sure, but the minute I

figure it out, you'll be the first one to know. Until then, can you live with a little uncertainty?"

I stared at him, realizing that I already did. "I told you I'm seeing someone, but it's not serious. We know that there will be a day where we'll say good-bye as lovers. I've never been too good at the commitment thing, not if it means marriage and family. Can you live with that?"

Killian broke into a grin. "I had a vasectomy four years ago. I think I can get used to the idea." He paused. "Do you love him—your boyfriend?"

Did I love Bran? He was freewheeling, fun, interesting, but was that enough? Was that the foundation of love? "I don't think so," I said slowly. "Not in that deep, unswerving way. I don't know if I really know what love is. I've never really been in love before, I guess."

"I can live with that answer for now." Killian slipped out of his seat, and I followed him into the building.

❧

By the time we joined Kyle, Manning, and Trish in one of the conference rooms, the fluorescents had already given me a headache. Kyle choked back a snort when he saw me in full light. "You look like death warmed over, Persia."

"Thanks," I said, raising one eyebrow, then wincing because it hurt.

Kyle waited until we were all seated, then turned on the cassette recorder. He recorded the date, asked Trish if she minded if we were present. She said no, that was fine. Then he asked her if she'd been read her rights and if she understood them, and she acknowledged that she had and did. Manning stated that he was present and that everything was aboveboard. We were ready to rumble.

"Trish, what do you want to tell us?" Kyle asked.

She took a deep breath, looked at Killian, who looked away, then leaned toward the tape recorder. "I want to confess to the murder of Sharon Wellstone. I shot her, nobody else was involved, and I take full responsibility."

Kyle took a deep breath. "Why don't you tell us what happened?" he said, folding his arms across his chest as he leaned back in his chair.

And she did.

❧

An hour later, Killian and I sat in Kyle's office. I produced the information that I'd taken from Bebe's desk. "This should go to the attorney general, I guess. They'll know where to direct it. Bebe's has been releasing dangerous products to the public, knowing full well they're a health risk. Along with the fact that she both kidnapped me and was planning on killing me, these should ensure that she's in jail for quite a long time."

"Shit, you guys are in a cutthroat business," Kyle said, shaking his head as he looked through the reports.

"Speaking of cutthroat, I also found proof that she was behind our computer getting hacked. And . . . I found my journal in Sharon's office. But I'm not giving it to you for evidence unless you really need it." There was nothing to charge Sharon with anymore. She was beyond justice on a mortal level, and wherever her soul walked, it was my guess that she was facing a tribunal for more than her petty crimes.

"Well, this puts an end to your problems at Venus Envy. Hell, I'll bet that your business skyrockets when this hits the papers," he said.

I shook my head grimly. "I hate to profit on the graves of others, but you're right. When Lydia Wang died, Venus

Envy's customer base soared. Curiosity seekers, and some of them stuck around after the novelty wore off."

Killian glanced at his watch. "I'm beat," he said. "Can I give you a lift home, if we're free to go?"

Suddenly weak in my knees, I nodded. Besides seeing Auntie, there was only one thing on my mind, and he could see it in my eyes. I glanced over at Kyle, who busied himself with his paperwork.

"You're both free to leave," Kyle said.

I told Killian I'd meet him out at the car and, after he'd left, I turned to Kyle. "Thank you . . . for coming to save me. Bebe was ready to dump me in the drink. I would have been fish food."

Kyle shook his head. "Killian saved you. Even though Miss Florence called me, I wasn't sure where you were. Without Killian's call, I'd still be searching for you. Next time, listen to your aunt."

I paused, my hand on the door. "Kyle—I'm sorry."

"Don't sweat it, Persia." He let out a short laugh, and as he looked at me, I could see that he was smiling gently. "I finally figured us out. You're my dream of freedom, of passion, of being able to do and say whatever I want to. You're the solitary wildcat. And me? I'm a wolf, the leader of the pack, responsible for order and decorum. I have rules to follow. I guess wolves and wildcats don't mix, do they?"

I gave him a slow smile. "No, but I like to think they can be friends."

Kyle pushed himself out of his chair and stretched. "Maybe they can at that," he said. "Just be careful. Wildcats may be elusive, but they can still be hurt."

"I know," I said. "Believe me, I know." And at that moment, I knew Kyle and I would be able to find our friendship. Solid, slap-on-the-back pals, watching out for each other as only friends can do.

~

Killian was waiting for me in the car. I slid in. "Auntie's expecting me," I said, hesitating, wanting nothing so much as to go back to his apartment and spend the next few days in his arms. He started the engine and silently drove me home, pulling quietly into the driveway to Moss Rose Cottage.

"We have a lot to sort out," he said after a moment.

I swallowed, my throat still raw from the pepper spray. "Yeah. I'm looking forward to it," I said, a sudden streak of fear racing through me. Did he really feel the same way?

He reached out and ran his fingers along my face, gently. "I've never known anybody like you, Persia. I can't get you out of my mind. I want to kiss you and hold you and stay up all night, talking and making love until we're punch drunk."

I caught my breath, shivering under his touch. "When it's time, Killian. I'll be waiting." The echo of thunder rolled as lightning split the sky and rain deluged the night. I leaned in, planted a long, slow kiss on his lips, then slammed the door and dashed for the house. After all these years, it had happened. I'd finally met my match.

Chapter Seventeen

The story had broken in the papers, and once again, I was a minor celebrity. Fame had its perks, I thought, watching as Tilda hurried off with our orders to get them right in. The BookWich was crowded as always, but a table had miraculously cleared when we showed up. I wasn't going to question it. I was starving.

Auntie was still in shock. "I still can't believe I almost lost you, Imp. Thank heaven you took Killian along. By the way, when do I get to meet this young man of yours?"

When I'd shown up at two thirty in the morning, Auntie was waiting, soup in hand. While I ate, telling her everything that happened, I could see her reading between the lines. Every time I'd mentioned Killian's name, she beamed.

Barb looked happier than in awhile. Theresa had forgiven her, and now her locks were back to their usual gorgeous copper. While her hair was ultrashort, she sported a sassy European style that suited her chic demeanor.

"Your hair looks great," I said. "Much better."

"I know. As Lady Godiva is my witness, I will never go

salon hopping again." Barb stirred her lemonade with her
swizzle stick, then asked, "So Trish confessed to everything?"

I nodded. "She did. She would never have let Janette
take the rap for something so heinous. Trish isn't . . . she's
not a bad woman—"

"A good woman doesn't go around killing off people
because they steal her work," Auntie interjected.

"No, but a good woman doesn't set out to ruin other
people's lives and drive them out of business either. I think
the whole mess with Bebe made Trish snap. She'd worked
on that cream for over two years." I paused. "What say we
stay out of the bigger leagues and keep Venus Envy a local
phenomenon?" I played with my iced tea. The morning
had broken cooler than in weeks. Our heat spell was almost at an end.

"What was the final straw that drove her to shoot
Sharon?" Barb asked.

I shrugged. Trish had left no question unanswered, and
we knew everything. "Remember the samples of new
products at the conference? Apparently, Trish suspected
that one was her cream—Janette confirmed that was the
product that they were working on through her snooping.
Trish asked Sharon to meet her after one of the late night
soirees. She confronted Sharon, and Sharon taunted her,
secure in the knowledge that she'd destroyed any records
that indicated that Bebe's Cosmetics hadn't actually discovered the formula. She took the opportunity to rub
Trish's nose in her defeat. Trish carries a gun for protection—according to Janette, she always has. I guess she
snapped, shot Sharon, then ran. She didn't realize that
Sharon was still alive, or she would probably have called
nine-one-one."

"So Janette didn't know anything about it?" I could tell that Auntie wanted to believe the girl had been innocent. While she knew all about the dark corners of human minds, she preferred to pretend that they were aberrations, uncommon. I'd finally realized that this was her defense mechanism to the voilence that permeated society. Unfortunately, I couldn't look past it. I was too much of a realist, which depressed me more than I liked to admit.

"I think on some level, she knew. But Trish is sticking to her story that she was the only one involved, and Janette is maintaining her innocence."

I shook my head. I'd been pissed as hell over my journal. In some cobweb-encrusted corner of my own mind, I'd had a brief desire to throttle Sharon, but I hadn't. What had kept me from acting on my desire? Was it the same factor that allowed Trish to go after Sharon? Was there something genetic that kept me from acting on impulse, while setting Trish free to pull out her gun, aim, and fire?

Or was it—and this I believed to my core—simply the fact that I'd made the choice to err on the side of right, and that Trish had chosen a darker path? In my heart, I believed it all came down to saying, "I may want to do this, but today, I will not act on my desire."

"What's going to happen to Bebe?" Barb asked.

"Well, you mean aside from the attorney general looking into the case, and her being charged with kidnapping, assault, and attempted murder?"

Auntie snickered. "You'd think that would be enough, but Kyle set the feds onto the news about her late husbands and the sizable insurance she managed to accrue through their deaths."

Barb blinked. "You mean—"

"Yeah," I said, nodding with a gleam in my eye. So sue

me for taking pleasure in Bebe's downfall. I had every right in the world to gloat. "They're exhuming her late husbands. She may be facing far worse charges than attempted murder and kidnapping." I flashed her a guilty grin. "Which makes me extremely happy. So, what about your niece?"

She grimaced. "She and her friends got off with a fine and community service. My sister has ordered her to either attend a private college—a very restrictive one—or to leave home and make her own way in the world. She's chosen college, thank God, though she'll go protesting all the way."

"Well, that's good news at least." I motioned to Tilda and asked for a slice of apple pie. "À la mode," I said, deciding to do it up royal.

"So," Auntie said after she and Barb mirrored my order for dessert. "I guess we go back to normal."

"I guess," I said, wondering what to do next. Almost anything we said or did would feel anticlimactic after the events of the past week.

Bebe's would close, of course, as would Donna Prima. Urban Gurlz would probably survive. They'd lost a spring line to Bebe's, but without the stigma of a murderer in their midst, they could recover. Janette was going back to school to get her doctorate so she could teach. Leila had moved on already, and Kyle said the cops were on the lookout for her. The attorney general was going to want to talk to her, that much was for certain. The Belles were all lining up for unemployment.

But at least Venus Envy would recover, though we had a lot of roses to replant and thirty acres to fence in. Kane had already promised his help to Auntie, and I had the feeling we'd be seeing a lot of him this autumn.

I'd collected my things from the apartment complex and said a fond farewell to Andy Andrews, cornering him in the hall to plant a big wet kiss on his lips. I left him speechless as I sauntered out of the building with the parting farewell, "Enjoy, babe, because that's all you're ever going to get out of me besides a TV buddy." He'd recovered enough to let out a long whistle as I waved over my shoulder.

And our computer was in one piece again. Andy had set it up with a security field that was locked as tight as a medieval chastity belt. He guaranteed that if we followed his instructions, nobody would hack into our system again.

"What about Bran?" Barb interrupted my thoughts.

"We'll stay friends. I think he wants to see more of Victoria, anyway. It's time to let the physical side of our relationship drop. I have so many questions . . . and no answers. Killian's gone to Seattle for a week," I added. "To wrap up all the details surrounding Donna Prima. When he comes back, we'll see what happens." With a rush of anticipation—mingled with a touch of fear—I realized I was looking forward to the journey.

"Did you still want to go to Port Townsend?" Auntie asked.

I nodded. "I need a vacation. Barb's going with me," I said, grinning at my best friend. "We're going to make it a real girl's week out. By the way Barb, did Dorian see the doctor yet?"

"Actually yes, and I want to thank you for encouraging me to have him go. Turns out, his lack of energy is due to a low thyroid. Now that he's on medication, he's going to be fine."

I glanced out the window. Another month until autumn, but I could smell the tang in the air that hinted at bonfires on the beach and storms raging in from Puget Sound. The seasons were changing, and so was my life. But this time, I wasn't running from anything. No, this time, I would stay put and face the transformations right where I was at. I took Auntie's hand in mine.

"Why don't we spend the afternoon figuring out how many roses we'll need to replant. We may have to wait a few years, but we'll have our garden back. And I plan on being around to see it."

Her eyes shone, and she let out a long sigh. "So do I, my dear. So do I."

From the Pages of Persia's Journal

Peace & Clarity Potpourri

After so much tension and worry, I decided to blend a potpourri to ease my stress. It's a fairly simple recipe and pretty to place in glass bowls around the house. I think we'll sell it at the shop, it's so easy and has a variety of uses. Besides keeping in bowls around the house, we can sew the potpourri into pouches, then slip the pouch into a larger pillowcase at night for restful sleep. Other hints for stress reduction:

- Practice gentle yoga or stretching about an hour before bed.

- Turn off the TV an hour before bed and listen to soft music instead.

- Take five minutes out of every hour to stretch, catch a breath of fresh air, or simply close the eyes and relax.

- Don't take on too many projects; learn to say no when you simply can't add another task to your schedule.

- Prioritize, and don't sweat the small stuff.

- Meditate at least once a day, or spend some time in silent prayer.

- Eat healthy food and plenty of it.

⋆ Drink eight glasses of water daily—it clears out the mind as well as the body.

3 cups dried rose petals
1 cup dried lavender
1/2 cup crumbled white sage
1/2 cup dried cedar needles
1 cup dried mint leaves
1/4 cup dried, powdered orris root
20 drops lavender essential oil
20 drops lemon essential oil
10 drops sandalwood essential oil

Mix all ingredients in a large bowl and lightly toss. Place in bowls or jars around the house, or use to stuff dreaming pillows, or you can put one cup in a cheesecloth or muslin bag and steep in 1 quart hot water, then strain and add the water to your bath. As always, avoid consuming this product, and keep out of reach of children and animals.

A REFRESHING DEBUT:
The New Bath and Body Mystery Series

Scent to Her Grave

by
India Ink

From custom blended oils to relaxing
spa services, the store Venus Envy takes care
of all the beauty needs of Gull Harbor,
Washington. Behind the counter is
Persia Vanderbilt, a woman with a nose
for mixing scents—and a mind
for solving murder.

"An appealing, credible heroine."
—*Publishers Weekly*

0-425-20533-9
**Available wherever books are sold or at
penguin.com**